T

Rye

Rooftop

Club

Summer Solstice

Mark Feakins

Books by Mark Feakins:

The Rye Series

The Rye Rooftop Club
The Rye Rooftop Club: Mother's Day
The Rye Rooftop Club: Summer Solstice

Stand Alone Books

Death and The Seagull

"Happiness is a gift and the trick is not to expect it, but to delight in it when it comes."

Charles Dickens

CHAPTER 1

The cone of shame, the pickle man and emails.

Spring in Rye is generally a time for residents to enjoy the arrival of daffodils in their window boxes, local Romney Marsh lamb on their Sunday plates and tourists peering through their windows.

For small beagle dogs such as Stanley, it was a time to race across the cobbled streets without fear of ice sending them skidding off track. Today he was a dog on a mission. He had been left behind for the last three mornings and forced to wear an annoying plastic cone around his neck for a reason that was beyond him, and he would stand for it no more. The moment the front door of the flat was open he managed to evade Ralph's frantic hands and legs, shrink to a quarter of his size and back through the tiny gap – the plastic cone scrapping noisily against the wood – and take-off up the High Street.

Ralph knew he stood little chance of catching up with him, since his ankle was only just feeling better after its recent fracture. He shouted after the little dog, whose bouncing tail and satellite-like collar could be seen disappearing round the corner ahead of him, but to no avail. He set off at a gentle jog past The Bookery - his pride and joy. He glanced in at the window display of books encouraging people back into their gardens (*Weeding the Wilderness Way*), their sheds (*Private Pursuits for the Modern Gentlemen*) and the great outdoors (*Short Walks from Teashop to Teashop*). Next door, Judy McMurray was in the window of Let's Screw, giving some colourful gnomes a quick wash and brush up, and he gave her a brief wave. Judy had become a familiar figure marching up the High Street in her starched blue overalls and running the DIY shop with military efficiency while Joe was away in Canada.

Ralph's ankle seemed to be doing well, so he upped his pace a little and cantered past the myriad of cafes, craft shops, comfy shoe shops and slick estate agents that made up Rye's High Street, before turning right down the steep hill of Market Road towards the station. He caught a glimpse of Stanley ahead, who had paused to make sure that Ralph was still playing the game.

"Stanley! Enough! Come here!" he yelled. But the little dog pretended not to hear inside the rotten cone he was being forced to wear and turned left towards Strand Quay.

As Ralph made his way beside the River Rother, he saw Stanley investigating the bottom of an iron lamppost outside the antique centre housed in an old fishing hut. The dog was engrossed in something particularly interesting at its base and Ralph slowed to a gentle, almost silent trot. As Stanley foraged behind the post, he suddenly got a sense of being watched and looked up. Ralph wasn't close enough to reach him, so

Stanley tried to turn, only to find that his humiliating cone of shame had trapped him between the wall and the metal post. He saw a beam of triumph cross Ralph's face, "Got you!". With a giant heave Stanley and the hated cone parted company and he shot up Mermaid Street heading for the top of the town. Glancing back, he saw Ralph standing with the limp curl of plastic in his hand and heard him shouting something he knew wasn't very nice, but he wasn't quite sure what the words actually meant. Never mind, this was fun and he barked a happy cry as he headed for the Mermaid Inn, where he knew delicious beery smells awaited the winner of the race.

Ralph plodded up the hill, his ankle now beginning to throb, with the cone over his arm. They'd managed to get Stanley to wear it for three of the six days the vet had recommended, during which time he had sulked, pulled it off twice, taken chips out of every door frame in the flat and smashed a vase, three mugs and a table lamp. The small patch of irritated skin it was there to protect had all but vanished, and Ralph wasn't sure that the flat, Stanley or his nerves could take any more. So, as he passed a dustbin he shoved the cone deep inside.

With the contentious item gone, he saw that Stanley sat down on the pavement ahead and quietly waited for him, "Alright, Stan. You win. Just wait there, my ankle won't take another long run." Stanley flapped his ears and settled down to enjoy the beer and cooking smells that wafted under the old timber door of the Mermaid Inn, one of his favourite places in town. Ralph shook his head and paused to catch his breath.

Mermaid Street was one of the most beautiful in

7

Rye, with dark timber frames holding together ancient white walls and tiny windows of a jumble of medieval houses. Flint walls and crooked gates hid neat pocket gardens from the prying eyes of tourists, who flocked each year to admire this and the other pretty streets and historic sites in the strange little town. The town that had provided Ralph with both sanctuary and the family of friends that had sustained him through a rollercoaster of adventures over the last six months.

When he reached Stanley, he grabbed the dog's collar and attached the lead, "Right, can we please go home now? I only wanted to go next door to see Anna, not do a marathon around town. Come on, Stan, we're going home."

Stanley had enjoyed the game but was ready for some breakfast and a snooze in his bed in the window of The Bookery, so was quite happy with Ralph's proposal. As they skirted the old church yard of St Mary's, they took a short detour past the town's most popular restaurant, which would soon be their new home. The white painted bricks that fronted the old warehouse gleamed in the morning sunshine, and Ralph looked above the glass front door to its red painted name - Cinque - Rye being one of the five twelfth-century harbours known as the Cinque Ports, that provided ships for the crown in times of need.

Above the sign, the first-floor windows looked foreboding, yet behind them lay a space he dreamed of almost every night. He hadn't come to Rye to fall in love, but the town had had other plans for him and he had fallen for Sam, the handsome chef and owner of Cinque. It was just a few metres from where he stood now that they had danced in the snowy street after what seemed like every possible obstacle, confusion and emotional muddle had been put in their way – like some ridiculous romantic comedy. But now they were planning to turn the floor above the restaurant into their new home and settle into a life that Ralph could not have imagined this time last year, when he was still married to Helen and living in a world of half-truths and confusion.

Stanley gave a pull on the lead and Ralph looked down at him, "Alright, Stan. Come on, we both need some breakfast. I have to see Anna first, though."

As the sun began to warm the cobbles of the High Street, his fellow shopkeepers arrived to prepare for the day ahead and he chatted to one or two as he made his way to The Cookery. The light was on in the cafe and the panel of stained-glass flowers above the door shone its reds and greens out into the bourgeoning day. He knocked gently on the glass of the door and the figure hunched over a laptop turned in her chair.

Anna's lemon-yellow silk kimono, round face and spiralling red hair looked like an avant-garde artist's impression of a sunrise as she peered through the glass. "Oh, it's you," she said, as she opened the door. "I was expecting the orange man."

"What orange man?"

"He brings the orange juice."

"You have a man who brings you orange juice?"

Anna stepped back to let Ralph and Stanley into the café, "Of course. He's actually the milk man, but I get my milk from the herb man, so he brings me the orange juice instead."

Ralph scrubbed his hands through his hair, "It's way too early to make any sense of that. I only popped in to make sure you were still alright to do the sandwiches for the book signing next door."

Anna picked up a scrappy piece of paper from the table she had been sitting at and started to read it, "Cheese and pickle, ham and pickle, salmon and cream cheese and no pickle, mini sausage rolls with optional pickle to dip in..."

"I don't remember asking for pickle," Ralph said, feeling tired all of a sudden.

"The pickle man came yesterday and left too much, so I'm on a roll pickle-wise for the rest of the week," Anna said, throwing the list back on the table.

"Oh, right, well, I'm not even going to ask who the pickle man is, I mean, he's probably the brother of the sausage roll man or something. The point is everyone is coming at two, so if I can collect them at half one, that'd be great."

"Yup, no problem. I'm going to start on them in a minute, I'm just finishing an email to Mum and Joe in Canada."

Ralph turned in the doorway, "Send them my love. Have you told Ruby about the fire yet?"

Anna pulled her kimono tight over her chest, "I'm doing it now, in this email. I've left it as I didn't want to spoil her fun, especially as it happened the day she ran off with Joe all loved up and everything. Plus, she's such a worrier. Talking of which, have you heard from Helen?"

Ralph nodded, "Oh, glad you reminded me, I got an email from her the other day and I need to reply. She's says she is the biggest pregnant woman in the history of pregnant women. I think she's a bit fed up, but she's still got months to go yet. The baby's not due until June and it's only April."

"Poor thing. Tell her to eat coal, apparently that's good for you if you're having a baby."

"Really? Are you sure?"

"I think so, coal or curries. One or the other," Anna smiled, waving her hand in the air. "Who knows, it's all a mystery to an aging spinster like me."

"You're only thirty-three."

Anna groaned, "Thanks for reminding me. Nearly forty and the highlight of my week is too much pickle from the pickle man. Right, clear off handsome neighbour with lovely hair and eyes and the town's most beautiful boyfriend, you're making me feel worse. I need to finish this email." She waved as she swung the door back into its frame, and Ralph and Stanley finally went home for their breakfast.

✳ ✳ ✳

To: rubyrose@beemail.com
From: annabanana@tallyho.co.uk

28th April

Hi Mum

How are you? Hope you had lots of Canadian Easter Eggs. Does the Easter Bunny travel as far as Canada?

Right, before I go on, I have to tell you something or I might pop a kidney (as Irene would say!). I haven't told you before because I thought you might panic and want to come home, but it's been 6 weeks since you and Joe flew off, so it's probably safe to tell you now. Someone tried to burn The Copper Kettle down. I know, I know, I should have told you before.

It happened on Mother's Day, the day we opened The Copper Kettle. You and Joe went off to the airport on your romantic elopement / escapade / frolic, I finished tidying up and went for a nice long walk around town to get my head clear after so much excitement. I met Dawa Singh, from Cinque, and we had a lovely chat (more of him later), meanwhile, someone was shoving something flammable through the letterbox of the tearooms. It was only saved by the hand of God - well, the vicar's hand, to be precise. Bob, the vicar, (not really the right name for a vicar, is it?), was coming out of the churchyard and saw the smoke. He ran back to the church, grabbed a bucket of sand and pushed loads of it through the letterbox and put it out. Luckily, Fiona wasn't upstairs in the flat or it could have been really nasty.

Because of Bob, the vicar, there wasn't a lot of damage. The door has scorch marks and the lovely new blue carpet has a burn hole in it, so the insurers are paying to replace them both. There was soot on the walls and ceiling, which we had to clean off and Ralph had to touch up his mural of the big copper kettle. We had to wash all the curtains and linens to get rid of the smoky smell, but everyone mucked in, as usual! The Rooftop Club were incredible, as usual!! I think I cried about every twenty minutes, as usual!!! So, we were able to open again on Tuesday, as planned.

Why would someone do that? On our opening day? It had all been so lovely, then you found Joe and did the most romantic thing ever and ran off together. I mean, honestly, if it wasn't for Ralph and everyone else, I think I would have locked myself in the cutlery cupboard and never come out again. (I don't have a cutlery cupboard, it's a drawer and I'd never get in it, but you know what I mean.)

The police came and had a look but didn't seem very interested. They thought it was kids messing about. If I caught them, they wouldn't be able to mess around with much for quite a while. Mind you, I went to see Psychic Sue in her shop, and she's got me convinced that it's not the last fire I will see this year. Apparently, my aura had a flaming ring or something. I hope she's wrong, she is sometimes; I never did meet a man with a motorbike and a big blue crash helmet. Anyhoo, it's all in the past now. The Cookery is still doing well, and Martin and Fiona are a great team in The Copper Kettle. Nothing for you to worry about.

Back to Canada! Tell me the picture you sent is not of you kayaking? Did you have to wear a crash helmet? I'd never get my hair in one! And axe throwing? (Is that actually a thing? Maybe it's a lumberjack thing? Have you met an actual lumberjack, yet? Yum!) Looks like you are having the time of your life. I'm so pleased.

It's brilliant that Joe is in touch with his family again; I had no idea they hadn't seen him for ten years. No wonder he was nervous of seeing everyone. His nieces and nephews sound fantastic, especially the one with green hair! (Don't you come back with green hair!) What else? Oh, Rosie's gone off with a rock band – don't ask! I'm getting a new waitress called Susan to help Fiona in the tearooms, she seems nice and is a friend of Judy. (The Judy who's running Let's Screw for Joe, not Judy Garland. Just in case you thought that. I would have done.)

Irene looks tired, I'm a bit worried. But she's like an old tank, isn't she? She'll just keep going through anything. If we had a nuclear war, I reckon the only things left standing would be her and the cockroaches. I won't tell her that though, she might take it the wrong way. I've found someone else to help her in the cafe full time too, she's Judy's sister. (Judy, is turning out to be very useful!)

I go out walking most evenings now, as I need some new knickers and I don't want to buy the big ones again. Sometimes I bump into Dawa when he's finished at the restaurant and we walk together. He's such an interesting man; did you know that all male Sikh's have the same surname – Singh? I had no idea, I just thought it was a really big family. Every day's a school day, isn't it? Like today, a customer told me that figs aren't vegan because wasps crawl inside and get absorbed into them. I had to Google it to make sure, and he's right! I won't be able to look a fig roll in the face again!

Enjoy your time but come back soon. Actually, come back when you are ready. I hope you are happy.

Love

Anna xxxx

* * *

To: helenh@woohoo.com

From: thebookery01@beemail.com

30th April

Hi Helen,

How are you doing? Sorry, for taking a while to reply, it's been busy now the sun's come out and the weather is better.

I'm sure you're making your baby bump out to be worse than it is. Can you really only see your ankles if someone holds them in the air while you lay flat on your back? I mean, you've still got 3 months to go! They'll have to roll you to the hospital like a barrel if you carry on like that. If it's going to be a massive baby, shall I alert the Guinness Book of Records, just in case? LOL.

Glad you are feeling less sick now, though, and it's working out having a housemate. She sounds great and I'm glad she's taking care of you. It sounds like you landed on your feet finding her. Not too long until you can go on maternity leave from the bank, is it? Good idea to stay, I reckon, and get the paid leave. You can decide what to do later when the baby is here. Everything will change then, won't it?

Sam and I are hoping to come up and see you soon.

I'm getting some proper help in the shop, it's crazy trying to do it on my own. Sam's got a good deputy in the kitchen at Cinque now, so we can take a few days off at the same time.

You won't believe it, but we are going to develop the empty floor above the restaurant and turn it into an apartment for us to live in. Yes, an 'apartment', Sam insists on calling it that. He says it's too important to be a plain old flat! He's so excited. Me too, although it's another massive change for me, so soon after - well, you know, after coming here and everything. Sorry. Sam put his house on the market, and it sold after three days for the asking price. He's moved in with me, so the sale can go through quickly. We're getting on so well, I love having him around all the time, as does Stanley.

Anna is still as bonkers as ever. She came in wearing a sort of fascinator in her hair the other day with a knitted Clanger on it. You know, the little pink space men things from the kid's TV programme? No idea where she found it. Luckily, Irene confiscated it when it nearly fell into someone's dinner.

She tells me Joe and Ruby are doing well in Canada, all loved up. It's brilliant. No sign of Fiona's evil husband, Andy. He's keeping his head down and their divorce should be through before too long. The sooner he crawls under a rock somewhere else the better.

Martin sends his love. He's settled into Auntie B's old flat, I think. It was so good to get him out of the homeless hostel. He looks a bit strained at the moment, but it might be working full time in the kitchen of The Copper Kettle. (I told you about the fire, didn't I?) Or it could be his divorce which is still dragging on. He has lots of secrets, I think, (being the Earl of Groombridge and something about stealing from the rich, for starters!), there is so much more to him than we know. I hope he decides to tell us one day.

Anyway, better go, a woman is in the shop and she has about 10 romance novels in her arms. Catch up soon,

Love,

Ralph

X

PS Stanley says, woof.

PPS. I hadn't forgotten that today was our wedding anniversary, but I didn't know whether to say anything or not. It's weird, isn't it? With the divorce going through and everything. Still, I've acknowledged it now and I'm so glad you are still a part of my life.

CHAPTER 2

Sam's bottom, Irene's second-best bra and a sombrero.

A few weeks later the gentle warmth of Spring was turning into a bright early summer, and Irene was trying out sandals for the first time in months. She'd decided not to rush headlong into bearing her toes so was still wearing her black winter tights as well, and it seemed to be working. Her toes were nice and warm.

It was early on Wednesday morning and she stood by The Cookery's old wooden counter and squinted. It had been a long time since she'd seen a man without his clothes on so she took her time, even though she had plenty to do. They opened for business in an hour and she had the new waitress to break in today, but she could do with the distraction from another low-level headache - so, she wasn't in a hurry.

She was awoken from her perusal by Anna charging down the stairs from her flat above, "Has the fat chicken gone off yet?"

"If you mean that plastic timer thing, not yet."

"Thank goodness. I had to change my trousers. Why I decided to wear white when I was making beetroot pies this morning, I don't know. I looked like a serial killer by the time I'd finished." She was now wearing purple and yellow tie-died loon pants and a shimmering silver Abba t-shirt under her raspberry kimono. She'd put her copper hair in tight pig tails and looked not unlike a child who had raided the back of her mum's wardrobe, but as always with Anna, it all suited her. "Have you been looking at Sam ever since I went upstairs?"

Irene adjusted her second-best bra, which didn't hold the tablets she liked to tuck away there as well as her best one, "Why not? He's only the seventh man I've ever seen naked." Irene quickly ran through the list in her head, "Hang on, no, there were eight. I forgot the farmer with the big tractor."

"Irene! How did you get to see him naked?"

"He had trousers held up by string. I had to buy him a belt in the end. Anyway, I'm a bit surprised by the size of this one."

"It's life-sized," Anna said, as she picked up the large, framed canvas and leant it against the door to her flat.

"I would think it is," Irene sniffed. "Why have we got a huge painting of him again?"

"Ralph painted it to go in their new flat above the restaurant, Sam has no idea. He took a sneaky photo of him one morning while he was looking out the window and painted it on the quiet. It's going to be a surprise."

"It'll certainly be a surprise to walk into your new flat and find your bare bottom on the wall above the telly," Irene said, tucking her glasses safely next to her tablets in her bra.

"If you didn't know Sam, would you know it was him?"

"Eh? Come again?"

"I mean, if you didn't know the painting was of Sam, would you be able to tell who it was?"

Irene peered at the painting again, "I shouldn't think so, I've never seen his bottom out of his trousers. How would I know it was Sam's bottom?"

Anna pointed, "From the face, Irene."

"Oh yes, that. But he's turned sideways looking out the window. All I can see is a tiny bit of his cheek and an ear. It could be anyone with long legs and a nice bum," she smoothed her dyed-black bobbed hair and headed around the old haberdasher's counter to the kitchen, where a timer in the shape of a plump chicken was tinkling on the worktop. She silenced it, then put on oven gloves to retrieve the contents of the oven.

Anna examined the painting, "I know, but if you look closely in the window there's a reflection of one of his green eyes. I'm not sure that's enough to identify him though, which is a help when it goes into the competition."

Irene poked a hot golden domed scone with a bony finger, "What competition?"

"Well, you know there's an annual painting competition at the Rye Art Gallery?"

"The one they do every year?"

"Yes, that'll be the *annual* bit."

"The one where you give away a free lunch to one of

the winners?"

"Yes, this year they get afternoon tea for two at The Copper Kettle."

Irene thought it was a waste of money giving things away for nothing, but apparently it was called marketing these days, "The dirty woman with cheese in her hair won it last year, didn't she?"

"It wasn't cheese it was.... well, whatever it was, artists don't worry about things like food in their hair. The thing is, I don't want Ralph to know, but I'm going to enter his painting in this year's competition. I'm dropping it into the gallery at lunch time. He thinks it's packed away safely upstairs where Sam won't see it."

Irene pointed her oven glove at Anna, "You'll get yourself in trouble. Sam hates being a celebrity and there he'll be, all exposed to the world."

"But you said you wouldn't know it was him."

Irene handed Anna the oven gloves, "The pies need coming out as well or they'll be like bullets. What's the prize if he wins?"

"The winning artist gets to paint the portrait of a celebrity."

"Who's that then?"

Anna started to take a tray of pies out of the other oven, "They haven't said yet."

"I bet it's that little fat fella who does the stars in all the papers. He'll do anything. I expect he'd like a free picture of himself."

"Ralph is always saying how he'd like to spend more time painting, but he finds excuses not to. I thought this might help him gain more confidence."

Irene waved a paper napkin at the painting of Sam, "Come on, take that thing away, we don't want everyone gawping at him in the nuddy. I'll put the pies on the rack, even though they look like they're bleeding."

Anna started to wrap the painting back in its large sheet of bubble wrap, "They're beetroot and mint. They've dribbled a bit."

"I'd dribble if you forced me to eat them."

"They are very popular with the vegetarians."

"So's tofu, but I'd rather lag my pipes with it than eat it. What time's the new girl due?"

"Girl? She's in her sixties, Irene."

"She might well be, but she's still the new girl."

"We'll get used to her. I'll miss Rosie though."

Irene massaged her temples and leant against the counter, "It was getting hard to keep up with her. First, she was a kind of black and white alien, then she became a hippy with plastic daisies in her hair. Where is she now?"

"Slovakia or Slovenia - are they the same country?"

"No idea, I don't think they'd been invented when I did geography."

"Pass me the sticky tape, will you."

Irene went round the counter to help Anna, "Here, let me do the sticking, last time you used this tape we had to cut a chunk out of your hair. I still don't understand why Rosie's gone there."

"She became a rock-chick. You saw her; lots of dirty

denim and leathery skirts. Apparently, she was a good drummer, learned it in her dad's shed when she was a kid. They bought her drums to help her work through her anger issues," Anna opened the door to her flat and dragged the painting up the stairs.

Irene called after Anna, "In my day kids didn't have anger issues; they were just miserable for a while and when they got fed up with that, they got themselves a paper round. I told her mum that, but she didn't want her handling the Daily Mail. What's Rosie doing in Slowveinika anyway?"

Anna came back into the café and put on her Magic Roundabout apron, "Well, she met some people who had a band. They needed a drummer, she showed them what she could do and, bang, she's an overnight rock-chick. They're on a tour of eastern European universities or something. That's why we've got two new waitresses; one up the road and I thought we should have one here too."

"Hmm, we'll see."

Anna was starting to prepare her Mediterranean couscous when the door of The Cookery burst open with a loud, "Cooey! New waitress reporting for duty, bright and early."

In the doorway stood a woman in her mid-sixties with a hearty face, hearty hips and an uninhibited laugh. Her hair was pure white, matching her white blouse, which rippled with yards of cream lace. Beneath that she wore a long black skirt that skimmed the top of a pair of chunky silver flip flops. "Not too early, am I?"

Irene eyed the cupcake-shaped clock on the wall to the right of the pith helmet and sniffed, "No, about right. Shut the door or the world and his lady friend will think we're open."

"Hello, Janet," Anna said. "Two ticks and I'll be with you."

Janet settled herself into a chair near the counter, "Don't mind me, mustn't stop the workers. Something smells yummy. We all love your pies, Anna. We've been here a couple of times me and the gang – my sister, Judy and our friends - ladies who lunch, you know. Causing chaos, I expect," and she let out a burst of raucous laughter. "You must be Iris. I'm Janet, but everybody calls me Jan."

"Not here they won't," Irene said, slamming the drawer of napkins.

"Beg pardon?"

Irene straightened her Dogs of James Herriot apron before answering, "You'll be Janet here."

"Oh, why's that?"

"We don't want anyone getting confused, do we? I mean we serve a lot of jam with scones and things. I can't be doing with someone shouting for jam and you come charging out at them. Or someone else asking for Jan and me wasting my time ferreting about for a pot of strawberry jam. So, it'll have to be Janet."

Janet looked momentarily lost for words, then started hooting with laughter again, "Oh, I can see we're going to get on like a house on fire. You're so funny, Iris!"

Anna took one look at Irene's face and quickly stepped away from her couscous, "This is Irene, not Iris. The Cookery wouldn't be able to survive without her, so she's in charge. She'll be showing you the ropes today.

Just follow her, Jan... I mean Janet."

"Of course, don't worry about me. I'm pretty quick at picking up new things."

Irene banged a cutlery basket on the table, "Well, pick up this lot and put them in the right holes." She indicated the myriad of different sized drawers in the old mahogany counter behind her.

Anna smiled at Janet, as Irene went to check the tables for crumbs, "Would you like me to show you where everything goes?"

"No, no, leave it to me. Did you know that my friend Pat is starting work next door at The Bookery? And Susan is going to be your new waitress at The Copper Kettle, isn't she?"

"Yes," Anna said. "I love that you all know each other."

"Well, it's thanks to my sister, Judy, of course. She's done marvels running Let's Screw while that gorgeous chap, Joe, is away. What she doesn't know about gardening and tiling is nobody's business. I said I'd love a little job to get me out of the house and Pat said the same, then Susan said she quite fancied it too. Oh, it was so funny," her laugh was suitably loud to show just how funny it had been. "Well, that was it, twenty minutes later Judy was running up and down the shops with a clipboard full of our names and numbers for you all. Once she gets a bee in her bonnet, there's no stopping her."

"Any news from the insurers, yet, about the fire damage?" Irene called from the front of the shop, attempting to stem the flow of Janet's chatter.

"Oh, yes, the carpet fitters come tomorrow."

Janet's hearty face attempted a look of serious concern, "I heard about the fire at The Copper Kettle. Do they have any clues as to who did it?"

Anna shook her head, "Nothing, not a single suspect or anything. It's a mystery."

Irene stalked into the kitchen, "It's a mystery to me how those knives and forks haven't found their way into a drawer yet."

"Oh, she's hilarious, isn't she? I have a feeling we are going to be a lovely team!"

* * *

A short distance away at the top of Lion Street, Martin was sitting at a linen covered table in the window of The Copper Kettle tearooms. He sighed as he sipped his third espresso of the morning and re-read the email he'd just written:

To: CountessG@fortnum.org

From: MartinRyeCook@zway.com

Wednesday 4th May

Grace,

Thank you for your letter via the solicitors. I will continue to reply directly to you as you are the one actually asking the questions.

Firstly, I have no opinion on your use of your title once the divorce is complete. Do what you wish. Secondly, no, I do not want any of the vases. Thirdly, you cannot have the Le Creuset pan back, I don't care if it was part of a set. And before you ask, the parrot never liked me, so he is all yours.

To answer your final question, the sooner this is all over the sooner we can move on, so my preferred date for finalising the divorce was yesterday.

I have one request. Could I please have access to the house to collect my belongings? As you know, I left with the contents of two bin bags only and, although they have served me well, I am ready for a change of clothes. I cannot imagine size eleven shoes and 34-inch waist trousers will be of any real use to you.

We were friends once. Great friends. I am sorry this is no longer the case.

Martin

His hand slowly moved the cursor over the send button, then with a swift motion he clicked, the email vanished and he slammed the laptop shut.

"Did you hear what I said?" Fiona asked, as she came through from the kitchen at the back of the tearooms.

Martin looked at her absently, "Hm? Sorry, old thing, I was contemplating the latest toing and froing with she who would like to be obeyed."

Fiona smiled as she sat in the chair beside him, cradling a steaming mug of tea in her hands, "Still no movement? Is it your wife – Grace, isn't it? - or the solicitor holding things up?"

Martin shrugged, "Both, probably. They seem to want every tiny detail sorted, in case she can screw a few more pennies from me. I shall have to sell the private yacht soon to make ends meet."

She laughed, "Where's it moored?"

"Behind the bus station, next to the bins. Still, I get seasick, so it's no loss."

"Is money a real problem?"

"No, dear thing, don't you worry. It's less about the money than my things. I would just like a decent pair of socks and my pyjamas. I don't ask much from the world."

"She can't deny you access to get things like that, surely?"

Martin chortled as he drained his coffee, "Oh, you haven't met the Countess Grace. The moment she threw me out, in her mind that house and everything in it became hers to do with as she wished. I'm not even sure my clothes and belongings are still in there."

"I'm sorry, but it all seems very unfair. You need them back and she shouldn't be stopping you. I mean, I let Andy take what he wanted from our house. He only took the expensive stuff, of course, but at least it got him out of my hair."

"You were very good to let him have anything in the circumstances. I still haven't ruled out the idea of your soon to be ex-husband having a hand in setting fire to this place on Mother's Day."

"Oh, I hope not," Fiona said, gripping her mug more tightly. "He'll get his share of the money from the house sale soon and then he's off to start a new life in Spain. I've tried to be as fair as I can. Why would he jeopardise it all by setting fire to The Copper Kettle?"

Martin sighed, "Men's egos are extraordinary things, dear lady. Your husband's took quite a bruising, didn't it? Your father left this place to you, but Andy had other more devious plans for it. You beat him fair and square when you sold it to Anna, which will be hard for him to swallow."

"I suppose you're right, but I don't regret anything we did."

Martin scratched his bushy eyebrows, "I am not saying you have done anything wrong. Far from it. I am merely pointing out that from his perspective he may have wanted to even the score a little before he heads off to the sunshine and dons his sombrero."

"I know, I know, but his crooked operation, as dodgy as it was, appeared to be far more sophisticated than pouring petrol through someone's letter box. Luckily, it seems to have been a one-off. So, it was probably some bored kids doing it for fun." Fiona stood and collected their coffee cups before moving into the kitchen.

Martin picked up the laptop and followed her, "Yes, you are probably right."

"How was your visit this weekend?"

Martin hesitated, "Ah, yes, I'd forgotten you were aware of that."

"I'm sorry, I don't mean to pry, but since my friend Claire told me she'd seen you at the nursing home, I've been concerned. That's all."

Martin nodded and reached for his long woollen coat, which hung on the back of the kitchen door, "And it is most kind of you."

Fiona watched him as he fiddled with the elastic

band that held his long grey hair at the nape of his neck. She looked at his hunched shoulders inside his old coat and wondered again how he had gone from being the Earl of Groombridge to sleeping amongst bin bags on the streets of Rye. She had really begun to care for Martin, he seemed so lost and yet tried his best to help everyone he could. He was a marvellous cook for The Copper Kettle, everything prepared with such care and precision. He'd even knitted her a neat black waistcoat for chillier days in the teashop that looked great with her traditional waitress ensemble.

"I don't know if I would be of any use to you," she said. "But if there is anything you ever want to talk about or anything I can do, then I am here. As your friend."

Martin coughed lightly, "How kind. Dear thing, you are exactly the sort of person that one needs as a friend, I can see that. But for now, things are somewhat complicated and... not easy to talk about. I have done many things in my life of which I am proud and many of which I am ashamed, and as a part of my recovery I am aware that I need to face them. Finally. May we leave it there, for now?"

Fiona laid a gentle hand on his arm, "Of course. But remember, we've all done things we wish we hadn't, but that doesn't make us bad people."

He looked into her eyes, "Have you killed a man? No, that would never even enter your head, because you are a good person. Now, if you will excuse me, there is a batch of miniature pork pies with our name on them down at The Cookery for our traditional ploughman's platters. I will return shortly." With that, he turned and left the kitchen, leaving Fiona in shocked silence.

CHAPTER 3

Gorgeous gorgonzola, roller-skating cats and proper friends.

The weather was mild for May, so, at the end of a busy day Ralph pulled on some shorts, slipped his bare feet into flipflops and dragged a sweatshirt over his head, his hair still damp from the shower. He'd spent a frantic day in The Bookery preparing for the next children's Beagle Book Club meeting, training his new assistant, Pat, and dealing with a whole host of bizarre queries about everything from TV newsreader memoirs to cookbooks that didn't include any mention of broccoli. Now he was looking forward to a quiet evening stroll around town with Stanley.

The little beagle dog waited on the landing eager to get going. Ralph grabbed a bottle of water and picked up the lead before starting down the stairs. He heard the front door open, "Only me," Sam called.

As he reached the hallway Sam smiled at him. An open, sweet smile, that lit his face and made his electric green eyes shine even brighter. It was a smile that took Ralph's breath away every time and made him say stupid things like, "Gorgeous."

"What is?" Sam said.

"What?"

"What's gorgeous?"

"Did I say gorgeous?"

"You did."

"Out loud?"

Sam laughed and leant his shoulder against the wall, "Yes, out loud. Were you thinking about me?"

Ralph could feel the blood rushing up his neck to his face, "No. You? Why would I...? Maybe."

"I love that you say what's in your head, but it's going to get you in trouble one day, when you say something you shouldn't to a customer."

"It's only with you. You fry my brain a little... in a good way. Right, I've embarrassed myself enough, I need to take Stanley out. I won't be long."

Sam pushed himself away from the wall and looked over his shoulder at the front door, "You are about to be ambushed, take care."

"Why? Who is it?"

"Anna, she's hanging around outside. I think she wants to go for a walk with you and Stan."

Ralph leant down and attached the lead to an impatient Stanley, "Is she alright?"

Sam shrugged as he opened the door for him, "Who knows with Anna?"

Anna bounced into view on the pavement, "There you are, I thought I'd come with you for a stroll, if that's

OK."

"Fine with me." Ralph turned to Sam, "See you later."

"Doesn't your *gorgeous* boyfriend get a kiss goodbye?"

"Gorgeous? I think you must have misheard; I'm pretty sure I said gorgonzola or gallbladder, something like that." He gave him a peck on the cheek and ducked out of the door as a laughing Sam slammed it behind him.

Anna pulled her yellow beret tightly over her curls as they set off up the High Street, "What was that about?"

"Nothing, me being an idiot as always. What's up?"

"Why should anything be up?"

"Well, you don't normally hover around outside to wait for me and Stan, that's all. Not that I mind."

"I'm on a keep fit thing. New knickers, all that."

"Oh, right. How was your day?"

"Fine, busy. Janet, the new waitress started today. She's lovely but seems to enjoy watching the customers rather than serving them. Oh, and she keeps calling Irene 'Iris'."

"Ouch, I bet that doesn't go down well."

"You can say that again. But it's early days, I'm sure she'll settle in. Didn't your lady start today? Pat, was it?"

"Yes, she's nice. She loves Stanley and wants me to call her Auntie Pat. She was good actually and bought six books, so if nothing else she's paid for some of her wages."

"Good, you need some help so you can do more painting."

Stanley had stopped at a particularly interesting lamppost, so they stood for a moment outside a charity shop with a window full of jigsaw puzzles, "I'd love to, but I won't have much time when the work gets going on the apartment. The builders start tomorrow, so I'll need to be over there a lot supervising them and sorting stuff out."

Anna clapped her hands together, her pink bat-wing jumper flapping like a flamingo contemplating flight, "It's so exciting, you and Sam getting your own place together. It's so romantic. Although I'm trying not to think about you not being my neighbour anymore and someone taking your place in the Rooftop Club."

Ralph hadn't thought about being replaced, "What? But we can still come up to the rooftop surely? I mean through your flat or Martin's?"

"Of course, but it won't be the same. I'm trying not to think about it. Let's talk about jigsaws or I might cry. Look that one's got cats on roller skates. I never knew they could do that."

Ralph looked in the shop window, "I think that might not be a real photo. The RSPCA probably have a rule about making cats roller skate for photos."

"That's good, because without helmets and padding it could really hurt them, even though they've got nine lives."

Ralph looked at his earnest little friend and shook his head, "Shall we move on?"

"Yes, those cats are upsetting me now."

"Come on, Stan, leave the post alone to enjoy it's evening. How's The Copper Kettle going?"

"Really good, Fiona told me it was ever so busy today. She is brilliant, you know. She got news that her son, George, has chosen to spend the Easter holidays with his criminal father, but she said it was what the boy wanted, so she couldn't complain. She was gutted though, I could tell."

"I would think she'd be worried that he'd pick up more bad habits from Andy. He was a proper little thug when he played for the Rye Rovers."

"Apparently, a term at boarding school has done him the world of good, thanks to Dew Drop Dobson's legacy. Rules and a strict timetable seem to have been exactly what he needed. How's the football team doing anyway? Won any matches?"

"Not since they formed the new club," Ralph said, pulling Stanley away from a sticky looking dustbin. "Come on, Stan."

"New club? I haven't heard about this."

"We must have told you about it. We've been talking about it on the rooftop for weeks."

"Nope, it's news to me. Mind you, now I'm in need of new undies I've been out doing my evening exercise, so I probably missed it."

"That's true. A little bird told me you'd been spotted walking with Dawa Singh a few times. Anything you'd care to share?"

"Which little bird? Oh, well, it doesn't matter, there's nothing going on. He's just a lovely man. So interesting. It's nice to have a proper male friend."

"Oh, thanks. What does that make me? Not interesting, not a proper friend or not a proper male?"

Anna linked her arm through his, "Don't be silly, you know what I mean. He's a gentleman, he's funny, interesting – did I say that, already? - and he has such a deep voice it makes my chest vibrate when he talks. I have to wear a sports bra now – although that's mostly because he has long legs and I sort of gallop along beside him."

"Sounds like there's romance in the air."

"No, not at all, and that's what's nice about it. He is so not available or right for me; he's a man of the world, sophisticated and very deep. I mean properly deep, he thinks about all sorts of things like... like the eco system. And social history, graves and plagues and... and the industrial revolution. I managed to throw in the Spinning Jenny the other night from history class at school. After that I just had to listen. He's brilliant, but it's just a friendship and it's nice."

Ralph gave Anna's hand a squeeze, "Well, good for you. It sounds like a very grown-up friendship. I'm proud of you; you might actually be starting to move out of puberty."

She giggled and put Ralph's hand firmly on her chest, "Oh, I hope so, these tits really don't need to get any bigger, do they? Sorry, I said tits... there I go again, can't stop myself. Maybe I'm not fully grown-up yet."

Ralph pulled away from her, laughing, "No, maybe you're not."

Anna skipped ahead and turned to face him walking backwards, "Tell me about the Rye Rovers, then. Have you sold the best players or something?"

"Well, you remember the council were making us

pay for the use of the pitch, so we had the fundraising fair? Well, they did the dirty on us and sold the land to property developers for flats. But the good news is that up the road the Winchelsea Wanderers were about to close down. Watch out, there's a..."

"Ouch!" Anna yelped as her bottom hit a metal dustbin. She turned her back to Ralph, "Is there a dent?"

"No, it's quite strong metal."

"Not the bin, idiot, my bum."

"How would I know? And leave your trousers up, please. Where was I? Oh yes, the team in Winchelsea had a pitch but no one to play on it, as their under-tens were down to three players. So, we've combined the two teams as the Rye and Winchelsea Rovers. They have a great pitch, with its own little club house. The guy who ran the team is really keen and has way more time than me, so my services are no longer required."

"Oh, they'll miss you."

"To be honest, it's a relief. I didn't have the time, with the shop and the apartment."

"But all those lovely children, Jillybean and Elliot, won't you miss them?"

"Most of them belong to the Beagle Book Club so I still see them in the shop. Some are getting too old now, like Joanne Ringrose. She's playing for an under-fourteen's team and is less keen on heading the ball in case it spoils her hair."

The town was beginning to get dark and the streetlights cast a warm yellow glow on the cobbles ahead of them. In the dim light a small black-clad figure caught Stanley's attention and he growled a warning.

They took no notice until they drew closer and could see what looked like smoke starting to seep out from under the door of Ethel Loves Me, the local arts and crafts shop. The shadowy figure appeared to be pouring or pushing something through the letterbox.

"It's a fire," Anna yelled. "They're setting Ethel's place on fire."

Her cries alerted the dark figure who took off down the hill with a loping run. Ralph grabbed Stanley's collar and unclipped the lead, "Chase, Stanley. Find them, boy."

The small beagle didn't need telling twice and set off after the would-be arsonist. Ralph hurried after Anna who was already at the door of the shop.

"We need to put it out. Look, it's starting to spread," she said, peering through the glass panels of the door.

"Wait a minute," Ralph said and took the bottle of water from his pocket. He pulled up the cap and pushed the end of it through the letterbox, squeezing the water out in a long stream onto the fire. Luckily, it was enough to dampen the beginnings of what could have been a much bigger blaze.

"You've done it," Anna shouted, clapping him on the back. "And here's Stanley."

Ralphed turned as Stanley trotted round the corner, his tail wagging, pink tongue hanging out of the corner of his mouth and ears bouncing, "Where are they, Stan? You were supposed to savage them and bring them to the ground."

"Can you really see Stanley doing that? I know he went for that knife wielding thug who attacked you and

Sam, but he thought you were in danger then."

"Never mind, Stan," Ralph said, stroking his soft head. "I'd better call the police, I suppose, and the fire brigade in case it's not quite out."

"Yes, good idea," Anna said. Ralph took his phone and dialled 999, as a large familiar figure appeared round the corner behind them.

Anna waved, "Dawa, thank goodness, we could do with some protection in case it all turns nasty."

"If what turns nasty?" Dawa said, his deep voice making Anna feel calmer already.

"Someone was trying to set fire to this shop. Ralph's on the phone to 999. Stanley chased him off, but they could come back."

Dawa looked up and down the street, "Which way did they go?"

Anna pointed down the hill, "Along East Cliff towards the town gate. They were small and dressed in black."

Dawa strode off along the route the arsonist had taken. He looked so big with his long legs and neat blue turban adding to his height, nobody would mess with him, she thought. After a few minutes he returned shaking his head, "No sign of anyone. Are you alright?"

"Just a bit shaken, I think. It could be the same person who set fire to The Copper Kettle. Do you reckon?"

"Possibly, but why would anyone do such a thing?"

"Hi, Dawa," Ralph said, ending his call. "Police and fire brigade are on their way."

"Did they say how long they would be?" Anna asked.

"Not really, but as the fire is probably out it's not top

priority."

She started to hop from one foot to the other, "Damn, I could really do with a wee. All the adrenalin, I expect, and that bump on the bum. Not to mention you feeling my tits."

Dawa's dark eyebrows shot up towards his turban.

"Wait, wait," Ralph said. "I did not... Dawa, she was..."

Dawa frowned, "Ralph, perhaps we should allow the police to settle this matter. If Anna wishes to make a formal complaint..."

Ralph's face turned red in the evening light, "But you don't understand..."

Dawa scratched his beard with care, "Ralph, I would advise you not to speak until you have a lawyer present."

Anna began to giggle, "Your face, Ralph! Honestly, don't you know Dawa's sense of humour yet?"

Ralph sighed, "Not as well as you, obviously."

Dawa smiled, "Sorry, Ralph, I couldn't resist it."

"Hm, it's fine. I suppose I'm still a bit wary of you, knowing how easily you can pick me up by the trousers."

"That was ages ago," Dawa said, shaking his head. "It's all forgiven and forgotten."

"Sure," Ralph said, who wasn't sure he'd ever forget it. "Why don't you guys head off, then Anna can have a wee. I'll wait for the police and fire brigade. I don't suppose you saw anything I didn't."

"No, just someone in black," Anna said, already starting back up the street. "They had black plimsoles, like the ones I wore to be a burglar. He was small, like a child... oh, perhaps it was a child?"

"Possibly, he certainly wasn't very tall."

"He had something in his hand, too, it might have been a paper bag or something."

"Really? I didn't notice that. I can tell the police though. Go on, off you go."

"Thank you," Anna said, picking up speed. "Come on, Dawa, we can nip into The George and have a drink and I can use the toilet, if you want?"

"Excellent, idea. Are you sure you'll be OK, Ralph?"

"Yes, I've got Stanley. When he's finished having words with that parking meter, he'll be on full alert for danger."

Dawa nodded seriously, "I'm sure he will. I hope you don't have to wait too long." He gave Ralph a brief bow and set off after Anna, who was scurrying up the High Street ahead of him.

"Enjoy your drink," Ralph shouted after them. "As friends," he added quietly.

CHAPTER 4

The history expert, a cupboard for wigs and a mystery begins.

Anna settled into the seat next to Dawa, "That's better, all sorted now. Thanks for the drink."

They were tucked into a corner of the Dragon Bar of The George Hotel, the refurbished sixteenth century coaching inn at the centre of the High Street. Only recently re-opened, it was welcoming locals and well-heeled tourists to its mix of old antiques and light modern décor.

"I haven't been here since they did it up," Dawa said, looking around. "It's good to scout out the competition for Cinque."

"It's supposed to be really nice, expensive though. They do weddings as well, apparently. Not that will be of interest to us confirmed bachelors slash spinsters."

"Why not? Dawa asked, innocently.

Anna felt a hot flush shoot to her cheeks, "Oh, well, I wasn't saying... I mean, you're not... and I'm not... it was just a comment."

Dawa grinned, "I'm teasing, Anna. Perhaps Ralph

isn't the only one who hasn't quite got the hang of my sense of humour yet. Sorry."

Anna breathed a sigh of relief, "No, maybe not. So, Mr History Expert, I bet you don't know anything about The George, do you?"

"Well, as a matter of fact, I know that three King Georges visited here, the ballroom was added in the eighteen hundreds for farmers to meet in town, and that little cupboard over there was used for people to put their wigs in, so they didn't get spoiled while they were drinking."

Anna sat open mouthed, "Is that all true?"

"Yes."

"Even the wig bit?"

"Yes."

"Blimey, you are so clever. How do you know all this stuff?"

"I read it on their website while you were in the toilet," Dawa said and hid his smile behind a sip of his coffee.

"You cheater," she laughed, picking up her glass of red wine. "But apart from that, you do know such a lot about history. How come?"

Dawa sat back in his chair and stretched out his long legs, "While I was born in this country, my parents were not. It always surprised me that they had so little interest in the history of their adopted home. They believed everything in the Punjab was far superior; the traditions, the food, the people, the clothes. I couldn't understand why they had come halfway around the world if what they had left behind was so much better. Anyway, I wanted to know what all these beautiful buildings were about and how things came to be. For instance, I was fascinated that the railways started here..."

Anna clicked her fingers, "Oh, yes, I know this one; Robert Louis Stevenson."

Dawa looked very serious as he tried not to smile, "Almost, I think he actually wrote Treasure Island. It was Robert Stephenson who invented the first steam locomotive."

"Well, you have to give me half a point, I was very close."

"You definitely deserve a point," he said. "It was almost right. Anyway, that's where it started, trying to learn about my country. The Punjab seemed so far away and alien, but England had everything I wanted and I needed to know more about it. It's probably a bit boring for someone as exciting as you, but I enjoy it."

"Exciting? Me? I don't think so. The most exciting thing I did today was chop beetroots while wearing white trousers. I wouldn't recommend it."

"I think you underestimate quite how interesting you are, Anna."

She tucked a curl of hair behind her ear, "Really? Are you joking again?"

"Not this time."

"Well, I'll drink to that. Two interesting people having a drink and talking about Stephenson's train and wigs in cupboards. People don't know what they're missing."

Dawa held up his coffee cup and she chinked her glass against it, "Cheers," he said and couldn't help but smile. He'd been doing that a lot lately, he thought. He found Anna charming and enjoyed every conversation they had together, she was so alive and full of life. He had not had many friends in recent years, since Sam's father Damien had been killed, and she was a breath of fresh air in what he realised had become something of a stale life.

"And thanks for rescuing me tonight," Anna said. "I can't believe they tried again. It proves setting fire to The Copper Kettle wasn't a one-off."

"We don't know if it's the same person, do we?"

"Well, it's a big coincidence if it's not. Two shops torched just a few weeks apart?"

"Yes, I suppose so. The police will be able to tell if it's the same sort of stuff used to start the fire, then we'll know."

Anna suddenly sat forward, "I've just remembered, Psychic Sue said I'd see more fire this year. She was right after all."

"Sue from the clothes shop?"

"Yes, it's called The Small Medium at Large. I get a lot of my things from there."

"I'm a little sceptical of psychic predictions. I mean, you were more than likely to see several fires this year, maybe a barbecue or in the fireplace here or another pub, for instance."

"That's true, but it's spooky, isn't it? I have a funny feeling about it, my feet are itching and that usually means something's up."

They sipped their drinks and Anna watched a couple across the bar start their second round of margaritas, "You see those two over there, by the wig cupboard?"

Dawa glanced across, "Yes."

"It'll never last."

"Really? How can you tell?"

"It's obvious, he's too handsome. He's not a keeper, but for now she's enjoying him. She'll see the light and move on soon."

"That's a little harsh, poor chap."

"Nah, he'll survive."

Dawa sneaked another glance at the young couple, "You seem like an expert on such matters."

"Not really. Although, I have had a fair amount of experience of blokes who are definitely not keepers. It's much easier to sort out other people's love lives than your own, don't you think?"

"Not my area of expertise, I'm afraid," he said, after a final sip of coffee. "So, any more news from Ralph about the fire?"

"Let me check. Yes, there's a new text from him. Ethel's arrived to open the shop. Only a lightly charred door mat, thank goodness. The police are there and are going to check CCTV apparently, but he was all wrapped up in black, so I doubt that'll do much good."

"It's very strange. Why would anyone want to burn down small businesses in a town like this?"

"No idea, but it gives me the creeps, knowing that a madman is running around town doing this."

"Well, I can walk you home when you've finished

your drink. I wouldn't want you coming face to face with him."

"Oh, that would be lovely, thanks. I would feel safer."

They sat in comfortable silence for a little while, enjoying their drinks.

"It's been a lovely spring, hasn't it?" Dawa said, after a while, regretting immediately how boring he sounded.

Anna, however, showed no sign of boredom, "Yes, I love the spring; I think it's my favourite season. Although I like winter, because it's got Christmas in it, and I love Christmas so much. Do you love Christmas? Oh Christ, I mean, oh Buddha, oh bugger, sorry. Do you do Christmas? Sikhs, I mean?"

Dawa chuckled, "I'm not offended, Anna. For a lot of western Sikhs Christmas is a happy time. We celebrate like everyone, not for religious reasons, but because it's fun. For other Sikhs Christmas is a more sombre time. For instance, on the 26th December, your Boxing Day, the younger sons of one of the Sikh gurus, aged seven and five, were bricked up alive for refusing to embrace Islam and give up their faith."

"No? That's awful."

"It gets worse. Hearing the news of their death, their grandmother, who had been kept imprisoned in a cold tower, embraced martyrdom and breathed her last, I think."

"You think? You don't know if Granny died too? Oh, Dawa, how can you know so much about British history and the black death and old Stephenson and not know the end of the story?"

He ran his fingers through his beard, "It's all a bit hazy

to be honest. I'm not a practising Sikh. I never really have been, so I've forgotten some of the stories."

"But you still wear your turban."

"I do, more as a sign of respect for my community than anything else. It's also habit, I suppose. I have always worn it. For some it's a spiritual practice, but I see it as simply preparing for whatever the day may bring. Especially when I was in the personal protection business, it felt like a piece of armour."

Anna stared at his immaculate blue turban, "It must be very thick. I mean, if someone conked you on the head it'd certainly cushion the blow."

Dawa smiled at her, "Were you planning on trying it?"

"No, I probably wouldn't be able to reach up there, you're ever so tall."

"Good, because I meant it as more of a metaphorical piece of armour."

"Anyway, it looks lovely, and I'm always impressed that you match it to the colour of your suit. Like tonight, how do you get the blue to be the same?"

"I have an excellent tailor. My suits are my one luxury in life, because of my size I prefer to get them made specially for me."

"Wow, that's amazing. Well, they are very beautiful. Imagine what your tailor would think if he saw me and my outfits," she laughed.

"He would probably tell me I should try something more adventurous, like you. My clothes are very boring."

"Boring? Beautiful, I'd call them. Immaculate, that's how I'd describe you. I couldn't imagine you being adventurous with clothes, it wouldn't be right." She pulled her hat out of her pocket and jammed it over her hair, "No, I can't see you in a yellow beret, like this one. I'd stick to your turbans, if I were you. Shall we make a move? I feel a bit guilty we've left Ralph to deal with everything while we are all cosy in here."

Dawa pushed his chair back and moved round to Anna's side of the table, "Good idea. Allow me," and he pulled the chair back behind her as she stood.

"You really do have the manners of a knight in shining armour, don't you?"

"I hope it doesn't offend you. I know some modern women feel it is a little patronising," he said, worry in his eyes.

"Blimey, no. You patronise away; move chairs, open doors, throw your cloak in puddles. The men I've known in my life barely wash, let alone treat a lady properly."

As they strolled back down the High Street, the road ahead seemed to be quiet and devoid of activity. Anna felt slightly disappointed, "Looks like all the fun is over. They weren't here long were they, the police and fire people?"

"I imagine there wasn't much to interest them, as so little harm was done."

They found the shop dark and quiet, as if nothing had happened, just a little smudge of soot above the letterbox betraying the earlier excitement.

Anna looked around, "Still, there must be some investigating to do. Would you like to investigate a little bit?"

"What did you have in mind?"

Anna led Dawa down the path the arsonist used to escape, "Well, he came down here. If he didn't leave any clues there's not a lot the police can do, I suppose, but it's worth a look."

"I would agree. I expect the police will increase patrols around the centre of town for a few days, which may put whoever it is off for a while. I can ask my neighbour, Phil, he's a police sergeant."

"Ouch, hang on. Something in my shoe," Anna hopped across the path and slumped on to a bench tucked against the flint wall that ran beside them down to the imposing town gateway. She removed her yellow plimsole, shaking it in the air, causing the pink silk flower sewn to the front to flap around like a butterfly.

"They are very colourful shoes," Dawa said, sitting patiently beside her. "May I?" he held out his hand to take it from her.

"You really are a proper gentleman, Dawa."

"I try my best," he felt himself blush, grateful that his beard covered a large proportion of his face. He felt around inside the shoe and flicked out a small pebble, "There, that should be better."

"Brilliant, thank you," Anna said, dropping the shoe in front of her and bending to stretch it around her heel. "Hang on, what's this?" She reached under the bench and pulled out a pale cone of paper, "It's what the arsonist had in his hand; I remember seeing it. I'm sure this is it. He was taking something from it and stuffing it onto the fire through the letterbox."

"Tearing up the paper to feed the fire, you mean?"

"No, something inside it, I think. It was all so quick." She peeled back the paper to reveal the dried silver green fronds of a plant, "It's weeds or something, all dried up. How strange."

"That's very odd. It has a very distinctive smell. Not unlike marijuana, but it doesn't look like it."

Anna grinned at Dawa, "Are there things in your youth you want to tell me about?"

"Far too many things, but not involving drugs I'm pleased to say."

"Now that sounds interesting, tell me more."

"Tales for another time, perhaps."

"Not you as well? That's what Martin always says. He teases us that he's stolen things and been a cat burglar, all sorts, then says he'll tell us more another time."

"A mystery always makes things more interesting, doesn't it?" he said, winking at her. "Anyway, we have a mystery right here to solve. What is this plant and why was the arsonist putting it on the fire they'd just started?"

CHAPTER 5

Intravenous tea, a grubby grey hat and artemisia vulgaris.

As Thursday dawned, Ralph and Sam were up, showered, breakfasted and waiting at Cinque bright and early. Stanley was sulking behind the bar, pretending to get some more sleep.

Ralph sat on one of the window ledges of the empty floor above the restaurant, and looked around the large bare space, "I can't believe it's actually happening. This is going to be our new home. It all seems so quick; I mean I was expecting all the plans and permissions to take months."

Sam was nervously pacing the old wooden floor, "Don't forget I got them when I bought this building as a rundown warehouse and started the restaurant. I concentrated on the business downstairs and never got as far as up here. So, it was just a case of checking in with the planning department and getting the architect's plans drawn up. Easy."

"Even though it's just a derelict space at the moment, we've talked about it so much I can see every room and where all the furniture will go."

"Me too. We're going to need some art for the walls, so you'd better get your brushes out."

"I'm sure we can find some proper paintings," Ralph said, looking out of the window.

"No, no, we're not having that. You always turn away and look out of a window when you find something difficult. It's the equivalent of what you used to accuse me of doing, hiding under the peak of my cap, and we know what happened to that, don't we?"

Ralph laughed at the memory, "I threw it off the rooftop."

"You did indeed. You still owe me fifteen quid for it by the way. Anyway, we must have something of yours on the walls."

"Maybe," Ralph said, looking away again as he pictured the painting of Sam safely hidden away in Anna's flat. He'd love Sam to like it, but he really wasn't sure it was good enough. He'd have to take another look at it, before he decided what to do. Putting paint onto canvas and creating a piece of art was one of the most exciting things he had ever experienced, but it was also terrifying. He felt completely exposed even when the subject, in this case Sam, was way more exposed than him.

"What time is it?" Sam asked. "Chaz said he'd be here at about eight."

Ralph checked his watch, "It's five to. How come he's starting on a Thursday, anyway?"

"He'd finished work on another building, so I managed to nab him to get going here quickly.

Normally, he'd give everyone a few days off, but he says he's got a new lad working for him, so he can get him started on the basic stuff, while the rest of his team start on Monday."

"I still haven't met Chaz," Ralph said.

"I know, but he's brilliant, you'll see. He did a great job on converting downstairs into the restaurant, so it seemed like a no-brainer to get him to do the apartment." Sam watched Ralph sitting in the early morning light and his heart felt full. This was going to be their home and he couldn't wait. He moved closer and put his arms around him, "It's going to be amazing. Our own place together. How do you feel?"

Ralph thought for a moment. It had all been such a whirlwind; Sam suggesting they convert the space into a home for them, then selling his house to raise the money for the works and moving into the flat above The Bookery. Then spending hours with the architect and pouring over plans to design the airy New York loft-style apartment of their dreams. He hadn't had much time to think how he felt about actually setting up home with Sam, but when he did it seemed like the most natural thing in the world.

"I feel like everything is fitting into place," he said. "You. Me. Here. The future. After everything we've been through since last year, we deserve this. I'm looking forward to it all being done and settling down to a normal life."

Sam laughed, "Normal? In Rye? I'm not sure that's possible, but I'm willing to give it a go."

As Ralph's watch ticked on to almost exactly eight o'clock, there was a loud knock on the restaurant door downstairs. Sam leaped down the stairs and Ralph could hear him welcoming people. Footsteps started back up the stairs and Sam appeared first. Behind him was a small man, at least half the height of Sam, but broad and burnt bronze by years of working outdoors.

"Chaz, this is Ralph. Ralph meet Chaz."

Ralph hopped off the window ledge and shook hands with Chaz, feeling the reassuringly strong, calloused hands of a man who built things for a living.

"Alright, mate," Chaz said. "Got yourself a beauty here - and I don't just mean Sammy-boy." He wheezed a little laugh at his own joke, "Bootiful room this, gonna be a cracking place to live. I'm gonna enjoy this one."

"I know, we're really excited," Ralph said. "So, how long do you think it'll take?"

Chaz sucked in his breath in the time-honoured tradition of all builders when asked their opinion on how long or how much things would be, "Well, now you're asking, Ralph. I've told Sammy-boy, that it might take ten to twelve weeks, but we're gonna give it a go for eight to ten. Gotta work round the restaurant, I know that. So, we'll crack-on early every day, knock off or do quiet stuff over lunch and be gone by tea time. Don't wanna upset the punters, do we? Keep the tea flowing and we'll get it done in no time."

"Ah, yes, tea," Sam said. "Are you ready for one now?"

"Always ready, Sammy-boy. You know me, I'd have tea fed through a drip in my arm if I could."

"Great, I'll get some and Ralph can run over the plans one more time with you, to make sure everything's clear," Sam turned back to the stairs, only to be confronted by the new member of Chaz's work force. "Hi, sorry, I didn't introduce you. This is Ralph, my other half."

Ralph came over and held out his hand to a thin young man who was leaning against the wall beside the stairs, half turned away with a grey beanie hat pulled low over his face. "Hi, and what's your name?"

There was a pause.

"Speak up, Jack, tell him your name," Chaz snapped.

With Chaz having done his job for him, Jack simply stuffed his hands deeper into his sagging jeans and mumbled, "Alright?"

Chaz shook his head, "He's Jack and he's no talker. I'm doing his sister a favour, friend of my daughter she is. Moved away though, left this one here at a loose end. Don't worry, he's not as useless as he looks. Come on lad, look lively. Help Sam with the teas."

Sam smiled at the skinny lad, who seemed to have turned even further in on himself, "Do you know the tea order? What Chaz likes?"

Jack nodded, "Yeah."

"Good, follow me, we'll get them sorted," and he headed down the stairs again into the restaurant.

Ralph watched the young guy hesitate, pull the grubby hat down over his ears and slink after Sam without looking back. Although he hadn't seen his face properly, Ralph had a funny feeling he knew him from somewhere but couldn't place him. A few seconds later all hell seemed to break loose below them. Stanley barked ferociously, crockery crashed, Sam shouted, Jack yelled and came charging back up the stairs slamming the restaurant door behind him.

Chaz stared at him, "What the hell did you do?"

The young man bent over with his hands on his knees, "Nothin'."

"Did you kick the dog or something?"

Jack rubbed his thigh, "No, he just went for me." He slowly straightened up and looked fearfully at Ralph from under the edge of his hat.

"I'm so sorry," Ralph said. "I don't know what..." he halted as their eyes met for the first time and he felt a flash of recognition, but Jack had quickly turned away. He couldn't place where he'd seen them, but he had definitely seen those hollow eyes somewhere before.

* * *

Stanley would not be placated, so Ralph brought the little beagle back to The Bookery. Once they were on familiar territory Stanley seemed less anxious and allowed Ralph to settle him into his bed in the window display.

Ralph sat with him for a few minutes, stroking his soft, brown ears, "What got into you, Stan? I know that kid was odd, but this town is full of odd people and you've not gone psycho before. Mind you, you're generally a good judge of character and I had a strange feeling about him too..." His thoughts were interrupted by a familiar pounding of feet coming past the window accompanied by a whirl of mauve kimono silk. He stood up as Anna charged in through the door, "Morning, hot stuff," she called.

"Morning."

Anna stood beside him, her red dungarees and kimono clashing contentedly with her lemon-yellow 'Go To Work on an Egg' t-shirt, "What's the matter with Stanley? He looks upset."

Ralph looked down at him, "I know, he went a bit bonkers with one of the builders at Cinque. I had to bring him home."

"Really? That's not like him. But we have other things to deal with - arson, being the main one."

"Not another fire?"

"No, calm down Fireman Sam, we have a clue," her face was alight with excitement and with a flourish she produced the paper cone of dried leaves from behind her back. "Ta da!"

"What's that?"

"I found it last night, thrown away behind a bench near where the arsonist disappeared. I'm sure he was trying to stuff bits of it through the door on to the fire."

"What were you doing behind a bench at that end of town? You went off in the other direction."

"Can we stick to the point, please? And that point is, we finally have a clue."

"OK, but what does it mean?" Ralph took it from her and gave it a sniff.

"No, idea. I was going to take it in to see Judy next door. She has a new herb section and is very knowledgeable about all that sort of thing, so she may know what it is."

"Well, I can tell you that; it's a load of mugwort," he

said, rolling the dried leaves between his fingers.

She snatched the cone back from him, "There's no need to be rude. You can't dismiss it so easily; it might be important."

"No, the name of it is mugwort; it's a herb. Mum used to grow it in the garden. Hang on," he disappeared to the back of the shop and returned a moment later with a *Know your British Herbs* book. "Let's have a look."

"I didn't even know there was a herb called Hogwart, I thought she'd made it up for Harry Potter."

"Mugwort," Ralph sighed, running his finger down the index list at the back of the book.

"Oh, right. How do you know about this sort of thing anyway? Is it a gay thing?"

Ralph looked at her, "What? How can it be a gay thing?"

"I don't know. You all seem to smell nice, in my experience. I thought it could be a fragrance thing."

Ralph shook his head, "Anna, be quiet and listen. Mugwort or artemisia vulgaris. It says here, it's related to ragweed and used as a flavouring for food and herbal medicine."

"What does it do for you?"

"Apparently, it's supposed to boost energy. So, you don't need any of this stuff, we don't want you having any more energy."

"Rude. Read on, Macduff."

"It also calms nerves, helps digestion and relieves itching, among other things. Oh, wait, it says it can be burnt as incense or smoked to put you into a trance-like state. It can smell a bit like marijuana when burnt."

"Yes, he said it smelt like marijuana."

"Who said?"

"Eh? Dawa, we were investigating together. So, why put it on the fire in the shop? I mean there was no one there to put into a trance, unless they were trying to slow the fire brigade down."

Ralph returned the book to the shelf, "If you're sure the arsonist dropped it, you'd better take it along to the police."

Suddenly, Stanley leaped up from his bed, barked happily and started jumping up at the door.

"Stanley, calm down. What are you doing? It's Pat, you remember? She started work here yesterday. Stop it," he waved Pat in. "Sorry about that, he doesn't usually do all that jumping about. He's gone a bit mad this morning."

"That's alright. I have a feeling it might be my fault," Pat said, looking a little embarrassed, as she removed her sensible mac and took a pair of sensible shoes out of a carrier bag to change into. "In a quiet moment yesterday afternoon, when you had gone to the bank, I was trying to teach Stanley how to open doors. I started to teach my Terence to do it, but it was a thankless task. Being a chihuahua he was never really going to be big enough to open anything except the cat flap."

"I see, well, I suppose it's a useful skill. You've met, Anna, haven't you?"

"Yes, yes. Lovely scones."

Anna grinned, "Not a euphemism, I hope. Sorry. Look

I can't stop, I have to go up to The Copper Kettle to see your friend Susan. She starts as a waitress today."

Pat straightened the long grey plait that ran down the length of her spine, "She's so excited. We all are, thanks to Judy for suggesting us to you."

"I know, it seems to have worked well for everyone. I'd better be off."

"Don't forget to take that into the police station," Ralph called after her.

"Yes, yes," she said, as she waved through the window. "I need to have a think first," and she was gone.

CHAPTER 6

The Dalai Lama, clipboards and extraordinary waterworks.

"**C**an I hang your coat up?" Fiona asked Susan, as Anna crashed through the door of The Copper Kettle.

"I swear that hill gets steeper. Mind you, a trot on the cobbles gets rid of your wobbles – or something like that. Morning Susan. Morning, Fiona. How's everyone doing?"

Fiona held out her hand as Susan slipped her anorak off her shoulders, "We're fine, thanks, Anna. I was just going to hang Susan's coat up."

"I'll take it," Anna said, tucking the cone of mugwort out of sight in the large pocket of her kimono.

"No, no, you're my new boss. I can do it, don't worry about me. Through here, is it?" Susan was a slightly stooped woman, with a long neck and a pair of bright green glasses hanging from a chain around her neck. She wore her dark grey hair in a tight bun and looked like she could have been born to work in either a library or an Edwardian teashop – which was handy, as this was her first day working in The Copper Kettle. She put her glasses on the end of her nose and gingerly made her way into the kitchen, returning equally cautiously a few moments later.

"I normally travel more quickly, but I'm trying out these new vari-focus lenses, so I'm cautious on unfamiliar territory," she said, looking around the tearoom. "I must say you've done wonders with this old place. It was rather run down, but now it's so bright and cosy."

"It took quite a bit of work, but I'm glad you like it," Anna said, then looked at Fiona. "Of course, your dad did his best..."

Fiona started polishing a pile of cutlery at the counter, "Don't worry, I know it was in a state. He'd neglected it for years. Thursday mornings are generally quiet, Susan, so we'll have plenty of time to run through everything before the lunch crowd come in."

"I'm glad to see you've got a black skirt and white top, Susan," Anna said, straightening one of the linen tablecloths. "You look very smart, just right. We try to provide a proper old-fashioned tea service here; people seem to really love it."

"I ironed your apron and cap this morning," Fiona said, pointing to the traditional white lace uniform hanging over the back of a chair.

Susan beamed at them, "You are all very kind. I cannot tell you how exciting all this is. Sitting around at home really doesn't suit me."

"Is there no Mr Susan?"

Susan frowned, "Sadly not. I was engaged three

times, but they all made other arrangements in the end. But there's still hope. One never knows what new luck might come your way," she said with a cheerful wink at Anna.

She put on her apron and neatly attached the old-fashioned lace cap to her hair, "There, do I look the part?"

"You really do," Fiona said. "Very smart."

Anna straightened the cap slightly, "Now, don't worry if you get a bit flustered today, it will take time to..." They all jumped when a thundering knock blasted from the front door.

"It's Judy McMurray, my friend," Susan said, waving at her through the window. "She works in the DIY shop."

"Yes, I know. Morning, Judy, come in," Anna said, as she let in the manager of Let's Screw. "How are you?"

"Good morning, Anna. I'm A-plus, thank you for asking," Judy said, patting her freshly coloured blonde hair back into place, after a few strands had become dislodged from its immaculate styling by the spring breeze. "Susan, were you on time?"

Susan opened her mouth but didn't have time to reply before Judy continued in a very different tone, having spotted Martin coming down the stairs, "Oh, here's Martin," she purred.

"Greetings, old thing," he said, before turning to Fiona. "I've tightened the joint, so there shouldn't be any leaks now."

"Trouble?" Anna asked.

"Just a leaky bath tap," Fiona said. "Martin

volunteered to take a look."

Judy took a step closer to Martin and tapped his elbow, "Has Susan won you over with her biscuits yet? You just wait until she's made a batch of her Melting Moments, you'll be begging her to marry you in minutes."

Susan tutted, "Now, Judy, stop."

Martin headed into the kitchen, "Perhaps you could show me the recipe one day, but in the meantime I shall be carving tomatoes into the profile of the Dalai Lama if anyone needs me."

Susan looked at Anna, "My goodness, that sounds complicated."

"I think he might be joking," Anna chuckled.

"I do like a man with a sense of humour," Judy said wistfully, then swiftly turned to Anna. "Now, Irene told me you'd be here settling Susan in. So, I popped up to see if you'd heard anything from Joe? He hasn't been in contact for ages. I send him the weekly figures by email, but he doesn't always respond."

"Yes, I had an email from mum a couple of days ago. They were travelling to Niagra Falls in a motorhome they'd rented. So, there's a chance they may not have constant access to the internet if they're in the wilds of the outback, or whatever they call it in Canada."

Susan sighed, "It's so romantic; an older lady finding such a nice young man, don't you think, Judy? I was saying to Anna that it's never too late for new luck to come your way, especially with summer coming..."

Judy frowned at her, "Yes, well, enough about all that. We've barely got over Easter and we have much to do before the summer."

"Yes, yes, of course. Sorry, Judy."

Although both women were the same age, it was clear that Judy was very much in charge. She was rarely seen without a clipboard in her hands and the starched boiler suit she wore for work every day reeked of military efficiency. She certainly seemed to have the ability to keep everyone in line.

"Did you hear about the attempted fire last night up the road at Ethel Loves Me?" Fiona asked, starting to lay the tables.

"No, I don't think so," Susan said. "Shall I help you?"

"Yes, could you grab the napkins and follow me round?"

Judy watched them go about their work with an appraising eye, "I popped in to help Ethel tidy up this morning. Poor thing, she was quite upset. I don't really see why, though, the fire wasn't very significant."

Anna stared at her, "Not significant? Someone tried to burn her shop down."

"Oh, well, yes, if you think of it like that," Judy mumbled, making a note against an item on one of her lists. "There was no lasting damage is what I meant. I understand you and Ralph saved the day."

"Yes, we were walking Stanley and we saw someone pushing something through the letterbox. The fire was already alight, but we scared them off and managed to put it out."

"Good heavens," Susan said, gripping her dangling glasses tightly. "How awful... I mean awful that it happened, not awful you were there to put it out."

Judy reached out and deftly removed Susan's fingers from the tight grip they had on her glasses, "Don't break them, dear. You know how you go through them when you get agitated." She smiled at Anna, "That's her third pair in as many weeks. Any news on the culprit? Were you able to give a description to the police?"

"No, not really. They were small and dressed in black, that was it really."

"Dear, oh, dear, what is Rye coming too? Probably some sort of troubled youth messing about."

Susan nodded, "Yes, troubled, I expect. Where next, I wonder? First here, then Ethel's place. Anywhere could be next."

Judy banged her hand on her clipboard, "Susan, don't go making a big song and dance about it. If it is youths, they'll soon get bored and go on to play with something else."

Susan was winding the chain attached to her glasses around her finger, "Yes, I mean, no. Sorry. Nothing to worry about."

"Glasses," Judy snapped, and Susan quickly dropped the chain back to her chest.

"Yes, of course."

"Well," Fiona said. "This has been lovely, but we are due to open soon."

Judy looked at her watch, "Leaping lizards, is that the time? I'd better dash. Good to know Joe is alright. Have a lovely day, and Susan... behave."

As Judy swept out of the shop, Susan squeaked again

and bobbed into what looked suspiciously like a curtsy to Fiona, "Have you been friends for long?" she asked, innocently.

"Oh, yes, years and years. We went to school together."

"Well, it's lovely you are all still close," Anna said. "Enjoy your first day. Any problems, let me know, otherwise I'll leave you to it."

"Yes, yes, I won't let you down," Susan said. "It's going to be such fun."

Fiona caught Anna's eye as she left and saw her wink as she called over her shoulder, "Good luck."

* * *

When Anna got back to The Cookery, Irene was stalking about the kitchen wielding a spatula, "Where have you been? A couple of minutes you said, that was nearly half an hour ago."

"What's the panic? Everything's ready and you've got Janet to help you."

"She's in the lavvy again. I've never known anyone like it. The doctor says my waterworks are something to behold, but she's in her own league."

"Let her be, it's probably nerves. Tell me something, Irene, and I don't mean to cause offence..."

"Which means you're going to," Irene sniffed.

"When women reach sixty or so, do they get a bit - weird? I mean Rye seems to be filled with the barmiest old women."

"Well, I'm glad you warned me you didn't mean to cause offence. Of course, we're not all barmy. Some of us are perfectly normal, despite our kidneys and waterworks. Oh, and while we're at it, who are you calling old?"

"You are seventy-two, Irene,"

"So?"

"Well, I mean, doesn't old start around sixty-ish?"

"Not in my book," Irene said, slamming the spatula down on the kitchen counter. "Aren't you satisfied with my work? Are you trying to get me out? Well, I won't go. I'll take you to a tributary for ageism. That woman from Countryfile did it to the BBC, who said she couldn't work with the sheep anymore. But she won, they said a woman of any age can work with sheep and John Craven."

"Irene, Irene, I wasn't saying that."

"I know I've been a bit peaky lately, it's these headaches. I think it's my new tablets, but it hasn't stopped me doing my job, has it?"

"No, not at all," Anna said. "What headaches? Why didn't you tell me? Should you stop taking the tablets if they give you headaches?"

"It's either take them or have kidneys that run amok."

"Well, I'm worried about you Irene, you've looked tired lately."

Irene waved a Hastings Pier tea towel at her, before fanning herself with it, "Don't you start, that's what my kids keep saying."

"Well, maybe you should slow down a bit. You're not

getting any younger."

Irene opened her mouth to reply, but no words came. Anna was mortified, was Irene about to cry? She touched her arm, but was shaken off, "Oh, Irene, I didn't mean to upset you. I'm so sorry."

"I'm not upset," Irene croaked, turning her back on her and scrubbing the fridge with the cloth.

"You know you're like a mother and grandmother all rolled into one to me. What would I do without you?"

"Shush," Irene said, producing a tissue from her bra and blowing her nose with it. "I'm not dead yet. Nothing wrong with me. Or there wouldn't be if I could get into the bloomin' loo once in a while."

"Ready for action," Janet called from the other side of the counter. "What are we talking about?"

"Death and waterworks," Irene snapped, as she stalked past her and into the toilet.

"On a Thursday morning?" Janet said, looking startled.

CHAPTER 7

Shepherd's pie, silk pyjamas and a difficult reunion.

By Sunday afternoon Martin was exhausted, so he turned the lights out in The Copper Kettle and sat in the soothing evening light at one of the empty tearoom tables. He eased off his leather brogues, put his feet up on the chair beside him and licked his lips as he considered having another cup of tea, but he knew what he really wanted was a proper drink. He shifted in his chair and planted his feet firmly back on the ground. No, that sort of thinking would not do. It was years of drinking that lead to weeks sleeping rough in the cold, which in turn led to his weakened, ageing body, and he was not about to go back there again.

Fiona stood quietly in the kitchen doorway and watched him in the dark. She had seen the tiredness in his eyes and the slump of his shoulders lately. She did her best to help in the kitchen when she could and make sure he took breaks in the fresh air. Her friend, Claire, had reported that she had seen him going to the nursing home three or four times a week, so she knew he wasn't at home resting properly in the evenings.

She approached his table and eased herself into a chair opposite him, "Do you have plans for tonight?"

Martin hesitated, he had planned another useless trip to the nursing home, but he wasn't sure he could face it, "I'm not sure. You?"

"Not much. I was going to make a shepherd's pie and wondered if you'd like to join me? It can get a bit boring eating alone every night."

"That's very kind, I am tempted, but..."

"Please don't say no, Martin. It's just supper, I think we both deserve it after such a long week, don't you?" she paused, not sure whether to go on. A quick look at his sad eyes gave her the answer, "Martin, it's none of my business, but I think you need a friend. One who makes a decent shepherd's pie, perhaps? One who is fed up sitting at home alone, who would be happy to go to the nursing home with you. For company. For someone to talk to."

Time seemed to stand still for Martin. The warmth of the tearoom and of Fiona's words drifted around him. Friend? He hadn't had a proper friend for such a long time. He had the Rooftop Club, of course, but they were all young and tied up in their exciting, complex lives, only needing to stop off at Auntie B's small iron table occasionally and vent a little to him.

His mind began to drift away. If Fiona came with him, what would he wear? On his own he never gave a second thought to his choice of clothes. His wardrobe was hung with a meagre collection of tawdry items gathered from the homeless shelter he had lived in before he'd moved into the flat above Let's Screw. He'd had plenty of clothes at his old home. Clothes for his teaching work, clothes for evenings and weekends, a whole range of pyjamas. He missed his pyjamas. When his drinking had gone beyond the pale and his wife had ordered his departure, he had taken what he could in two large binbags. His choice of leather shoes and some cooking pans had made sense with nearly a litre of brandy inside him, but now he wished he'd had the capacity to choose more carefully.

He still hadn't been allowed access to the marital home to remove any of his belongings. It wasn't that he wanted much. A couple of photographs perhaps and the small wooden box at the back of his wardrobe. Oh, and his pyjamas. He really missed buttoning up a pair of crisply ironed pyjamas every night. He thought he might sleep more easily if he had them.

"Martin? Are you OK?" Fiona's voice brought him back to himself.

"So sorry, old thing. How rude, I floated off for a moment," he sat upright, catching a glimpse of himself in the mirror on the wall. Look at what he had become; a bedraggled shadow of a man. But he couldn't change, not yet. His long, motheaten coat still served to hide his tired body, while his old tartan hat covered his lank hair and troubled head. He so wanted to cut his hair, to buy a new coat - something practical, that weighed less on his shoulders. He was desperate to fully embrace his new life as a cook and a friend to all these marvellous young people and feel that he truly deserved to be a member of the extraordinary Rye Rooftop Club. But he couldn't. Not yet. He had one final duty to perform. He had to face his past. Explain himself. Then he might be free to start again. But it felt so hard. Harder even than kicking the booze.

"...Kicking the booze," he muttered.

"What was that?"

"Sorry, old thing, what I meant to say was that I would be delighted to join you for supper," he surprised himself by saying. "But I fear it would be a wasted journey for you to come to the nursing home, you will not be permitted to come into the room to meet my friend." This was a lie. He made it sound like the home wouldn't allow it, but it was him who couldn't let anyone else into the room.

"Oh, the journey out to Kent would be enough. Some fresh air and different scenery. I wouldn't dream of imposing with you and... whoever you are visiting. I'd be happy with a cup of tea and some company."

While Fiona made the pie for supper, Martin had time to return home to his flat and make the best of himself – as much as he could. He spruced up his old coat with a clothes brush he had found in Auntie B's neat wardrobes. He put on one of his home-knitted waistcoats in maroon and gold, and some second-hand green corduroys. He used a piece of paper towel to bring a dull shine to his shoes. He tucked his hair into the old tartan hat, which was a little damp from his attempt to rinse out some of the lingering smell of the street. He didn't look in the mirror, there was no need, he knew who he was.

Fiona had been right, a friend who made a very decent shepherd's pie seemed to be exactly what he needed. It was delicious and she was an interesting and amusing companion. After they had washed and dried the dishes, humming along to a Mozart concert on the radio, he made one last attempt to dissuade her from going with him.

"I'm sure you would much prefer to put your feet up this evening than have me drag you halfway across the county, wouldn't you?"

Fiona, reached for her coat, "Not at all, I'm looking forward to it. That dinner is going to sit heavily on me if I don't get out and walk it off. Come on. Do you get the bus from down the road?"

It was a warm evening making it a pleasant walk to the end of the High Street and they stood by the bus stop outside a purple-coloured clothes shop.

"I'm just going into the newsagents for some mints," Fiona said. "Do you want anything?"

"No, I'm fine, thank you."

"I won't be a tick," she said and popped over the road.

Martin glanced briefly behind him at the clothes shop, noting it's unusual name – A Small Medium at Large. He turned back to watch for the bus when he noticed the owner fussing around in the window, finishing off a new display of bright green and yellow clothes. He heard her bang on the glass behind him. He had got used to ignoring people who asked him to move on. She banged again. He just looked up the road for his bus.

"Mr Martin," a voice called from behind him. "Martin?"

He roused himself and turned, "I'm sorry, were you talking to me?"

The little lady, with bright white hair and huge round

glasses, smiled, "Of course. It is Martin, isn't it? You live in Auntie B's flat, don't you? I've heard all about you from Anna, she buys a lot of her clothes from me."

Martin looked over her shoulder at the clothes on display in the window and nodded, "Yes, indeed, I can imagine she does. They are... fantastical."

The little lady laughed, "Well, they've never been called that before. I like it."

Martin nodded, "Was there something you wanted, dear lady?"

She looked a little taken aback, "No, I just wanted to say hello. I've seen you toing and froing between the cafes, that's all. I'm Sue. You may have heard of me, I'm known as Psychic Sue."

"I'm so sorry, of course. Hello, Sue, it's very nice to meet you. I'm sorry for being rude, we are on our way to... ah, here is our bus."

"Oh, good, that was quick, wasn't it? The universe must be looking out for you. I'm sure we'll meet again, and if you ever want your aura taking a looking at, just let me know," and she hustled back into her shop and closed the door.

Fiona came running over the road as the bus pulled up, "That was good timing," she said, waving at Sue through the window. "Did you meet Sue? She's great fun, I've bought a few things from her. I haven't been brave enough to wear most of them yet, but I will one day."

"Yes, I can imagine a little courage might be required," he said with a smile and escorted her on to the bus.

Forty-five minutes later, the bus dropped them over the Sussex border in the pretty Kentish town of Tenterden. Fiona waited while Martin stopped at a small supermarket and bought a box of After Eight mints and a copy of Homes and Gardens magazine. It was almost dark by the time they reached the gate of a large timber framed house, that had been extended several times with modern brick wings to either side.

"Oh, it's lovely," Fiona said. "Some of these modern care homes can look quite bleak, can't they?"

Martin rang the bell on the intercom at the gate and waited, "Yes, it was a manor house once upon a time, part of a much larger estate."

"Hello?" a disembodied voice said through the small silver speaker.

"Hello, Erin. It's Martin. I know it's a little late, but..."

"Martin, how lovely. Come in."

A buzzer sounded and the gate clicked. He pushed it open and they made their way up the narrow concrete path, waiting again at the front door of the house to be let in. A few moments later there was another click and the door was pulled open.

Erin, a cheerful redhead in a smart nurse's uniform smiled and stepped back to let him enter, "Evening, my love. Come on in, he's all ready for you."

"This is Fiona, she has accompanied me for some fresh air. I don't suppose a cup of tea could be rustled up for her while I go in?"

"Of course. Hello, Fiona. Tea or coffee? We also do a lovely hot chocolate, if I can tempt you."

"Well, a hot chocolate would be lovely, if it's not too much trouble."

"Not at all, pop yourself down in the lounge over there and I'll bring it through to you," Erin said, as she disappeared down the corridor.

"Now, don't worry about me," Fiona said to Martin. "I'll be quite happy here with my drink. Take as much time as you need."

Martin smiled at her. It had been comforting to have company during the journey, which felt much longer when he was alone, but from here he was on his own and a leaden feeling settled in his stomach.

Fiona watched him walk slowly down the pale green corridor, his body seeming to get heavier with every step. She saw him hesitate outside the door. Then he turned and looked at her. She smiled encouragingly, although her heart was breaking for him. It was obvious he didn't want to be here or go through the door. She put her hands on the arms of the chair and started to stand, but he waved her back into her seat. He took a breath, tucked the After Eights under his arm and pushed the door.

Inside the room the light was soft. It came from a couple of table lamps, with carved wooden bases and pale cream shades, over which sheer orange scarves had been thrown to spread a diffused golden glow around the large square room. Although it was functional, in a nursing home it had to be, the room felt both homely and luxurious. The bed sat in the middle of the far wall and was hospital issue, but the throw over it was damask. The single armchair which sat beside it was upholstered in a deep blue velvet, with a plump purple cushion at the back of the seat. The walls were painted a warm apricot, complemented by yellow and pink paisley curtains. There were paintings of all sizes covering the walls, he hadn't counted them but there must have been thirty. Landscapes, seascapes, flowers, country scenes. One large portrait hung directly opposite the bed, so it could be seen at all times by the occupier. Martin didn't look at it, he looked at the man in the bed instead.

He was very thin and pale against the white linen, as if he might fade away into it. His delicate arms, encased in blue silk pyjamas, lay neatly at his side on top of the sheet. His breathing was slow but regular.

Martin placed the chocolates and the magazine carefully on the bed within reach of the man's left hand, withered and twisted with age like ancient tree roots. After a moment the hand moved slightly and touched the chocolates, feeling the square shape of the box, "Thank you," the voice gentle but weak.

Martin removed his hat and his coat and hung them on the hook on the back of the door. He then sat in the blue armchair. Silence hung in the air.

The man opened his eyes and looked at Martin with a smile, "Would you like a chocolate?"

Martin shook his head.

"Would you like to talk, Phillip?"

Martin shook his head again.

"That's fine. It's lovely to see you. We can talk when you're ready," and the man laid his hand on top of

Martin's.

They sat like that for an hour, as they had each time before - Martin's head bowed, the frail man lightly holding Martin's hand.

Eventually, Martin could stand it no more. He stood, took his coat and hat from the hook, turned and said what he always said, "I'm sorry, Robin. I will talk next time."

Robin nodded, "Don't leave it too long, I won't be here forever."

Martin opened the door and hurried into the corridor. He always left more quickly than he arrived, embarrassed and not wanting to stay a moment longer than he had to.

He walked down the green corridor, pulling on his hat and coat as he went. He didn't see the young man swing round the corner in front of him until it was too late, and they collided at some speed.

"Shit," the young man spat. "Watch it, moron."

"That's enough," the voice of Erin, the smiley nurse, cracked across the corridor. "It was an accident. Are you alright, Martin?"

"Yes, fine. I'm very sorry, my fault, my fault."

"Whatever," the young man grumbled, pulled his grey beanie hat low on his head and ran out of the front door and down the path.

Martin watched his back as he ran away. A back and a voice he knew very well.

CHAPTER 8

Unlocking old stories, coconut liquor and the Summer Solstice.

The last bus of the day chugged along the dark country roads. A strong blue moon lit the hedge rows and made dark silhouettes of the trees. But the bus windows were steamed up, so Martin and Fiona failed to see the beauty on their return journey.

They had stood in silence waiting for the bus outside the nursing home. Fiona had chosen two quiet seats towards the back when it arrived. She could feel that Martin wasn't in the mood to talk as he sat slumped inside his large coat. His friend must be quite ill, she thought, as his mood had change considerably since they shared the shepherd's pie earlier in the evening. But she was glad she was there with him, sometimes simply having company was enough.

After another ten minutes Martin pulled himself up in his seat, "I must apologise, I have been a very dull companion."

"Not at all," Fiona said. "It's been a lovely evening. Erin, was very nice, she even found me a couple of biscuits to go with my hot chocolate."

"Good, good. She's a fine woman."

"Did you have a nice chat with your friend?"

Martin twisted his tartan hat into a ball in his hands, "I must confess that we didn't speak."

"Oh? Aren't they able to speak?"

"Oh, he can speak, it's me that can't find the words. It's ridiculous and mortifying."

Fiona stayed silent, allowing Martin to go on in his own time if he wanted to.

"I haven't seen Robin for many years. Not since he started the business. I had no idea that he was now a patient there until recently."

"So, it's his nursing home?"

"Yes. I gave it to him."

Fiona turned to face him, her eyes wide, "You gave him a nursing home?"

"It wasn't a nursing home then, of course. It was part of the Groombridge estate. My inheritance," he said, with what sounded to Fiona like a great deal of bitterness. "It was the least he deserved."

Martin fell back into silence, folding and unfolding his old hat.

Fiona gently prompted him, "Is Robin a relative of yours?"

Martin gave a deep chuckle, "He worked for my father, for a while, and then he fell in love with the wrong person. No, the right person, but... it is very hard for me to explain."

"I see."

"No, you don't, old thing. But he is a good man, a very good man. Thanks to our family he was robbed of everything he ever wanted, which wasn't much. Some happiness perhaps. I gave him the old manor house, which had been in our family for generations, so he could have a new future. That and... well, some of our ill-gotten gains."

"Martin," Fiona said, rescuing the crumpled hat from his long fingers. "Please don't stop there. You always get so far with certain information and then stop. You told me you'd killed someone, now you had some sort of ill-gotten gains. I know it's not any of my business, but please tell me the story."

Martin smiled at her, "But that's just it, dear thing. I can't bring myself to talk about it. I discovered Robin was unwell, on his way out as it were, so I went to visit him. Finally thinking that he and I could talk about what happened. I have locked it all away you see, ignored it and him for so many years. But I seem unable to unlock it again. When I see him, I have no idea how to begin and the thought of trawling back through everything that happened seems so awful that I jam up. Can't say a word."

Fiona leant across and took one of his long hands in hers, "That means you're not ready yet. You've taken the first step, to come and see Robin. When the time is right, you'll be able to talk about it."

Martin looked at his tired hand laying in her fresh, smooth one, "How kind you are. I hope you are right. Might it be too much to ask you to come with me on another occasion? Having someone else here does seem to have helped. I've said more to you than I have said to anyone for decades."

"Of course, I'd be happy to come. Any time."

He looked up to see her encouraging smile and he felt something shift. If only he had been blessed with children, perhaps his daughter would have been like Fiona. But he could never have been a father, look at him and the mess he had made of everything. He wearily looked out of the window at the moon and then down to the lights of Rye glowing ahead of them.

"Good heavens. Do you see that?" He pointed to a bright spot in the centre of the town's lights.

"What?" Fiona asked, peering through the clogged-up windows.

Martin took his hat back and wiped the glass with it, "There, right in the centre of town. It looks like smoke and bright lights of some kind?"

They looked at each other, "Not another fire?" Fiona said, panic in her voice.

"I am very much afraid so, old thing."

* * *

Martin and Fiona left the bus as soon as it reached Rye and followed the light and smoke to the High Street. Ralph was standing opposite the purple exterior of Psychic Sue's clothes shop, watching the fire brigade carefully putting away their hoses and equipment.

"Ralph, what's happened? I was here talking to the owner a few hours ago. Is she alright?" Martin said.

"Yes, she wasn't hurt."

"Was she inside?" Fiona whispered, looking around.

"No, she'd gone out to the supermarket. Anna's looking after her at Cinque. The fire got a hold but the fire brigade came quickly. Luckily, it was mostly smoke and there doesn't seem to be much damage. It could have been a lot worse. I'd better go and tell Sue the fire's out."

"I'll stay for a few more minutes, see if there is any more information," Martin said.

When Fiona and Ralph reached Cinque, Sue was tucked into a corner sofa in the bar area with an untouched cup of tea in front of her. She stared at it, occasionally saying something to herself that no one could hear.

Fiona rushed straight over to her, "Oh, Sue, I've just heard. It's Fiona, do you remember me? I've bought some clothes from you, with butterflies on them."

Sue looked at Fiona and it took a moment for her to register who it was. Then her face crumpled and she burst into tears, "Oh, Fiona, Fiona."

Fiona sat beside her and held her while she cried, rocking her gently. Ralph joined Anna and Dawa at the bar. Anna too was crying.

"It's alright, Sue. The fire is out now, it's all over," Fiona said. "You'll have the shop up and running again in no time. Don't you worry." She looked up at the others, "We've had some lovely chats in the shop lately, she's been so kind to me. She took me out to supper last week."

Sue sniffled into a tissue, "Nearly choked on a scampi,

85

didn't I? Fiona was marvellous, she came to my rescue with the old heave-ho in the tummy and the scampi shot across the room and bounced off the glasses of an old man who was doing the crossword with his wife. We had a lovely evening, didn't we, Fi?"

Fiona smiled, "We did, Sue."

The others stood quietly and when Sue's tears began to subside, they moved to the table.

Ralph sat beside her, "The fire brigade say they have it under control. It hadn't spread upstairs, so it's just the shop itself that's been damaged, mostly by smoke. The chief said he'd come up when they had done all they could, to talk to you. It seems it was started deliberately."

"We'll clean it up and you can start again," Fiona said.

"No, no," Sue said, pushing her cold tea away. "Not if it was started on purpose. The energy in there will be all to-pot."

"We knew it was the arsonist, didn't we, Dawa? It had to be," Anna said. "The third one."

Dawa looked at Ralph, "It does seem to be becoming a problem, doesn't it?"

"I don't understand what's to be gained from it? Why would anyone do such a thing?"

Anna took the seat beside Fiona, "Sue, being a psychic and stuff, does mugwort mean anything to you? It's a herb..."

"Yes, it's a very powerful herb," Sue said, pushing her glasses up her small nose and peering at Anna. "It's often used to ease you into a deeper meditation, but it has to be dried and burnt for that."

Anna nodded, "Dawa and I have been talking about it and we wondered whether some local kids have been using it to get high or something, then doing stupid things."

"Unlikely, dear. It's not really a herb to make you high. They say it opens a more direct channel to things like lunar magic. Oh, and it's ever so good at stopping itching. I once had this terrible patch of skin..."

"Wait," Anna said. "Lunar magic? What's that?"

"Does this bar stock that coconut stuff, Malibu, by any chance? Tea is going to do nothing for me."

Dawa smiled and headed for the bar, "Yes, it certainly does. I'll bring some. Hello, Martin."

Martin came into the bar and beckoned to Ralph, who joined him, "The police will be here in a minute. Definitely arson. They're not saying much, but I heard the sergeant say it looked like the same MO as the other fires. MO being modus operandi, I assume."

"Yes, that's what I heard too."

"Dawa's nice," Sue whispered to Anna. "Is he yours?"

She felt herself begin to blush, "No, we're just friends."

Sue squinted across the bar, "Shame, he's got a lovely aura. Purple, which is for royalty, you know. Nobility and spirituality too, plus a hint of mystery – which can be a good thing or a bad thing."

"Wow," Anna said, transfixed. "That's amazing. That fits him perfectly."

"I can see it all, dear, now the shock of the fire is

passing."

"Good, let's talk lunar magic," Anna said. "If you're up to it, that is."

"Oh, yes, it'll take my mind of everything. Oh, here he is, our purple nobleman," she smiled up at Dawa as he brought a glass of Malibu and ice to the table.

"I'm sorry?" he said, setting the glass in front of her.

"Nothing, Dawa," Anna said, quickly. "Sue is going to tell me about the lunar magic."

Sue took a sip of the sweet liquor and smacked her lips, "De-lish! Now then, lunar means the moon, of course. So, it's magic that is usually only available at night. Basically, people believe they can cast spells of different strengths depending on the phases of the moon. The mugwort sends them a bit doo-lally, and they reckon it helps channel the magic and witchcraft better."

Anna gripped the edge of the table, "Witchcraft? Like real witches and things?"

Ralph and Martin looked startled as they joined the table, "Witches?" Martin said. "Now, I've heard it all. First it was fairies, then pixies, then the devil himself, not to mention some vile gossip about immigrants. This really must stop."

"I know what you mean, Martin," Sue said, throwing back the remainder of her drink. "That didn't take long, did it?"

"Another?" asked Dawa.

"I shouldn't, but I have had a nasty shock, haven't I?"

"I'll top it up for you," he said, returning to the bar.

Sue pointed at Martin, "I agree with you. Most of it is a load of old nonsense, really. But there are all sorts of things we don't understand in this world. I mean, I speak to my son regularly, even though he's passed, but that's because I've got the gift. Proper Pagans have the gift too, and they can call on the moon for powers and so on. Especially around the Summer Solstice, that's a very powerful time for them."

"The Summer Solstice?" Anna said, looking up at Dawa as he brought Sue's new drink back to the table. "Isn't that an ice cream?"

Dawa smiled, "I believe it's Midsummer Day. A sacred time for pagans. Am I right, Sue?"

Sue took a sip of the Malibu, "Ooh, that'll grease the joints! Yes, it's the middle of June, only a few weeks away. It's time for rebirth, but there are those who use it for mischief. The naughty ones."

Fiona looked at Sue wide-eyed, "What sort of mischief?"

But Sue ignored her as she stared deep into her glass as if she had forgotten all those around her.

"Sue?" Fiona said, rubbing her arm gently. "What is it?"

"Well, either it's trapped wind from the Malibu, or I'm having a psychic episode." She gave a little burp and mumbled, "The Summer Solstice is when it will end."

"When what will end?" Anna whispered.

Sue looked up at her with blank eyes, "What, dear? "

"You said it will end at the Summer Solstice."

"Did I? I wonder why?"

CHAPTER 9

Early risers, solicitors and baby Pugwash.

To: rubyrose@beemail.com

From: annabanana@tallyho.co.uk

15th May

Hi Mum (& Joe)

Sorry it's been a while. It's been a bit manic. We've had brilliant weather so the tourists have flooded into town. I think I baked about 200 pies last week (the old favourite - sausage, mash and beans all crammed into one pie – was a big hit, until Janet gave one to a vegan from Bournemouth and all hell broke loose.)

Other than that, Janet's working out well. She's stopped spending hours in the loo and is getting the hang of things and of Irene. I don't think Irene is warming to her, though. She says there's something suspicious about her. No idea why.

Irene sits down a lot now. I don't know if she is trying to make Janet work harder or if she's struggling. She won't tell me and I don't want to upset her again, so I keep an eye on her from a distance.

What else? We've drawn a blank with the arsonist thing. We think they've been feeding the fires some sort of dried herb called mugwort. It's all very strange. Psychic Sue's shop was the latest one. Lots of smoke damage, which has ruined all her fabulous clothes. It's tragic. She's too upset to go back to her flat above the shop, so she's staying with Fiona some of the time and then with a friend in Bexhill called Destiny. Isn't that an amazing name? I'm thinking of calling my first born, Destiny. (Don't get excited, you aren't going to be a granny for a long time yet – unless immaculate conception makes a comeback.)

Anyway, the arsonist used this mugwort again on Sue's shop, but Sergeant Phil isn't convinced it's anything other than something that burns well. An accelerant, he called it. I'm not sure. Sue said it's all about the Summer Solstice, she saw it in her Malibu and ice. She's very spiritual and psychical (is that a word?). Her son died and she talks to him all the time, so the others reckon she's a bit unhinged, but I think there's something in it. It has me properly spooked; I have to sleep with the little green rabbit lamp on in my bedroom now. It's been a week since Sue's fire and there haven't been any more, thank goodness. We've run out of clues, but something very odd is going on.

I've found a lovely lady who will cover for Martin when he has some time off from The Copper Kettle, so I don't think he'll die any time soon. He looked shocking last week, absolutely dead on his feet. I'm not sure what's wrong with him, he won't tell us. Fiona says she's keeping an eye on him, which is a relief. She is lovely.

You know I said I'd secretly entered one of Ralph's paintings into the annual art competition? Well, it's results day next week and I'm trying to get the Rooftop Club to go with me. Ralph will defo be there, as he's giving some book tokens as prizes for the winners of the kid's section. I can't wait to see his face when his picture of Sam wins. I know it will. Do you think I'm a bit psychical too?

I'm doing at least 10,000 steps a day now. I don't have a fancy watch or anything that tells me what I've done, but I did try and count them one night when I was out with Dawa. He kept interrupting and I got a bit lost and had to start again a couple of times, but I'm sure it was at least 8 or 9,000. He's lovely and easy to talk to, plus he also thinks there's something more to these fires than meets the eye. It's so frustrating the police won't take it more seriously. Anyway, it turns out that Dawa is an excellent cook. He's popped into The Cookery a few mornings when I'm baking, (he's an early riser, he says) and he's a dab hand with a rolling pin. I've bought him his own apron, it's got the Thunderbirds on it. He loves it... I think.

Thanks for the photos. The one of you and Joe in the big yellow rain macs at Niagra Falls is hilarious. You both look like drowned Wombles (Oh, Psychic Sue gave me a new Wombles t-shirt from the shop, with only a bit of soot on one arm. She sends her love and hopes your aura is holding up – or something like that.) Where are you going next? Can't wait to hear more about your adventures.

Love

Anna xxxx

PS Rosie doesn't like Slovakia and wants to come home, but her mum won't let her. She says she signed up to the band and she can't abandon them in the middle of a foreign country. I suppose she has a point.

* * *

To: helenh@woohoo.com
From: thebookery01@beemail.com

17 May

Hi Helen,

How's the bump? It can't be any bigger, can it? Are you sure you're not having twins? Anna wants to know if you've chosen a name yet? She suggested Pugwash or Destiny last night and she wasn't even drunk!

The Bookery's still busy, so I'm really pleased to have Pat now. She's turning out to be a real asset. She's got the hang of everything and has even reorganised some of the shelving and suggested new books that people of her age want to read. It also means I'm getting a bit of time off. I've even started painting again. I do it down in the basement, the little window at the back gives some light and I've put in one of those daylight bulbs, so it's fine. Sam makes such a fuss about my paintings and wants to hang everything on the wall and show it off. He means well, but if I know he's going to show everyone I don't paint freely, if you know what I mean. If I'm left on my own and think no one is going to see what I'm doing I can paint what I like and how I like. Anyway, Anna's looking after the big picture I did of Sam, and I'll give it to him as a housewarming present when the apartment's finished if I think it's OK when I see it again.

The builders are doing a great job, they've only been there ten days but they've started putting in new electrics and the plumbing, and they've cleaned up and sealed the old brickwork, which looks amazing. It's really exciting. Stanley still hates, Jack, the young guy who Chaz is training up. He's a funny lad, he's always hiding in corners or disappears when I go to see how they're doing. I have a very strange feeling about him, but I don't know why. Maybe I'm getting psychic – or psychical, as Anna insists on calling it.

She's getting obsessed about these fires around town and is being egged on by Psychic Sue about it being to do with magic and spells. Honestly, it's crackers. The funny thing is she is so obsessed with it all that she hasn't realised she's falling for Dawa Singh. You remember him from Cinque, don't you? The scary Maitre D'? She says they're friends and I think she really believes it. They're always strolling round town together and he's started 'popping in' to the café first thing in the morning to help her do the baking. Who gets up at half past five to help someone else bake pies?! If she didn't have magic on her mind, she would have noticed that he's smitten too. (Smitten? That's the sort of word Pat would use, in fact, I may have got it from her.) Sam thinks he is too. He's asked Dawa about it, but he claims it's just a friendship as well. Watch this space.

What else? Say hi to your parents, although I

don't suppose they've forgiven me yet. My parents are cruising round the med, so Mum will be the size of a house when she gets back and will have to join Slimming World again. Dad refuses to go with her, although he eats as much as her and finishes off her plate usually when she's had enough. Nothing changes.

Anyway, keep well. Keep eating your greens.

Love,

Ralph

X

* * *

To: CountessG@fortnum.org
From: MartinRyeCook@zway.com

May 20th

Grace

Thank you for your letter, via the solicitors. To answer your questions in order:

The drive was resurfaced three years ago.

I don't know where the hoover attachment for cat hairs is. Ask the bloody cleaner.

No, you cannot deduct the cost of the Le Creuset pan from the divorce settlement. You have never cooked in your life.

I will not reply via my solicitor, because it costs a small

fortune every time she puts pen to paper and she only writes what I tell her to anyway. So, you can have it all from the horse's mouth via email, and forward it on to your own solicitor so he can charge you an arm and a leg to read it.

I would like to fix a date to come and collect my things. You cannot get someone to put them all in bags and put them outside the door as you suggest. I need to be there. Please do not go through my wardrobe, leave it all exactly as it is and I will come and pack it up. It will only take an hour or less. I have asked very little of you, but I am asking for this.

Martin

CHAPTER 10

Sherlock Holmes, the Day of The Dead and scorched earth.

The end of May brought more fine weather and plenty of visitors to Rye. Parking places were scarce, as were seats in the myriad of tea shops, so minor scuffles would break out as frantic games of musical chairs began every time a table or parking space became free.

Anna gathered a large cake box into her arms and weaved carefully through the café to the door, "Irene, can you open the door for me, please?"

"Only if you shift out of the way, I'm not twisting today - my kidneys are up," Irene said, rubbing the small of her back.

Anna allowed Irene to open the door, then edged through sideways, "Ta. It's only an hour or so until closing and I should be back in half an hour, so you'll be alright, won't you?"

"If the happy hippo over there pulls her finger out and does some work," Irene grumbled.

"Irene, I've told you before about body shaming. If

Janet hears you, she'll be ever so..." but Anna never got to finish her admonishment as Irene swung the door shut in her face. "Irene!"

Anna watched Irene's back stalking into the kitchen and shook her head, "You get worse and worse. Honestly!"

She turned away and set off down the High Street. As she reached The Bookery she found Pat working with Stanley by the front door of the shop.

"Hi, Pat, what are you up to?"

Pat was on her knees, holding Stanley by his collar, "I am attempting to train Stanley to open the door, but he seems to be taking an awfully long time to get to grips with it. Largely because my cardigan pocket is full of treats, I expect."

Stanley barked at something inside the shop and shot off to investigate, "Looks like lessons are over for today," Anna laughed.

"It would appear so," Pat said. "What's in your box?"

"It's a birthday cake for a party at the cemetery... don't ask! Anyway, I need to get going or I'll be late. See you later."

Pat watched her go down the street and turn the corner, before giving her attention back to her new beagle friend, "Right, young Stanley, come out from behind that counter. If it's a spider, leave him be."

* * *

Rye Cemetery sits on a hill overlooking the Romney Marshes, which cover about a hundred square miles of wetland around Rye. Long ago people lived there, but when it became a breeding ground for malaria no one was too keen to hang around on a permanent basis, so for centuries it was left to smugglers and sheep to make the most of it. More recently people had returned in the shape of bird watchers, canal enthusiasts and the occasional local having a picnic.

Anna pulled her little pink car into the cemetery car park and carefully manoeuvred the cake box from the boot. As she headed for the small group of people, holding balloons and champagne glasses in the far corner, she saw a familiar figure crouching under an apple tree.

"It's a bit soon to be choosing a plot for yourself, isn't it?" she said as she approached Dawa, who was on his hand and knees brushing moss off a crooked gravestone.

He smiled up at her, "This is the last place I expected to see you."

"I could say the same to you. I'm delivering a cake to that lot over there. It's a birthday party for someone who died."

Dawa looked over at the partygoers in little paper hats, "Really? Ah, Día de los Muertos?"

Anna blinked at him, "I never expected bad language from you."

"It means Day of the Dead. It's the big Mexican festival when families celebrate the departed and visit graves to decorate them."

"Oh, well, it might be. I just thought they were a bit nutty, to be honest. It's an old school friend of mine...

well, I say friend, I couldn't stand her. Josie got her boobs before everyone else and she thought that made her special. Now she has this perfect life, with babies and a big house and a cock-a-dooddle-poo dog and she smells of ginger nuts and icing sugar and her hair is shiny like conkers and... and.."

"She sounds like a monster."

"YES! Yes, she is. I knew you'd understand."

Dawa grinned at her, "But she pays for expensive cakes from you?"

"She does. I always add on a bit though, because it's her, but I tell her she's got a discount. I'm a terrible person, aren't I?"

"Not at all, it sounds like she can afford it. After you've delivered the cake have you got time for a quick stroll?"

"Oh, yes, I'd love that. Hang on," she scuttled between the headstones, nearly losing her footing a couple of times and threatening to throw the cake across someone else's grave. So, she slowed down, smiled politely at Josie and her family and swapped the cake for an envelope of cash. When she got back to Dawa she waved the envelope at him, "I feel like a spy in one of those boring dramas on TV when everything was in black and white. People used to go to graveyards and exchange things for brown envelopes, didn't they? I never understood it all. Talking of things I don't understand – why are you in the cemetery?"

Dawa straightened up and pointed at a row of graves in front of them, "It's such a lovely day, I actually came down for a walk, but I got caught up looking at these.

There are five graves, all from the same family. Look at this one; Eliza was only a few weeks old in 1840-something, I can't read the rest. Then she has three brothers and a sister here, all dead before they were six years old. Imagine that. Terrible, terrible. The last one is for her parents." He stood with his head bowed for a moment.

"We think we have it bad sometimes, but it's nothing like that. Was it the plague, do you think?"

Dawa shook his head, "More likely to be the flu or something equally simple. Awful. But you're right, it's good to remember how lucky we are. A nice walk through the countryside is perfect after seeing this. Shall we?"

Anna pointed ahead of them, "Yes, there's a gate over there. I've only got about an hour, then I need to be back. Oh, wait, I've got the wrong shoes on."

Dawa looked down at Anna's feet, which were currently housed in a pair of red leather clogs, with blue windmills painted on the front, "They're very pretty."

Anna felt herself blush, "Oh, thanks. I like them. I've got some wellies in the back of the car, two ticks." She skipped over to her car and perched on the edge of the boot while she swapped her clogs for a pair of rainbow-coloured boots. "That's better," she said, as she returned to him.

They walked through the cemetery gate and into a wide field following a path across its centre. Anna tried to surreptitiously look at him as he walked beside her. Eventually, he caught her and stopped, "What is it?"

She felt herself blush again, "Nothing, well, I was

interested in what you were wearing for a country walk. I mean, I've seen your lovely suits and when you pop into the café you have very nice jeans, all ironed and everything. Which reminds me, I wonder where my iron is? I had one once, I'm sure."

Dawa tried not to show his shock, "You don't iron anything?"

Anna threw her arms wide, "Erm, have you ever looked at me. Would you iron this lot?"

He took in her loose pink silk trousers, a Wombles t-shirt and her favourite flowing tartan kimono in red and black, "No, I see your point. So, what did you think I'd wear?" he said, walking on again and squeezing through the gap in a hedge. He held his hand out to help her through, which she took without thinking, then froze. She'd never touched him before, and it felt... lovely. He had lovely hands, long and brown and ever so soft.

"Tell me," Dawa said, looking at her intently.

"What?"

"Don't be embarrassed, I want to know what you thought I'd wear to walk in the countryside."

"Oh, I see, well," she took a breath as he helped her gently through the narrow gap. On the other side he could have simply dropped her hand, but he didn't, he held it.

"Are you OK?" he said. "You look worried."

"Me? No, never better. Worried is my best look. Worried and interesting that's me. Erm, I think we go that way," she pointed diagonally across the field with her other hand. Touching him for the first time seemed to have had a very strange effect on her, she didn't know what it was, but she felt different. *They* felt different.

"Oh, right," he looked at his hand holding hers, seemed to think about it for a moment and then let her go. "After you. So, did you expect me to wear a suit to impress the sheep?"

"I'm not sure. I mean, you're always so sharp. I think I'm the opposite of sharp, don't you?"

"Yes, I think you probably are, Anna."

"Oh, really?" she was disappointed.

"Everything about you is soft and fluid. It's wonderful," he stopped talking and looked ahead. What did he say that for? But it was the truth, she really was the softest person he'd ever met and that was genuinely a wonderful thing. "You still haven't said what you thought I'd be wearing?" he said, recovering himself.

"Didn't I? Well, I suppose I thought you'd wear some very smart wellies – which you're not. Nice walking boots, by the way."

"Thank you."

"And maybe a deerstalker hat, like Sherlock Holmes."

Dawa stopped short and turned to her, laughing with a rumble from deep within his chest. Anna began to giggle too.

He adjusted his turban, which was making his head itch in the warm sun, "Would I wear the deerstalker over the turban?" he asked.

"I don't know, I hadn't thought that far. But you look great, just perfect for the country. Jeans, walking boots, a puffer waistcoat thing. You look great."

"Thank you, but do I really look like a man who'd wear a deerstalker?"

Anna grimaced, "Maybe? But a nice one." She started to walk towards a flock of sheep that were watching them from the next field, "Do you have turbans to match every outfit?"

Instinctively, Dawa reached up to touch his turban, just as Anna flung her hand out to swipe a fly that was buzzing around her and their hands clashed in mid-air.

"Ouch," she said. "Sorry."

"No, I'm sorry are you OK?" He took her small hand in his large one again and looked into her eyes, where he saw a flicker of something he hadn't seen before. He was quite rusty in these matters, but he could have sworn it was desire. But they were friends, she wasn't interested in him. Before he could think any further, a pheasant shot out of the undergrowth beside them and made Anna scream.

They both dropped their hands as if stung.

"Blimey, it frightened the life out of me. Nature's creatures are all very well, but honestly, they need to learn some manners, don't they?"

"Erm, yes. What were we saying?" Dawa was more startled by what he'd felt and seen in Anna's eyes than the bird.

"Hats and turbans, I think," she said, her cheeks feeling the heat of a blush, so she looked down at her rainbow wellies. "We were talking about Sherlock Holmes' hat or something... wait, what's this?" She crouched down and peered closely at the ground, "Better yet, smell this."

He bent down beside her and looked at a square patch of burnt grass and weeds. It was a small area, no more than the width of his hand span, as if something very hot had been laid or a small fire had been lit there.

"I can't smell anything," he said.

"Closer," she said.

He put his head almost to the ground and sniffed, "Marijuana?"

"Not marijuana, mugwort! Look at this," and she held out a few sprigs of dried herb that exactly matched the ones they had found in the arsonist's paper cone. The sprigs were charred and she pointed to more spread around the scorched grass, "They've been putting mugwort on a fire."

"Who?" Dawa asked, looking around.

"Well, it's not the sheep. I bet it's the same people or person who's been setting fire to our shops."

"There's more than one," he stood up and pointed behind him. "There are five burnt patches, all the same."

Anna crawled across the field to the different squares of scorched earth, "Yes, and there's mugwort on all of them. What do you make of that, Mr Holmes?"

"I have absolutely no idea, Dr Watson. We appear to have a mystery on our hands, perhaps we could talk about it over dinner this evening?" He hesitated as he waited for her reaction, but it was instant.

"Oh, yes, that's a great idea. We can work out what on earth is going on and if these fires are really connected to the ones in Rye."

He looked away, she wanted to talk about the fires.

Of course she did. What was he thinking? Why would someone like Anna feel anything other than friendship for someone like him? It must be the combination of heat and a tight turban putting foolish thoughts in his head, "Excellent," he said, wiping the perspiration from his forehead. "We have some sleuthing to do then, Dr Watson."

He turned and started to lead the way back to the cemetery.

CHAPTER 11

Toad in the hole, satanic symbols and a chase begins.

The small flat above The Copper Kettle had rarely seen visitors when it had been the home of Dewdrop Dobson, but since his daughter Fiona had moved in it was quite a different place.

She had gradually redecorated with light colours and softer furnishings which made it a pleasant place to spend the evening. Something Martin had learnt from regular suppers there in the last few weeks. He and Fiona had been back to the nursing home a few times and he had managed to make some progress. He had started to tell Robin a little about his current life and his friends in the Rye Rooftop Club. They hadn't strayed into the past, which was still too hard for him, but at least they had talked.

Tonight was toad in the hole, mashed potato and peas, with onion gravy, of course. Psychic Sue, who was still staying with Fiona until she decided what to do with the shop, had told her she loved toad in the hole. But when they had finished, Fiona saw the sausages still laying on her plate.

"I'm sorry you didn't like it, Sue," she said. "I thought you said it was one of your favourites?"

"Oh, it is. It was lovely, but I've got to be in the mood for the toad bit. I always love the hole, so I eat that every time." She smiled as she turned back to Martin, "So, you knit them yourself? I wish I'd known; I could have sold them in the shop. That tank top is marvellous and the purple shines like a ripe plum."

Martin fiddled with the hem of his jumper, "Many thanks, old thing. It keeps my mind occupied, where brandy would have previously filled the gap. It's good for dexterity too, keeps the old fingers agile."

He got up to clear the plates, as the sound of a doorbell came from the hallway, "Were you expecting anyone, Fiona?"

Fiona pushed her chair back, "Not tonight."

"Allow me," Martin said, and delivered the plates to the kitchen before heading down the stairs and into the tearooms below. He could make out two figures through the glass of the door, one tall, one short.

"Martin, it's me," Anna called. "I haven't got my key with me."

He unlocked the door, "Evening all," he said nodding to Anna and Dawa.

"Sorry, Martin," Dawa said. "Anna and I were talking and we thought it might be useful to have a chat with Psychic Sue, if she was here. But we don't want to disturb your evening."

Anna pushed past Martin, "Actually, we do, because we think we've found a clue. About the fires."

"That sounds intriguing. Fiona is upstairs with Sue. We have just finished a delicious toad in the hole supper."

Anna led the way up the stairs, "How funny, we've had posh sausage and mash in The Mermaid Inn. Oh, Dawa, remember to tell Sam that. It's a good idea, he could have sausage nights. They'd be a hit."

Dawa looked over his shoulder at Martin and smiled, "She has an awful lot of ideas, doesn't she?"

"She does, old thing, she does," Martin chuckled.

Anna bowled into the living room, "Hello, so sorry to interrupt your evening."

"That's alright," Fiona said, clearing the last things from the table. "Would you like a coffee?"

"No thanks, we've just had one. I'll be buzzing all night if I have another."

"I have decaff, I've just made one for Sue."

"No honestly, Fiona, we're fine," Anna said, then looked at Dawa. "Sorry, I mean I'm fine, not we. I didn't mean we're a we or anything. You can have a coffee. Obviously, if you want."

Dawa laughed, "I'm fine too, thank you. Shall we ask Sue what we came for, then leave these people to their evening?"

Anna tucked some curls of copper hair behind her ear, "Oh yes, good idea."

"Me?" Sue said, pushing her large glasses up her nose.

Anna moved a chair closer to her and sat down, "Yes, it's about the fires. The thing is, we found some small burnt patches of grass where fires had been lit in a field

109

near Romney Marsh this afternoon. They were in a big circle. There was a pheasant too who nearly gave us heart attacks, just appeared like a ghost out of this big hedge..."

Dawa, who was standing behind Anna, leant down to her, "Back to the fires," he said, gently, his deep voice rumbling in her ear.

"What? Oh yes," Anna said, fiddling with her hair again.

Martin and Fiona exchanged small smiles.

Anna pulled her phone out of the pocket of the dungarees she had changed into for dinner, "I took a photo of them, would you like to see? Each one had burnt mugwort in them or around them?"

Sue sat forward, "Interesting. You say they were in a circle?"

Dawa scratched his beard, "Yes, we've been going over and over it all evening, but we can't make a connection back to the shops that are being burnt, except the mugwort. We wondered if you could think of anything."

Martin lowered himself into a chair next to Anna, "May I see the photograph?"

"How many fires had there been?" Sue asked.

"Five, I think," Anna said.

Martin nodded in confirmation, "Yes, I can see five. Quite equally spaced."

Sue reached down beside her chair and started to rummage around in a large patchwork tote bag, "Draw them for me. In exactly the positions you found them. I have a pencil in here somewhere."

Dawa reached into his pocket and pulled out a pencil, "Here," he said.

Sue was still upside down in her bag, "And I swear there was some paper in here too. Or some loo roll, maybe."

Fiona went to her father's old drawing board in the corner of the room, something she had not yet had the heart to dismantle, "Here's some paper, Sue."

She laid the flimsy paper out on the table and they all gathered round. Anna then drew five dots in a wide circle around the edge of the paper, according to the layout of the fires as shown on her phone. Then she pushed the paper towards Sue.

Sue peered down at the five dots, then reached out silently to Anna, who put the pencil in her hand. Everyone watched closely as she began to draw. She started with the first dot in the centre of the top edge, she then drew a straight line diagonally to the dot in the bottom right-hand corner. From there she continued the line back up and across to the dot in the middle of the left-hand edge, then straight across to the middle of the right edge, then down to the left-hand corner. Finally, she drew her final line back to the first dot at the very top of the paper.

Anna gasped and everyone stood back.

"I don't understand," Fiona said. "That's a..."

Sue dropped Dawa's pencil in her tote bag, "Yes, dear. It's a five-pointed star, often known as a satanic pentagram."

Fiona shuddered, "A satanic pentagram?"

"The fires are not laid out in a circle, they are laid out in a pentagram. Now to be fair the way I've drawn it the point is at the top, which makes it represent good. I was going for the dramatic when I said it was satanic. The five points refer to fire, water, air, earth and spirit. When the single point is upwards it's a sign of goodness and spirituality. But," and she slowly turned the paper around until the pentagram's top point was facing downwards. "If it is reversed it's thought to be the sign of the descent of the spirit and of satanism."

"How do we know which one this is?" Anna asked, frantically turning the paper round and round.

"Well, we don't dear. But if it's connected to the arson attacks, as you suggest, it can't be being used for good, can it?"

Fiona looked around the group, "I don't really understand this, but it seems like the police should know about it."

"I'm not sure," Dawa said. "It all seems a bit farfetched, doesn't it? Satanic symbols, mystic herbs that call down magic from the moon. It's one step away from the pixies causing the fires."

"I would agree," Martin said. "Sue, from your experience as a psychic, would you say that the authorities might be sceptical of this sort of thing?"

"I should say so. You won't have much luck with that lot when it comes to the spirit world."

Anna was staring intently at the pentagram, "Hm, we need to do some more research and thinking about this. Leave it with me and Dawa, we found the circle of fires, so we can do a bit more digging. Not on Romney

Marsh, I don't think you're allowed to dig there or have barbeques, let alone mugwort barbeques."

"What were you doing on the marshes anyway?" Martin said, with a gentle smile, which earned him a kick under the table from Fiona.

Dawa looked at Anna, "We bumped into each other and went for a quick stroll."

Anna frowned, "Yes, I was delivering a dead cake to a grave person. I mean..."

Fiona went to an armchair and picked up Martin's long coat, "Ignore him, Anna. Martin, you have a bus to catch, don't you?"

Martin shifted in his chair, "Oh, well, I may not go tonight."

Fiona moved to behind his chair and started to pull it away from him, "Oh, no, you don't. I may not be able to come, because Sue is here, but you agreed you would still go."

"I suppose so," Martin said, standing and taking his coat from her. "Shall we go out together?" he asked Anna and Dawa.

"Yes, good idea," Dawa said.

"Thanks so much, Sue," Anna said, kissing her on the cheek. "That's really helped. Now we know it's some sort of satanic ritual, probably all leading up to the Summer Solstice."

"You need to work out what it is they want, dear. What do they need from these burnt shops for their spell?"

Anna called down to Dawa, who was already at the

bottom of the stairs, "Sherlock, did you hear that?"

"Yes, I heard," he said. "Every time we find something out it just leads to more questions."

Anna shrugged, "Maybe we need to have a little walk and talk about it," she said with a shy smile.

He held the café door open for her, "Maybe we should. Good night, Martin."

"Good night, old things," Martin said, watching them walk away into the church yard. He smiled and straightened his purple tank top. As he turned down the hill, a dark figure slid out of a shop entrance ahead of him. They were in dark grey clothing, with their hood up and head down.

"Wait!" Martin called, but the figure began to jog down the hill. He turned back to shout before hurrying after them, "Dawa, Anna! Quickly." He paused as they came running towards him, "I'm not sure if there may be a problem, a fire perhaps in the hairdressers?"

Dawa looked over Martin's shoulder and saw the dark figure running away, "You check, Martin, I'll go after him."

"No, no, leave this to me. I can handle him," and he began to lope over the cobbles, doing up his flapping coat as he went.

He got to the bottom of the hill in time to see a familiar thin back disappearing in the distance. Martin followed discretely, sensing he knew where they might be heading. The hooded figure jumped on a bus at the end of the High Street, and at the last moment Martin slipped through the closing doors and took a seat at the very front, while the young man sat huddled at the back. It would seem his hunch was right.

CHAPTER 12

*A school reunion, Samurai warriors
and tea with two sugars.*

Martin had guessed correctly. They both got off the bus in Tenterden, Martin waiting patiently for his prey to alight first before he quietly followed him.

They went along the familiar route until they reached the nursing home and the young man rang the intercom. He was swiftly granted access and Martin waited five minutes until he too pressed the buzzer.

"Hello," said the cheerful voice.

"Erin, it's Martin. I know I'm not expected, but may I come in?"

"Yes, of course. Come in."

Once Martin was inside, Erin was full of apologies, "I'm so sorry, Martin. No one told me you were coming, Robin's not ready for you."

"Thank you, dear lady, but I am here to see someone else. There was a young man who came in a few minutes before me?"

"Yes, he comes most nights at about this time. Do you know Jack?"

"I believe we have met a few times. Where would I be able to speak with him?"

"Well, I shouldn't say, but he's in the dining room. He's such a lost little soul. He comes every night and he's never eaten anything, so I've started to feed him. We have a hot meal ready for him before he goes to see his dad. I wouldn't want that repeated though, Martin, if you don't mind. It's not in the budget, you see."

"Yes, of course, old thing. How generous. May I go through?"

"Yes, it's at the end of the corridor, down there."

He pushed his way through the doors of a large pink dining room and they banged behind him making the hunched figure alone at a far table jump and turn. Jack immediately leapt to his feet ready to run. Martin held up a hand toward him, "Sorry to startle you, old thing."

"Who are you? I ain't done nothing."

Martin took a step towards him, but Jack backed away, knocking over his chair, "I've a right to be 'ere."

"Yes, visiting your father, I believe."

Jack instinctively pulled his beanie hat lower over his forehead and looked around him for the nearest escape route, "Who are you?"

"You didn't ask my name when you kicked me as I slept under Rye Tower before Christmas. Nor did you ask again when you tried to throw my belongings into the river. But my name is Martin."

Jack began to shift from foot to foot, "That wasn't

me. And that weren't you, that was some old drunk, a tramp."

"One and the same, old thing. I don't have it with me, but you may remember a certain tartan hat? Red, green and yellow, with flaps..."

"What?" Jack said, recognition spreading across his face. "That was you? Well, I didn't, I mean... it weren't..."

"We have also met before my time on the streets, but you would have called me Mr Martin then."

"Eh? I don't know a Mr Martin... 'cept at school, but that was some posh, lanky teacher... Jeez! Was that you too?"

"When I was lodging on the streets of Rye, I thought I had fallen about as low as I could go, until you came along."

"What do you mean?" Jack said, edging slowly to the side of the room, assessing his chances of making a swift exit through the dining room door.

"Well, I thought I was in a pretty poor state, but then this young twit started turning up, usually drunk or high on something, causing all sorts of damage to property or people. He was clearly in a worse state than me - deeply lost, hurting and powerless. So, he took his anger and frustration out on the few people in society he considered to be lesser than himself. People like me."

Jack shook his head and moved a few steps closer to the door, "What you on about?"

Martin sighed, picked up a chair and placed it in front of the doors. He sat down and crossed his legs, as if he was settling in for a chat with an old friend.

"Oy, you can't keep me in here. This is kidnap."

"Is it?" Martin asked, pleasantly. "Good heavens, how awful for you."

There was a heavy silence in the room, as Martin started to pull at a loose strand of purple wool from the bottom of his jumper, "So, you barely troubled me at school because you were hardly ever there, if I recall. However, you had turned into quite a bully when you found me on the streets. But worse still, you chased my friends with a knife. Twice, I believe - getting a good bite from Stanley for your troubles, along the way. Did he leave a scar?"

Jack started at the mention of the little dog and turned his back on Martin, "Aha, so you remember them."

Jack spun round, "I didn't do nothing to 'em. It was me got attacked, knocked out cold."

"I have to say I was never very good at sports at my school, but the one thing I could do was bowl a cricket ball. So, when I launched my bag of pots and pans at you it was a pretty accurate throw."

"It was you?"

"It was indeed."

Jack took a menacing step towards him, but Martin's look was enough to bring him to a halt.

"What do you want, old man?" he asked, sounding braver than he felt. "I'm sorry if I upset your friends, right. I was drunk. I was drunk most of the time then. Not now though. I'm clean, got a job."

"That is good to hear. Where?"

"I'm a builder, learning anyway. Chaz is showing me stuff."

"Chaz? Not the same Chaz who is currently working on the floor above Cinque and turning it into an apartment?"

Jack bit his lip, fearing that he may have said too much.

Martin nodded, "It is. Well, well. Have you apologised to Sam and Ralph for frightening the life out of them? Or haven't they recognised you yet?"

Jack pointed an unsteady hand at Martin, "They don't need to know nothing. I'm not doing anything wrong. I'm doing what Chaz says, that's all. He's given me a chance and I don't want it messed up. Please."

Martin looked at the miserable lad for a long moment, assessing the genuine distress he could see in his face, "Sit down."

"What?"

"Sit. I want to talk, that's all. You can begin by answering one question. I'll know if you're lying."

Jack crossed his arms over his chest, refusing the order to sit, "What?"

"Did you burn the clothes shop and try and set fire to the hairdressers tonight?"

Jack's jaw dropped, "Eh? I ain't burned nothing. I told you, I don't wanna mess up this job. It's the only good thing I've got going for me."

Martin studied Jack's thin face and could see genuine shock in it, "Fine. Please sit down while we talk, then you can go and see your father. He'll be wondering where you are, I expect."

Jack shrugged, "Doubt it." He picked up his chair and slowly sank into it.

"Why do you doubt it?"

"Got Alzheimer's, ain't he. He's no idea who I am."

"Tell me about your dad."

Jack was still, except for the slightest bouncing of his left knee. Martin waited. His years of teaching had taught him that troubled young people often needed more time than you imagined gathering their thoughts. Some simply chose to ignore you and test your resolve, but he suspected that Jack wanted to tell something of his story.

It took several minutes before Jack finally spoke, "He's old. Older than most dads, I suppose. He's been here three months. We had 'im at home before then."

"We?"

"My sister and me."

"That must have been difficult."

Jack shrugged.

"Do you still live with your sister?"

"Nah, she's moved away. Couldn't get a job 'ere. Plus, she said she couldn't be around Dad no more. That's when she asked her mate to see if Chaz would give me a job, so I could look after myself. That's how I got to work with them friends of yours, the queers."

Martin frowned, but let that pass, "Did you get on with your dad?"

Jack looked directly at Martin, "He was a shit."

"Ah, I see. And your mother?"

"Sod knows. She disappeared when I was about two. So, it was just the three of us. Paula, that's my sister, kind of brought me up, she's a bit older. He never did nothing, left it all to her. Never said thank you nor nothing, but he never bullied her neither. Probably knew she'd tell him to f-off and he wouldn't get no dinner."

"And he bullied you?"

Jack shrugged, "Yeah. I got used to it."

"Jack, you shouldn't have had to get used to it, you were a child. You know that don't you?"

"Yeah, I do now. The shrink said it was something about trauma and what-not that got me into trouble. Being angry with everything, drinking and stuff. Like having a go at them queers."

Martin leant forward, "Before we go any further, please answer a question for me."

"What?"

"Is there a name that your father called you that you hated, that was particularly unkind or cruel?"

Jack swallowed and looked away.

"Look at me Jack, please."

He did.

"Was there a word?"

Jack nodded, his leg starting to bounce again.

"I want you to think of that word now and hear your father saying it to you. Are you doing that?"

Jack shrugged, then nodded.

"Think of how that word made you feel when he said it. Now remember that you make someone else feel exactly the same when you use the word queer or anything similar. Do you understand?"

Jack nodded.

"Words are weapons in the wrong mouths, Jack. Like your father's. I assume, as you don't like him very much, you don't really want to grow up to be like him?"

Jack looked at the floor and shook his head, "Nah."

"Then please think when you use words that you know very well are designed to hurt."

"She said that too. The shrink."

Martin sat back, "Are you still seeing her?"

"Nah. Last time I was in trouble with the police my solicitor got me off if I went to see her. That's all finished now."

"I see, and was it useful?"

"Yeah, I s'pose so. Paula said I was nicer afterwards."

"Good, then I commend you, Jack. Changing one's behaviour is hard. I couldn't stop my drinking and that is why you found me on the streets."

"Really?"

"Oh, yes, I was a proper drunk. Not angry like you, just unable to function efficiently. Lost my job, my wife and my home. But I'm getting better now."

"Do you still drink anything?"

Martin raised his bushy eyebrows, "Tea. Lots and lots of bloody tea."

Jack paused then stood up, "Want one now?"

"That's very kind. Two sugars, please."

Jack went to a counter at the side of the room and dropped tea bags into two mugs and poured water on them from a hot water urn, "Why are you 'ere? Who you seeing?"

"All in good time, old thing," Martin said. "Let's finish the tale of young Jack first. I'm interested in why you visit your father if you think of him as a bit of shit?"

Jack grinned as he heard Martin's refined voice use that word, "He always said I couldn't do nothing. He never took no notice of anything I did at school, not even the stuff I was good at." As he stirred the milk and sugar into the tea he used his other hand to feel for something under his jacket at the base of his back. Once he was satisfied it was still there, he brought the mugs back and handed one to Martin, "But I've got a proper job now, and it ain't too bad."

"Thank you."

Jack returned to his seat and flopped down, "I show him photos of what I'm doing at the queers... I mean, Sam and Ralph's place. I put some pipes in today, plumbing stuff and I wanted to show him what I done."

Martin nodded slowly, waiting for more.

Jack's leg began to bounce again, "He looks, but he don't really take in what he's seeing. The nurses say sometimes he's more like his old self. So, I come every day in case he's more normal and can know what I've done."

"And what do you want him to say when he is more his old self?"

Jack responded without hesitation, "Well done, son.

As soon as he says that I ain't coming back. That's it, I'm done with him. I just want him to know that I can hold a job, I can pay my way and I'll be alright."

"Yes, I believe you will be, Jack. More than alright. You make a decent cup of tea, for a start."

"Ta." Jack grinned at him, "Sorry about the stuff when you was on the street. I didn't know what I was doing most of the time." He reached round to his back again, an unconscious movement that had not gone unnoticed.

"I hope that whatever is down the back of your trousers is not a weapon, Jack? You told me you had put all that behind you."

"Nah, don't worry, old man. It ain't nothing like that, it's something I do. Nothing special. Bit of drawing stuff."

"May I see?"

Jack's hand lingered on his back, "I ain't no artist."

Martin frowned, "You are an artist with a tea bag, so I'm willing to take the risk."

Jack shrugged, then carefully pulled a rolled up A4 notepad from the back of his trousers. The cover was curled back and he tried to smooth it between his hands, "It's probably not your thing. It's kind of a graphic novel."

"Interesting. I had an interest in Japanese Manga for a while, when a promising student was creating dystopian graphic novels." He put his tea mug on the floor and held out his hand, as Jack stared at him open mouthed.

Slowly, Jack came forward and placed his notepad in Martin's hand. Martin set it gently on his lap and wiped his hands on his trousers to ensure they were clean. He smoothed the cover as Jack had done and carefully peeled it back to reveal the first page. It was a blaze of activity. A series of four panels were neatly outlined on the page and exquisitely detailed drawings of Samurai warriors roared their way across them. Martin tried not to show his surprise as he turned the page to find the story develop in further panels of carefully drawn and inked artwork.

Although the notepad was tatty it was clear that Jack had spent hours poring over each meticulous panel telling the story of a young Samurai servant, forced to fight in place of his master. Halfway through the notepad the panels stopped and there were blank pages.

"What happens next?" Martin said, flicking gently back through the pages of drawings.

"Don't know yet," Jack said, sinking his hands deep into his pockets.

"Who taught you to do this?"

"Erm, no one, I just mess about with it."

"I can assure you this is far from messing about. This is quite brilliant. Such a shame you didn't come to more of my art classes at school, I was always on the lookout for talent like this. Is this your first story?"

"Nah, I've got a few more at home. Paula used to love them, so I drew them for her and told her the stories. She weren't so good at reading, she liked seeing the pictures."

Martin handed the notepad back to Jack, "You have a

talent, young man. Congratulations. Perhaps one day I could see some of your other stories?"

Jack scratched his head under his hat, "Yeah, if you want to. I'll have to find them, they're in the flat somewhere."

They both jumped as Erin, the smiling nurse, tried to open the dining room doors but banged into Martin's chair. "Sorry, dear thing," he said, moving aside.

Erin pushed the door open and stuck her head through, "I just wanted to let you know we're going to be getting everyone ready for bed soon. So, if you want to see your dad, Jack, you'd better come now."

Jack sighed, "Alright, ta, I'm coming," and stuffed his notepad roughly down the back of his trousers again, causing Martin to wince at the casual treatment of such beautiful work.

Martin stood and Jack collected the mugs and his plate of cold steak and kidney pie and took it through to the kitchen. Martin heard him washing them under a running tap and smiled.

Jack returned and they both headed out into the corridor, "Erm, don't suppose you wanna meet my dad, do you?" Jack said, looking embarrassed.

"Would you like me to?"

Jack did his usual shrug, "Up to you. I don't mind or nothing, but sometimes I wonder what he's gonna be like. I mean, I wanna show him what I've done when he's normal, but at the same time..."

Martin put a hand on his shoulder, "He can be difficult when he's his old self?"

"Yeah, something like that."

"Very well, let us face him together. Lead the way, old thing."

CHAPTER 13

Showtunes, the tartan hat and a countess.

P sychic Sue went to bed early, as she tended to rise with the sun and do some meditation that involved chanting and banging of small cymbals. Fiona wasn't quite sure it followed any particular discipline, as she'd heard Sue singing showtunes in amongst the chants on some mornings. But she was a pleasant and easy guest who needed a friendly home until she sorted out what to do with her shop and the flat above.

In order not to disturb Sue, who was snoring quietly in the guest bedroom, Fiona had the radio close to her with the volume turned down low. She sat under a reading lamp, mending Martin's old tartan hat that had started to come apart at the seams. He tried to protest when she took it from him, but she had insisted she would enjoy trying to piece it back together.

After an hour in the quiet, humming along to music as she worked, it was something of a shock to hear a sharp knocking on the door of the tearooms downstairs. She checked the clock, it was gone ten o'clock. Perhaps it was Martin wanting to collect his hat. She turned off the radio and put the hat on the side table, before heading down the stairs. The knocking came again, three hard bangs on the door.

She thought it might be good to start to get friends to use the back door, so she could ignore unknown callers to the tearooms, "Who is it?"

"The Countess of Groombridge," a shadowy figure called back through the door.

Fiona froze. Martin's wife? Visiting her in the middle of the night? Had something happened to Martin, had there been an accident?

"Is he alright?" Fiona asked, as she quickly unbolted and opened the door.

"You tell me," came the haughty reply. The countess stood tall and straight in a tightly belted grey Macintosh, an expensive handbag held defensively in front of her. She had blonde hair, the colour clearly not of nature's doing, piled high on her head with force and a wall of hairspray. Her eyes were grey and dangerous as they took Fiona in from head to toe.

"It's very nice to meet you, I'm Fiona."

"So I believe. I realise it's late, but am I to be invited in or shall we conduct our business on the doorstep?"

Fiona stepped back, "Oh, I'm sorry, do come in. Has something happened?"

The countess didn't answer. She stepped into the tearoom, looking around her carefully, as if fixing every detail in her mind. "Hmm," she said. "Where are the living quarters?"

"Upstairs. Would you like to come up? I can put the kettle on."

Before she had finished, the countess was climbing the narrow stairs, leaving Fiona to follow in her wake.

When she got to the top her visitor was standing stiffly in the middle of the living room, her face pinched with haughty distaste. Fiona found herself apologising, "It's my father's old flat. It's only temporary, but it's convenient for work. Would you like a cup of tea or coffee?"

The countess looked at her, "He's not here?"

"If you mean Martin, no. He left after supper."

"When will he be back?"

"Back? I don't know, he comes for supper a few times a week. If you need him, I can point you towards his flat, or take you down there if you like."

"Let us not waste time on pretence, Mrs Hawkins," the countess said, as she tucked her coat carefully around her bottom and sat on the edge of an armchair, clasping her handbag tightly on her knees.

"Grace, I really don't know what you mean. And how do you know my name?"

The countess flinched slightly at the use of her Christian name, but never took her gaze from Fiona's face, "I have people who can find out these things. I've been keeping tabs on my husband ever since I told him to leave the house, knowing that every piece of information would be useful during the divorce. A woman needs to have her wits about her in such matters, I'm sure you will agree in your current situation. Your husband was not the easiest, I understand."

Fiona stiffened, "I don't know what you think you know about my situation, but it is really none of your business."

"Oh, but it is, Mrs Hawkins. If my husband is being supported by another woman then it has an impact on the divorce settlement. Why anyone would want a drunken fool like him is beyond me, but I suppose if you are desperate..."

Fiona rarely raised her voice, but since freeing herself from Andy's coercive control she had promised herself that she would no longer be brow beaten by anyone. She realised this was exactly the moment to fulfil that promise, "Stop it, Grace. Martin and I work together. We are friends, nothing more."

"That is not what I have been told."

"Well, you have been given very poor information. And... and..."

Grace's grey eyes were looking steely now, "And?"

Fiona had so much she wanted to say but didn't know where to begin or even if she should. She looked at Grace, tightly buttoned up, angry, tense, full of righteous indignation but also hurt. She sat on the armchair next to her, "And... I understand what you must be going through."

Grace forced her shoulders back, "I don't need your sympathy, young lady."

"Well, then perhaps you might appreciate some honesty. Your husband is a charming man, with a troubled past. That can't have been easy to live with. He has told me something of his troubles with drink, but he is doing very well putting it behind him. I can't imagine what he went through, sleeping on the streets every night for weeks. I also can't believe that if you did keep tabs on him, as you say, you would have left him there."

Grace reached for the pearls that were stretched around her throat, "He had brought the situation on himself."

"You knew he was sleeping rough and you did nothing to help him?"

"Why should I? He had drunk himself into the ground most days, so now he could sleep on it."

"That is cruel. I know what it's like to be in a marriage that is unhappy, I really do, but I would never see anyone brought that low. Never."

"Then you have quite a different outlook on life to me." Grace's tone was sharp as she tried to change the direction of the conversation, "Do you deny that you and my husband are in anyway interdependent?"

"Interdependent? What an awful word. We are friends, no more. Martin needs friends more than ever, and he has plenty in Rye."

"Does he really? Then the people of Rye have lower standards than I had realised," she stood, but instead of heading back towards the stairs, she grabbed the tartan hat on the table next to the chair.

"So, you are not in any sort of relationship with my husband? And yet here is his hat, what's left of the disgusting thing."

Fiona jumped to her feet, her fists clenched tight at her sides, "It's here because I was mending it for my friend. He has worn it every day through the cold winter, trying to keep warm as he slept on benches and behind hedges. What is disgusting is that you will not let him collect the rest of his clothes and other belongings, so he can have some dignity back."

"Dignity? You dare talk to me about dignity. You have no idea what I have suffered with a drunk for a husband. The invitations dried up; my friends abandoned me in droves. It was bad enough that he worked as a teacher in a comprehensive school, instead of something more in keeping."

"In keeping with what?"

"With our status."

"It was in keeping with Martin, with the man he is. He loves art and the power it has to help young people. That's why he was a teacher. You must have heard him talk about the great masters and what they have to offer new generations of young people, freeing their creativity and allowing them to view the world from different perspectives. He is so passionate and inspiring."

Fiona looked at shock cross Grace's face and realised that, no, perhaps the countess had never heard her husband speak that way, "I'm sorry, Grace, but the Martin I know doesn't seem to be the one you are familiar with. Or perhaps you have forgotten the real him."

Grace's jaw tightened and she threw the tartan hat on the floor, "Don't you dare tell me what I have forgotten about my own husband. Don't you dare. Perhaps you have been charmed by him, he could do that once upon a time. But there is an awful lot about him that you don't know. How he treated his poor father, shamed the family, let the Groombridge estate be taken from him. The man is a failure, always has been. I may accept that you are not in a relationship with him; you seem to have a spark in you that might prevent you sinking to that level. He is old enough to be your father, if not grandfather, after all. I will leave now and would appreciate you not talking of our conversation with anyone. We women must stick together." She spun around and marched towards the stairs, her back stiff.

"Wait," Fiona said and Grace hesitated, but did not turn. "Women should only stick together if they know they are trying to do the right thing. You are not. You are trying to hurt Martin. I know he is not perfect and his past is complicated, but he is doing his best to deal with all of that. He needs our support, not our judgement. It may be too late for you, but I can see the man he is underneath this tatty tartan hat. Grace, if you can find anyway to remember what he must have meant to you once, please allow him some dignity and let him collect his belongings."

Grace listened to Fiona's words but said nothing. Too many walls had been built around her over the years to allow a stranger to illicit emotion from her. She tightened the belt on her coat and descended the stairs. She opened and closed the door with barely a sound and walked down the hill to the waiting taxi. As it pulled away, she looked back at the small window above the tearooms with its warm yellow glow, and envied the young woman starting her life again behind the glass.

CHAPTER 14

Savoury surprises, lifeboats and Dawa makes a mistake.

The next day was Saturday and for the locals it was a big day, as the winners of the annual Rye art competition were to be announced at 7.30pm. After moving the last customers out and closing the café, Anna only had a couple of hours to prepare the catering for what could be as many as fifty guests.

Dawa had been dragooned into service and was wearing the Thunderbirds apron Anna had bought for him.

"I don't want to sound ignorant," he said. "But why are we pushing whole roasted garlic cloves into these little scones?"

"They're my Savoury Surprise Scones. Instead of the usual boring cheese ones, these are parsnip and garlic. The parsnip is the savoury bit and the garlic is the surprise in the middle."

"Amazing," Dawa said, smiling at her enthusiasm and creativity. "I would never in a million years have thought of that."

"Me neither. I hope they taste alright."

"You mean you haven't made them before?"

"Nope, I forgot to buy cheese and had loads of parsnips in the fridge, so needs must and all that. You look nice today, by the way. Did I say that already?"

"Erm, no, but thank you."

"I think blue turbans look really good on you," she kept her head down over the tray of scones, feeling the intimacy of them both working next to each other warming her skin. They were trying to carry on as normal, but she was conscious that since the walk on the marshes things had been far from normal between them. She tried to sound casual as she asked, "Is it true Sikhs started wearing turbans to signify that everyone was equal?"

"Yes, where did you learn that?"

Anna felt herself blush a little, "I looked it up. I also learnt that Sikhism is the fifth largest religion in the world and has twenty-seven million followers, at last count. Sorry, but I was interested."

"Don't apologise, it's charming that you made the effort."

"Well, thank you, kind sir," she said, bobbing a curtsey and staggering against the counter. Dawa put out a hand to save her. She turned to see him laughing too, not at her but with her. She was amazed that such a serious looking man could have such a lovely laugh. Then there was that smile. Those teeth. The lovely deep eyes... She shook herself, "Anyway, where were we? Oh, yes, you'd had a thought about the fires."

"It's more of a question really. The pentagram has five points and if your theory is right that each one matches a fire in the town, that means two more shops have to burn before... before what?"

"I don't know, but I know they have to be connected. I mean it can't be coincidence, can it? It's just a working theory, my dear Watson."

"I thought I was Sherlock Holmes and you were Dr Watson?" Dawa said, starting to wash up at the sink.

"Oh, yes, I forgot. The main point is, who's next?"

Without thinking, Anna leant across Dawa and rinsed her hands in the sink. She was very close. He looked at the pretty freckles sprinkled across her nose. He could see her breath moving a few strands of copper hair that had fallen across her cheek.

"Anna?" he asked.

She stepped back and dried her hands, "What is it?"

"I... well, I wanted to say how much I enjoy our time together."

"Oh, me too. I feel like I can tell you anything and you won't laugh at me or think I'm daft. I love talking to you."

"Do you?"

"Dawa, what's the matter? You look a bit funny. Are you allergic to garlic? Are your lips going to turn blue, is your throat closing? Oh, my god, I've killed you with garlic."

Dawa didn't know what to do. Anna's voice was rising in hysteria. He knew he should say something or do something. This was a moment that required action on his part, but he had no idea what that was. So, many thoughts ran through his mind at such a speed he couldn't find one to hang on to. So, he kissed her. He pulled her to him with his wet, soapy hands and kissed her.

The moment he felt her soft lips against his he knew he'd done the wrong thing. She tensed and tried to step back. He stared at the shock in her eyes, as her beautiful, freckled face turned red. He'd done the one thing he'd told himself he must not do; he had ruined their friendship. The best thing that had ever happened to him.

He stepped away from her and with a tight throat apologised, "Anna, forgive me." Then he practically ran to the door, ripped it open and fled.

Anna stood in the kitchen, the feel and taste of Dawa Singh still on her lips. She stayed like that for ages, not wanting to break the spell. Then a feeling rose from her green plastic sandals to the top of her head. She punched the air and yelled, "YES!" at the top of her voice.

* * *

Ralph was waiting on the pavement for Sam to lock the blue door of their flat when Dawa came flying out of The Cookery and ran towards him.

"Everything alright, Dawa?"

Dawa looked startled as if he didn't recognise him, then he stopped and shook his head, "No, I think I have done something very wrong."

Sam grinned, "Well, you forgot to take your apron off, for a start."

Ralph looked at Dawa, who was clearly not in a joking mood, "Shut up, Sam. Dawa? What's happened?"

Dawa hesitated, he wasn't sure whether he should confess or not, Ralph was Anna's best friend after all, "It's... well, I seem to have... I don't know."

Sam unlocked the door again, "I think we should take this up to the rooftop, this situation looks like it needs a drink. Come on."

They led a dazed Dawa through the flat and on to the roof terrace.

Dawa went to the low wall that overlooked the town and sighed, "This is beautiful. I've heard about the rooftop and your club, but I've never actually seen it."

Ralph went to the bar for some beers and Sam moved Dawa over to a chair and pushed him down into it, "I can't believe you've never been up here; you are always welcome."

Dawa kept his eyes in his lap and Sam saw the strong man's shoulders slump, "I'm not sure I will be welcome now."

Ralph placed the beers on Auntie B's little iron table.

Sam pushed a bottle in front of his old friend, "Dawa you need to tell me what's going on. It can't be as bad as you think it is. If Anna's kicked off about something it's just part of her way. You need to let her calm down and it'll be over in a couple of hours – that's what we do."

"I doubt you ever forced your unwanted attentions on her though, did you?"

Ralph wasn't expecting that and he choked as a sip of beer went down the wrong way. Dawa jumped up and thumped him firmly on the back, which made Ralph cough even more.

"Sorry," Dawa said. "I'm stressed, that was a little harder than I had meant to hit you."

Ralph's eyes watered as he shook his head, "No... no. It's fine. I'm fine. But maybe don't hit me again."

"Understood," Dawa said and sat down. "Sam, Ralph, I must tell you, women are something of a mystery to me. I watched them throw themselves at Sam's father, a very handsome, virile man. They were unrepentant and I may even describe some of them as rampant, if that is not misogynist."

"No, I don't think so in that context. Women are allowed to be rampant, I guess," Ralph said.

"I then watched them try to worm their way into your life, Sam, when you were forced into the world of celebrity by Jane Scott. Another woman who is, shall we say, single-minded? I have a mother and aunties who were in complete control of our family throughout my childhood. They would feed and coddle and bully you from dawn to dusk."

"Good grief, it sounds like a horror film," Sam said. "But there are kinder, gentler women, Dawa."

"I know. I have met a few. I was engaged for a short while."

Sam sat up, "I didn't know that. What happened?"

"She was very sweet. We were promised to each other from a very early age, our mothers were friends. We had no knowledge of it or say in it. Suddenly at eighteen we were told it was time to marry."

"Blimey, that must have come as a bit of a shock," Ralph said.

Dawa took a sip of his beer, "You could say that." He didn't know why he was telling them all this, but he found he couldn't stop talking, "We were friends, but we didn't want to marry one another. There was no spark or chemistry, or whatever is needed for a relationship such as marriage. We fought our parents, but they insisted. We both refused, so a stalemate was reached. It lasted for a month, neither side budging until Alisha disappeared with a boy from the supermarket. He gathered trolleys and the like from the car park. He was a very nice lad. They eloped. I was freed of my obligation."

"That sounds like a lucky escape. What happened to them?" Sam asked.

"I believe they are still together, somewhere in deepest, darkest Essex," he managed a brief smile. "She deserved to be happy, she was a very pleasant person."

"So, when you say you forced yourself on Anna," Ralph said, moving back to the main point, conscious that he and Sam were due at the art gallery. "You don't mean anything bad, do you? I'd be very surprised if..."

"I kissed her. Without asking or getting consent or her opinion or permission or..."

Ralph and Sam looked at each other and sighed with relief.

"Dawa," Sam said. "Anna would have been over the moon that you kissed her."

"Of course, she would," Ralph added.

Dawa was stunned, "What? Over the moon? How do you know?"

"It's been obvious," Sam said. "She's been as giddy as a kipper for the last few weeks."

"Because of me?"

"Of course. She's been on about your clothes and your eyes and your lovely teeth..."

"You do have great teeth by the way," Ralph chimed in.

"And she's obsessed with the quality of your shoes, for some reason."

"But, why didn't she say something?"

Sam leant in to Dawa, as if things needed explaining in simple terms, "Well, you've both been so wrapped up in this paranormal, witchy, solstice stuff that neither of you saw it coming. We did. We all did. Plus, I mean, you can be a bit of a closed book, can't you?"

Dawa picked up his beer and took a long drink, "I have never had a woman as a friend, I was enjoying it. Enjoying it too much to spoil it by falling in love with her. Everything changes then, doesn't it?"

Sam looked at Ralph, "Well, yes, it does tend to. But not for the worse, Dawa, it gets better."

He looked astonished, "Does it?"

"How many women have you actually dated in your life?" Ralph asked.

"Four."

"Four?"

Dawa looked up at the sky and sighed, "I can honestly

say I have absolutely zero understanding of good women. Monsters, I manage reasonably well, I have Mama Singh and Sam's mother, Jane Scott, to thank for that. But as for the special ones, like Anna, I have not got a clue."

Sam smiled, "Well, you are in the right place, my friend. The rooftop is exactly where you need to be to begin to understand the world of love and romance. Boys, girls, beagle dogs, we love them all equally and we are experts at ridiculous relationships, as well as the best ones you can possibly imagine."

"So, you really don't think I have behaved inappropriately?"

Ralph laughed, "Knowing Anna, she's downstairs now making heart-shaped biscuits and practicing writing Anna Singh in icing across them."

* * *

"You need to pull yourself together, you've gone barmy," Irene declared as Anna twirled across the kitchen with a tea cloth wrapped across her head like a veil.

"But you have no idea what it was like," she said. "He was so strong. He was washing up and it was passionate, it came from nowhere, he just pulled me in to him and kissed me."

Irene pulled a chair into the kitchen and sat down heavily, "Tell me who it is then. I've heard about the kissing and him mauling you about with his big, strong hands and all that. We've all been there and done that, but you haven't said who."

"I'm not sure we're ready to go public yet," Anna said, pouring herself a glass of orange juice. "Do you want a drink?"

"Not today, I'm retaining fluids again. I'll need a lifeboat soon if I hang on to this much water," Irene sniffed. "But you can tell me, I won't tell a soul. I have no friends, you know that, well, not any I like anyway."

"No, Irene, I need to sort things out with him first. I think he was a bit frightened by the passion of it all. He left pretty quickly. He may be back soon with flowers or something. Do you think he'll be back with flowers? What if we've gone over to the gallery? I'll leave a note on the door, maybe. It was funny, he left so quickly he forgot to take his apron off. It was a Thunderbirds one, I..."

"Oh, it's Dawa Singh," Irene said.

"What? How did you know that?"

Irene adjusted an awkward bit of hanky in her bra, "I saw him talking to Ralph outside the bookshop and I thought it was odd he had a pinny on."

"Well, you mustn't say anything to anyone. He's a very private person. He's ever so deep too."

"What's he doing with you then?"

"Excuse me, I can be deep."

"Daft, not deep, you mean."

Anna ignored her and hung her Brighton Aquarium tea towel veil back on the hook, "Look at the time. We need to get all this food over to the gallery. Grab that pile of boxes, I'll bring the rest."

CHAPTER 15

Expensive owls, Angela Lansbury
and surprise guests.

Martin and Fiona were enjoying a stroll around the Rye Gallery ahead of the competition results, "His drawing skills are extraordinary," Martin was saying. "You would never have thought him capable of a coherent thought to look at him, let alone anything like a graphic novel. Samurai Warriors too, of all things. Here is my dilemma, dear thing. He is working on Sam and Ralph's new flat. Should I tell them and potentially jeopardise Jack's new start, or keep quiet and let them have their homophobic attacker quietly plumb in their bathroom?"

Fiona leant her shoulder against a white column, "If it were me, I wouldn't tell them. I would find a way of persuading Jack to tell them himself and apologise."

"Yes, that would certainly be worth a try," Martin said, laying a steadying hand on her shoulder. "One other tiny thing... don't move."

Fiona froze, "Why? What is it?"

"That column you are leaning on appears to have a

large ceramic owl attached to the top with a price tag of nearly a thousand pounds."

Fiona began to panic, but Martin held her still, "What do I do?"

"Slowly and I mean *very* slowly, start to lean towards me. No sudden movements."

Fiona did as instructed and millimetre by millimetre took her weight away from the column, which gave the smallest of wobbles, but the owl stayed attached to its perch. She sighed with relief, "Thank goodness. Imagine if you hadn't seen it and..."

"It would have been a very expensive evening followed by quite a few nights with a magnifying glass and a large tube of glue putting it back together again," Martin chuckled.

Fiona moved away, "Look, Anna's arrived. Shall we see if she needs a hand?"

"Good idea."

They crossed to the front of the gallery, where a large table covered with a white cloth had been set up for the food. Anna and Irene were beginning to lay out plates and platters.

"Thank goodness," Irene said. "Two healthy specimens. She's in love and not firing on all cylinders, it's all hands on deck."

"I am absolutely fine," Anna said, as she disappeared under the table. "Just need to deal with the fairy things," she shouted from behind the white cloth.

"See what I mean," sniffed Irene. "Martin, you're on plates and napkins. Fiona, start doling out them mini scone things and the sausage rolls. They're vegetarian, but I had one and they didn't taste much like grass."

As they began their allotted tasks a string of fairy lights flew up from under the table and looped themselves over Irene's arm, causing her to stagger against the table, "What are you playing at?"

Anna crawled out from under it, "I told you; I was looking for a socket to plug the fairy lights in. They'll look nice draped around the food."

Irene untangled herself from the wires, "Gave me a proper fright, you did. No wonder I'm holding on to water in every crevice. I'm part woman, part mermaid."

The gallery door opened and Ralph and Sam hurried in, "Sorry we're late," they chorused, exchanging looks and sniggering.

"They're drunk," Irene said, waving a daisy patterned napkin at them. "That's all we need. Two tanked up wotsits..."

"Irene, behave," Anna said. "Can you help Fiona and Martin? Everyone's arriving and they announce the winners in about twenty minutes. We need to fill people's faces with as much of this food as we can before then."

Fifteen minutes later, the gallery was heaving with an excited crowd, all enjoying the food and looking at the competition entries.

"Where's Sam bum?" Irene whispered loudly to Anna.

"Shush, they still don't know. See those two big easels with the sheets thrown over them? Well, they're the top two, which they'll reveal in a minute. Ralph's painting is not on the walls so it must be under one of the sheets.

He's going to win, I knew it!"

Irene crossed her arms over her chest, "He's going to go mad, you know that don't you?"

"No, he'll be fine," Anna said, checking for any newcomers. "You did stick the note to the café door, didn't you? So Dawa knows I'm over here."

"I did, but you won't see him for dust. He's had a taste of you, so he'll head for the hills now. Grizzly bears do the same when they've had half your leg."

"Oh, they're going to start, come on."

Paul, the gallery owner, called order and everyone gathered around the covered easels in the middle of the gallery. Anna and Irene squeezed through the crowd to stand with Ralph, Sam, Fiona and Martin, "It's so exciting, isn't it?" Anna whispered.

"It'll all end in tears," Irene sniffed.

Paul introduced the Mayor of Rye, who wore his chain of office at a slightly crooked angle, but his wife's large hat prevented her from noticing and putting it straight.

"We will begin," Paul said, after the polite applause for the mayor's welcome speech had died away. "With the junior competition winners. All entries had to be by young people under the age of fourteen. There will be a winner and a runner up, who will each receive book tokens kindly donated by The Bookery just along the High Street." Paul gestured to Ralph and the crowd applauded enthusiastically.

"I am afraid that our very special celebrity guest is running a little late, so the mayor has agreed to present the prizes to our young artists. Now, the runner up is..." He reached behind the first easel and pulled out a large sheet of cardboard, on which the familiar face of Captain Pugwash had been rendered in dried pasta shapes. "Laura Panter and her ingenious portrait in pasta of Captain Pugwash!"

There was more applause and little Laura Panter stepped forward to claim her tokens from the mayor.

"Didn't she win your competition for the Beagle Book Club with the same picture?" Martin said to Ralph out of the corner of his mouth.

"I don't think it could have been the same one, as all the pasta fell off, if you remember."

"Ah, yes, indeed," Martin said, with a chuckle.

Paul then reached for the winning picture, "And the winner is, Elliot Village, with his painting of Broadway legend Angela Lansbury in a tea pot. A reference to her role as Mrs Potts in Beauty and The Beast, I imagine."

There was a big cheer and the small nine-year-old with plastic glasses and a sequined bow tie, who everyone knew as the Rye Rovers' goalkeeper, stepped shyly forward to shake hands with the mayor.

"The judges were not only impressed by the quality of Elliot's art, but with his knowledge of Broadway history in one so young."

Everyone applauded again and Elliot waved at Sam and Ralph, who cheered their young friend back to his place beside his mum, Amanda, who had chosen a particularly revealing top for the evening as her husband had left her last New Year's Eve and she was determined not to be alone for the next one.

"Now," Paul said, hushing the crowd. "In the adult section, there is a runner up who wins a delicious afternoon tea for two at the beautiful Copper Kettle Tearooms." Anna stepped forward and curtsied to acknowledge the applause. "The winner, however, will receive a paid commission to paint our very special celebrity guest. I wonder if we should take a break, while we see what has happened to them? They may have got lost."

As he spoke the door to the gallery slammed open behind the crowd and a voice quite used to addressing a large audience rang through the gallery, "Darlings, you must think I'm awful to be so late." Everyone stared at the vision draping herself across the doorway, before spontaneously bursting into the loudest applause of the night. Except one small group of people who all looked at Sam, "Mother?" he groaned.

"Ladies and gentlemen," Paul shouted above the noise. "Please welcome our very special guest, Britain's favourite Hollywood actress, Miss Jane Scott."

Jane held her pose for a moment to give everyone the full impact of her deep blue velvet dress and famous curvature, before sashaying towards Paul through the crowd that parted like the Red Sea in front of Moses.

"The lovely man who drove me thought we were going to Ryde, not Rye," she said as she arrived in front of her audience. "Luckily, I spotted his error before we actually got to the Isle of Wight Ferry," she tipped her head back and gave a full-throated operatic laugh, which set the crowd off again.

She looked around the room, assessing the numbers and best angles for photographs, but stopped dead as she saw Sam, "Samuel! Darling, how did you know I'd be here? It was supposed to be a surprise. Come kiss your mother." She flung her clutch bag at Paul and held her arms wide.

The audience strained to see Sam, Jane's famously handsome son. He kept his head down and his position in the crowd.

"I think you have to go and kiss her," Ralph whispered to him, pushing him forward.

"I don't want to," Sam hissed back.

"It has to be done, old thing," Martin said, eying Jane Scott carefully, remembering their previous encounter when he used all his persuasive skills to prevent her selling her son to the highest tabloid bidder.

Sam reluctantly slouched towards his mother and disappeared inside her elaborate embrace. "Why are you here?" he said in her ear.

"We're filming up the road and I've been trying to get a free portrait done for years. Do you know how much they cost?" she whispered back, before pushing him away from her and fussing with his hair in a theatrical but motherly way. "I swear you get more handsome every time I see you," she said, swinging him round to face the crowd. "Don't you think so everyone?"

The crowd did think so and whooped and whistled as Sam quickly escaped back into the centre of the Rooftop Club who closed protectively around him.

"Well, perhaps we should find out who has won the right to paint my portrait," Jane purred. "Oh, are you the mayor? How sweet, I didn't know they still had those. Good lord, now that's a hat we'll all remember in the morning, Mrs Mayor," and she hooted with laughter.

"Shall we reveal the winners of this year's Rye Art

Competition," Paul said, hurriedly. "Ms Scott, if you could pull the cover off the smaller painting to the left, please. This is our runner up."

Jane expertly revealed a small oil painting of a seagull floating through the breeze above Camber Sands, a small child below reaching up to try and touch it.

"How cute," she muttered, before slinging the sheet back over it. "But who's going to paint me?"

Paul handed her an envelope, "Perhaps you could present the afternoon tea vouchers to our very own local police sergeant and artist Phil Logan, who painted this charming local scene."

"If I must," she mumbled, as Sergeant Phil came forward and shook her hand. They had their photo taken and he returned to the crowd.

"And so, now the big moment," Paul began, but he got no further as Jane stepped up to the larger easel, grabbed the top of the sheet and pulled.

"The artist who will paint my portrait is..."

There was a gasp from the crowd swiftly followed by genuine and prolonged applause for Ralph's portrait of Sam.

"W-what the..?" Ralph stuttered, turning furiously to Anna.

"Surprise," she sang.

Jane was looking anxiously around the noisy crowd, "But who won? Who did this?" she called.

Anna and Irene took Ralph by an arm each and thrust him towards Jane, as Paul announced, "The winning painting is entitled Morning View, by Ralph Wright."

Ralph and Jane faced each other, "Ralph?"

"Hello, Jane."

"You did this?"

He swallowed hard, "Erm, yes."

"But... it's beautiful," she said and turned to gaze again at the painting.

"R-really?" Ralph managed to say.

"I had no idea you could do something like this."

The crowd had fallen silent by now, everyone looking at the large painting of Sam's naked back. Jane took a step closer to the picture, peering intently at it. Eventually she turned, "I would know that green eye anywhere. Can you see it in the reflection everyone?" The crowd leaned in to see. "It is identical to my own. Eyes that launched a thousand sighs, one critic famously called them. I have also seen that bottom many times in my life, often hovering over a potty, I will admit. This is my son, isn't it? This is a portrait of Sam!"

The crowd gasped again, something they were beginning to enjoy, and turned to look at Sam. Martin took a discrete step forward and turned to Sam, partially blocking everyone's view, "It's a shock, but it is also a stunning picture," he said, quietly.

"Yes," Fiona added, stepping beside Martin, blocking Sam from the rest of the crowd. "You must be very proud of Ralph."

Even Irene could see what was happening and took a large tray of sausage rolls and drew people away from Sam, "Nothing to see here. He's got a lovely bum, we can all see it over there on the easel thing, not here. Come on, who's not had one of these miserable vegetable things?"

Ralph pushed his way through the crowd as they turned their attention back to the painting, "I didn't know about it," he said to Sam.

"But you painted it."

"Yes, I did, as a surprise housewarming present for the apartment. Anna was supposed to look after it for me until we had moved in. I had no idea she would do this. I'm going to kill her."

"Not if I kill her first."

"I'm sorry. I thought it would be a nice gift, you looked so beautiful that morning, watching the sun come up. It was a perfect moment and I wanted to try and capture it for ever."

Anna appeared between Martin and Fiona, her hands firmly on her hips, "I wanted Ralph to be prouder of his work. You should be proud too, Sam. Of him and of yourself. So, I'm not going to apologise."

Everyone looked at Sam, waiting for him to explode, his face was red and a frown deeply etched across his forehead. Instead, he started to shake his head and laugh, "Ralph keeps saying to me we need to face the world and not hide anymore. But I never thought I'd be doing it arse-first."

Anna grinned at him, "Well, it's a very nice arse. So why not?"

"Here, here, old thing," Martin said, starting to laugh along with Sam. "I'd be delighted if anyone even took a passing interest in painting me in the altogether."

Sam put his arms around Ralph, "Congratulations and thank you. It's beautiful and you are very, very clever. Now, who said he wanted our life to settle down into something normal?"

"Hmm," Ralph said, managing a brief smile. "You did say it was unlikely to happen in Rye."

Sam looked at the circle of friends who had attempted to protect him, "Come on, there must be some champagne in this place to celebrate with. I need a drink before I face the woman I have to call my mother."

"I think that drink may need to wait a few minutes," Ralph said, pointing towards the door of the gallery.

They all turned and saw the entrance being blocked by the large presence of Dawa Singh and an elaborate basket of flowers.

"Hello," Anna said, tucking a curl of copper hair behind her ear.

"Hello," he said from the doorway and held out the basket to her. "Ralph seemed to think you might like some flowers. I wanted to say sorry for what happened."

"I should think so," Irene said, passing with her tray of sausage rolls. "That Thunderbirds apron is the property of The Cookery. We could charge you with theft."

Martin took hold of Irene and moved her gently but firmly to the back of the gallery.

Dawa looked down at the apron he was still wearing, "Oh, I'm sorry, I forgot all about it."

"Don't worry," Anna said. "I bought it for you. It's yours."

"Thank you."

Anna took the flowers from him, a brilliant display of bright yellow dahlias, purple irises, orange roses, and long, pink gladioli, "I don't think I've ever seen anything so beautiful. Thank you."

"I'm sorry I didn't give you any notice of kissing you," Dawa said. "I am aware that's not how a gentleman should behave. It won't happen again."

"Oh yes it will," Anna said, dumping the basket of flowers on the floor, grabbing his Thunderbird apron and pulling him down until his lips were low enough for her to kiss.

CHAPTER 16

Mother Theresa, The Chippy Chipper
and the pentagram leads the way.

An hour later, Ralph made his way up to the roof terrace. He had spent the last forty minutes alone with Jane Scott as she took him through a file full of photographs and written instructions in painstaking detail, to ensure that he painted exactly the portrait she wanted.

Martin spotted Ralph and waved him over, "Congratulations, old thing, on your much-deserved win. There is a well-earned beer awaiting you here. I hope you appreciate the spirit behind Anna's surprise."

"Yes, I think I'm over the shock now," Ralph said, settling himself next to Sam. "Where are the love birds?"

"They went for a walk," Fiona said. "But they said they'd come up and see us before they went out for dinner – on their first official date. Isn't it sweet?"

Martin raised his glass of lemonade, "It certainly is. What a night."

"Yes, yes," Sam said, waving at Martin. "No need to go

on. I'm tyring to forget I exposed myself to half of Rye tonight."

Ralph turned to him, "The painting was meant as a surprise housewarming present, but we don't have to put it up."

"Of course we're putting it up. If my rear is so highly regarded, then I want it to be admired by everyone who visits us. But you are all forgetting the big issue."

"Which is?" Martin asked.

"Ralph now has to paint a portrait of my mother."

"Oh, hell," Ralph said, slumping low in his chair. "You should have heard her. She's desperate to be painted as a cross between Princess Diana and Mother Theresa. She thinks it should go in the National Portrait Gallery in London. I mean, who does she think I am? Is there any way I can get out of it?"

"No, you're not getting out of it," Anna's voice called from the door to her flat. She hurried on to the terrace, dragging Dawa behind by the hand. "Please don't. Paint her how you like, she's not paying for it. Put horns and a tail on her or something."

Ralph sat up straight, "And cause even more trouble? You got us into this mess, don't try and make it worse."

"I was trying to do something nice," she said, taking Dawa to the bar to get themselves drinks.

"I know, but it'll be a disaster, I just know it."

"Don't do yourself down, old thing," Martin said. "She was quite taken with your work, Ralph, so I wouldn't worry."

Fiona sipped her gin and tonic, "Will she have to sit

for the portrait, or will you use photos?"

"Photos, thank goodness. She's left Rye already."

Sam felt his mood lifting, "Has she? She's gone?"

"Yes, she only has one day off from filming whatever it is she's working on. She only came to get a free portrait done of herself. She's given me loads of photos of her through the years – all massively airbrushed, of course. And a huge list of dos and don'ts."

"Well, that's a relief," Sam said. "Put it all in the bin and we can get that girl, Laura, to do a picture of her from macaroni and spaghetti."

"I think the gallery pay me a bit to do it, so I'm sort of obliged," Ralph said, miserably, and the group lapsed back into silence.

Fiona smiled at Anna and attempted to lighten the mood, "Those were beautiful flowers, Anna, weren't they?"

"They're amazing," she said. "I can't remember the last time anyone bought me flowers. It's so romantic. We're going out for dinner in a minute, it's our first proper date."

Sam grinned, "Dawa Singh, the romantic."

"Not to mention Dawa Singh, the detective," Anna said, pulling up a deckchair. "Before we go, we should talk about the fires. We think they may be related to the Summer Solstice on the 21st of June, which is less than a month away. That's when all the witchy things come to a head. So, we think there's going to be a couple more arson attacks before long."

Dawa pulled Psychic Sue's drawing of the pentagram

from his pocket, "We think each point on the pentagram could represent a fire in the town. We have had three, so we are expecting two more fires over the next few weeks, leading up to the longest day. But where? Whose business is going to burn?"

Fiona blinked at him, "Gosh, it sounds serious when you put it like that."

"I think it is serious," Martin said. "Have you considered there might be something specific about the location or type of shops that have been targeted?"

Dawa nodded, "We've been over and over that, but can't think of any real connection between them."

Martin's brow furrowed, "Ralph, would you be so kind as to pop into my flat and you will see a piece of glass on the side table. It's from one of Auntie B's framed paintings that fell and broke. Would you bring it out, please, but take care the edge is sharp. Also, there is a marker pen and a town map in one of the drawers."

"Yes, of course," Ralph said and disappeared inside.

Anna shook her head, "It can't be what the shops sell; a café, a craft shop and a clothes shop. There's no pattern there... oh, except they all begin with C. Wow, that's it, I've cracked it."

Sam crossed his arms, "Not if you call them a tea shop, a gallery and a dress shop."

"Oh, yes, well, I suppose you could call them that."

"Nice idea though," Dawa said, squeezing her hand. "It's that sort of lateral thinking that we need if we are going to break through this puzzle."

Anna looked up at him in wonder, "Is it?"

"Absolutely."

She beamed, desperate to kiss him again, but she didn't want to embarrass him.

Ralph returned with the piece of clear glass, the map and a pen. He handed them carefully to Martin, "What are you thinking?"

Martin sat forward and unfolded the map on the table, placing the glass over it, "Well, it's just an idea. Let's see."

He started with a cross marking the fire at The Copper Kettle, he then drew a line across the glass from there to Ethel's gallery, then another to Psychic Sue's shop.

Anna gasped, "It's the beginning of the pentagram. Each of the fires is at a point on a Pentagram!" She picked up the drawing and laid it next to the piece of glass.

Martin sat back, "It would appear so. It could just be coincidence, but it does seem odd."

"And if you finish it off and put in the final two points, where would they sit?" Dawa asked, quietly.

They all remained silent, staring intently at Martin. When he had completed the next line, they all leaned forward to see where his pen had stopped, "Now bear in mind, this is not one hundred percent accurate, but it could be somewhere here near the Quays."

"The Chippy Chipper," Anna said, stabbing the spot on the map with her finger. "It's mostly houses now, but right where that point sits is the fish and chip shop."

"Good lord, you're right," Martin said.

Fiona leaned over Martin's shoulder, "Imagine if someone set fire to a chip shop? It could burn the whole street down. Surely no one would be so stupid."

Ralph had been staring intently at the map, "And the final point, where would that be?"

Martin returned his pen to the glass and began to carefully draw the final line of the pentagram. The Rye Rooftop Club collectively held its breath as the thin black line travelled across the map.

"No," Anna breathed.

Ralph turned away, "I thought so."

"What? I can't see, move your hand Martin," Fiona said, leaning forward.

Martin slowly lifted the pen from the glass and the completed pentagram. The last point of which sat directly on top of The Bookery.

"Now, remember, this is just a theory. If I had drawn the shape slightly to the left or to the right, it would have been a different location."

Ralph nodded, "Yes, like The Cookery or Let's Screw. Either way, if this is right, one of our shops is next to burn."

Dawa stood and pulled his phone from his pocket, "I'll tell Sergeant Phil of our findings, the police need to know." He stepped away as he made the call.

Ralph looked up at the sky and took a deep breath to steady himself, "Forewarned is forearmed, I suppose. We can increase our security, put in CCTV or something."

Sam peered at the map again, "Well, maybe Martin's

pen's a bit off, it might not be The Bookery."

"But if it's not it could be The Cookery," Anna said, choking back tears.

Martin rose and clapped his hands, "Now, look, this can't be right. I'm sorry I even mentioned it. The best we can do is hope that we have pinpointed the general area of the next attacks, so we can protect the properties as best we can."

Dawa returned to the group, "I've spoken to Phil. He's still not convinced, but he has promised to get more patrols to come past the chip shop and along here over the next few weeks."

"Will that be enough?" Anna asked.

"It depends how determined they are," Sam said, grimly.

"So, what do we do now? Set up someone to be on guard over night? Sleep in our shops?" Anna asked, panic starting to set in.

Ralph turned back to the group "Well, the first thing I'm going to do is nail up the letterbox. Then get an intruder alarm, so if someone tries to fiddle with the front door I'll be alerted. You can do the same."

"That sounds, sensible," Dawa said. "We don't need to have dinner at The Mermaid, Anna, if you'd rather stay here this evening."

She looked at him then shook her head, determined not to let some madman with a match spoil such a special night, "No, this is important. It's our first proper date, we must go."

"We'll stay," Ralph said. "Don't worry."

"Erm, maybe not," Sam said, looking at his phone. "Message from my mother. Her limousine has broken down, she's panicking she won't be back at her hotel to get enough sleep before an early start on set tomorrow. She can't get a taxi, she says. Brian must be having his tea or something. She wants rescuing."

"Damn."

"It's fine, I'll go on my own," Sam said, looking like it was the last thing he wanted to do.

"I could stay," Martin said.

"Absolutely not," Fiona said, firmly. "You're off to the nursing home. Your friend is expecting you. You also need to talk to that young man, don't you?"

"Yes, you're right, dear thing. As always."

"Listen," Ralph said. "This is crazy. We all have other things we need to do. It's getting late and the other attacks all happened before this time in the evening, so I reckon we're safe for tonight. Besides, the police will be keeping an eye out. We can sort everything tomorrow. Dawa, can you pop in and see Louise at The Chippy Chipper and tell her to be alert?"

"Yes, we can go in on our way to The Mermaid."

"Excellent, I can call Judy about Let's Screw while we get Jane. Then she can be prepared for tomorrow too."

"Are you sure?" Anna said.

"Yes. There have been enough surprises for one night, I really don't think anything else will happen tonight," Ralph said, and took a firm grip of Sam's hand for comfort, hoping that he was right.

* * *

Irene missed everyone leaving by only a few minutes as she stalked up the High Street to The Cookery. She was annoyed with herself. If she hadn't left her glasses in the napkin drawer, she wouldn't have got this headache and she wouldn't have had to drive herself back into town.

She didn't bother to put the lights on in the café, she knew her way around with her eyes shut, besides, her head was feeling fuzzy and the bright light would have made it worse. As she pulled open the little drawer, a shadow crossed the window behind her. Irene turned in time to see a small figure dressed in black, with the hood of their jumper up - just like the person Anna had described who set fire to Ethel's gallery.

Irene made her way back to the door and opened it quietly, not wanting to draw attention to herself. She'd learnt enough basic technique from Midsomer Murders to know what she was doing. She peered carefully around the edge of the door frame and saw the back of the suspect hurrying past The Bookery. Then she saw them hesitate. Irene knew that trick, so she quickly pulled her head back out of view, assuming they were checking the lie of the land around them. After a moment Irene slowly stretched her long neck forward and looked back down the road.

The would-be arsonist was crouched at the bookshop's door stuffing something through the letter box. It was not a late-night postal delivery that was clear, because a moment later a flame appeared and that too was forced into the shop. Irene gasped, she was not a woman to be shocked easily, but her headache tripled as if a thunderbolt had struck her. She staggered back into the shop, the door closing behind her with a bang.

Irene's thoughts were confused. She knew there was danger, but also dizziness and a numbness. Where was the numbness? Her face, but just one side. She tried to put a hand to it, but the hand wouldn't respond. "Fire," she tried to say, but her mouth refused to make the shape required to form the word. She staggered towards the counter and gripped it with the hand that still seemed capable of normal operation. *Fire*, she kept repeating in her head, trying to pull herself together. *Fire. Fire.* Until another word replaced it and a final terror went through her just before she hit the floor. *Stroke.*

CHAPTER 17

Fire engines, extinguishers and Stanley's sixth sense.

Fiona was thinking about getting a dog. She'd never had one as a child, her dad had told her they were dangerous and unpredictable. Her husband, Andy, called them a waste of money and wouldn't even discuss the idea. But she had always harboured a dream of having a companion of her own, maybe a labrador. So, she was thoroughly enjoying her night of dog-sitting Stanley, while Ralph and Sam went out to rescue Jane Scott, Anna and Dawa had their first official date, and Martin went to the nursing home.

It was so lovely that Anna had found Dawa, she wouldn't have put them together immediately, but she could see how it might work. She really hoped it would work; Anna deserved a little bit of love in her life.

She was approaching The Cookery with Stanley leading the way, assuming he was going home. She was happy to let him lead for now, she'd turn left in a minute and head up the hill to her flat, where he'd be staying to watch some TV until Ralph picked him up later.

As she passed The Cookery, she glanced in. It was dark and quiet, so she moved on. The coloured lights that illuminated the window display of The Bookery were shining out on to the pavement a little brighter than normal, she thought. They were so pretty; it gave such a warm glow to the street.

"Steady on," Fiona said to Stanley as he shot forward with a loud bark. She pulled him back, "Come here, heel. You're not going home yet, we have to turn up Lion Street, you're coming to mine... Stanley, stop it." He was pulling and jumping against the lead until it hurt her shoulder, "Stop it."

But Stanley would not stop, he pulled her forward until she could see into The Bookery. It wasn't the window lights glowing more brightly, it was dancing orange flames beginning to engulf the shelves of books inside. "No!" she cried, as she ran to the shop door. But the fire was raging so strongly the door handle was too hot to touch. "Ow," her hand burned the moment she touched it. "Stanley, come back, come back."

She pulled the barking dog backwards across the road and tied his lead tightly to a lamppost, before she fumbled her phone from her coat pocket. She dialled 999.

"Fire brigade," she shouted at the dispatcher who answered her call. "Sorry, sorry, I didn't mean to shout. Fire brigade, please, and police. There is a fire in The Bookery, the bookshop on Rye High Street. Please tell them to hurry, it looks bad, really bad."

By the time she'd finished the call, the whole of the inside of the shop was lit as if all the lights had been switched on, such was the fury of the flames. Fiona knelt to comfort Stanley, "It's alright, Stanley. Your dad's aren't in there. Oh, I need to call them."

As she pulled out the phone for a second time a figure darted out of the door of Let's Screw, "Judy," Fiona called, waving frantically. "Judy, take care, there's a fire."

Judy looked at Fiona on the opposite side of the road, "I know," she yelled and lifted the heavy fire extinguisher she had tucked under her arm.

Fiona made sure Stanley was tightly tied to the post and ran across to her, "Thank goodness. Do you know how it works?"

"I do," Judy said, confidently. "I am fully trained in basic fire prevention and control. Stand back."

Fiona did as she was told and Judy set the extinguisher on the pavement. She fiddled with the pin at the top to break the seal, all the time repeating to herself, "Pin, aim, squeeze, sweep. Pin, aim, squeeze, sweep."

"I can't hear you, Judy. What are you saying?"

"Pull the pin. Aim the hose. Squeeze the handles and sweep from side to side."

"The door is too hot, Judy, you won't be able to get in. It's too dangerous."

"I can get this in the same way the fire got in," she said and started to lift the flap of the letterbox. She staggered backwards as the heat shot out towards her, "Hang on," she yelled and hurried back into Let's Screw.

Fiona stood and looked in horror as the books on the shelves with Ralph's beautiful paintings on them started to burn, "Hurry, hurry," she called, as she ran to the DIY shop door.

Judy appeared immediately, wearing a large pair of

gardening gloves, "Keep clear, I'll try again."

"Be careful, maybe we should leave it to the fire brigade."

"No need for them," Judy said, picking up the extinguisher. "I'll have this sorted in a jiffy."

"I've already called them, they're on their way."

Judy looked at her with fury, "No need for that, I can put out a little fire." Then she turned and tried to push the nozzle through the letterbox, but the size of the gloves impeded her and she just couldn't get it through as the heat and flames started to push her back. "No, no, no," Judy shouted, as she battled.

Fiona grabbed the back of Judy's navy overall and tried to pull her away, "Leave it, it's too late for that. We have to wait for the fire engine. Listen, I can hear the sirens."

They both stopped as the distant wail of the emergency services reached them. Fiona helped Judy across the road and stood with Stanley, who was beside himself. Pulling at the lead that tied him to the lamppost, he jumped and lunged in the air.

"That dog is going to do itself a mischief," Judy snapped. "You need to control it."

Fiona undid the knot and pulled Stanley back towards The Cookery, "Come with me, it's alright. We'll stand out of the way up here. I must call Ralph, I forgot. Come on, Stanley, we're going to get Ralph back."

* * *

Sam and Ralph were nearing Jane Scott's luxury

country hotel on the outskirts of Rye when the phone rang.

Sam glanced at Ralph, "Who is it?"

Ralph was listening intently, "Yes, we're on our way. Thanks."

He took the phone from his ear but didn't move or speak.

"Everything alright?"

Ralph looked at him, "The Bookery is on fire. It's burning down."

"What?" Sam said, swerving the car to the side of the road and slamming on the breaks. "Are you kidding?"

"That was Fiona, she's there now. It's burning. She says the fire brigade aren't there yet, but she can hear them coming."

Sam was starting to turn the car around, then he hit the breaks again, "Shit, shit, shit – Mother!"

Jane Scott quickly unclipped herself from her seat belt in the back, "Don't worry about me, the hotel's up ahead. I'll walk. It'll be fine, darling, they'll put it out. That's what firemen do." She opened the car door, "Hurry, but don't drive stupidly, Samuel. Do you hear me?"

"Yes, Mum, and thank you."

She hesitated with her hand on the door, "It will be alright. Text me," and she slammed the door.

Ralph felt numb, he couldn't bring himself to speak as Sam roared away back to town. He closed his eyes. He knew that his beloved bookshop would be gone by the time they got back to Rye.

* * *

Fiona put the phone back in her pocket as a fire engine roared up the cobbles of the High Street. The crew quickly took control and those who had gathered to watch in horror were ushered away. Fiona found herself standing in front of The Cookery, tears running down her cheeks, "Oh, Stanley, Stanley." She bent down to caress the distressed dog's ears.

But Stanley would not be comforted, he knew something was very wrong and he was afraid. He put his nose to the ground and sniffed left, then right. He could detect the tang of something that smelt of danger and heat, but he already knew about that - there was something else. He moved closer to the wall, where there was the usual concoction of scents. He followed the wall to the doorway and sniffed at the cool air coming from the gap at the bottom. He whined; he'd found what it was he could sense - more danger. He whined again and began to scratch at the door.

"Stanley, whatever's the matter? Leave the door alone, The Cookery will be fine. The fire people are here, come back out of the way," Fiona tried to pull him away from the door. But Stanley knew danger when he smelt it and the little dog pulled back with all his might, barking to draw attention to what he had sensed.

A fireman came running over, "Is there someone inside this place? The flat or the café?"

"No, she's out tonight," Fiona said. "It's empty."

"Are you sure?"

"I'll ring her now, but she went out for dinner."

"And there can be no one else in there?"

"No, Anna lives alone and the café's empty."

He nodded briefly, "Let me know as soon as you confirm that she's not inside," and ran back to help with The Bookery.

Fiona's shaking hands nearly dropped the phone, not helped by Stanley continuing to pull and worry at the door, "Right, that's enough, Stanley. Come on, we're going over the road."

She pulled and dragged him back to the opposite pavement, as he barked and struggled to warn her that something was wrong in The Cookery.

"Anna, it's me," Fiona shouted into the phone, over the noise of the chaos around her. "It's Fiona. Can you hear me? You need to come home, it's so awful. The Bookery is on fire. Please come back. Yes, the fire brigade is here, but... but... oh, please come back. Yes, yes, Ralph's coming back too. OK."

She finished the call and stood watching the firemen break into the shop and start pumping gallons of water inside. Her heart broke as she wept for all the books, all of Ralph's artwork that had brought the shop back to life, the incredible objects suspended in the air to form The Ceiling of Curious Things, Ralph's new life in Rye and even Stanley's soft, little bed in the window – all of it ruined. All of it gone.

CHAPTER 18

Smoke, Stanley's new skill and a cold hand.

Dawa reached the High Street first and skidded to a halt as he looked at the scene in front of him. Two fire engines were now parked at acute angles across the road. Police were controlling the crowd of locals and escorting people from their properties along both sides of the High Street. He could barely see The Bookery under the pall of smoke that covered it. He looked up at the flat above it, but it seemed intact and the curtains hung calmly at the window as if nothing untoward was going on below them.

Anna appeared at his side, red faced and breathing hard, "No, no," she moaned, clutching Dawa's arm. "Ralph's beautiful shop. Who did this? How could they?"

Dawa pulled her to his side and put his arms around her, "I think it's just downstairs. I can't see any flames in the flat. It doesn't look like it's spread. Your place hasn't been touched."

Anna pushed away from him, "I don't care about my

place. The Bookery was everything to Ralph. It was his life, everything."

"I know, I know. There's Fiona, with Stanley. Let's go and see what she knows. Come on." He took her hand and led her across the pavement.

"Oh, Anna, this is terrible," Fiona said, her eyes red from smoke or crying or both, she was no longer sure. The two women hugged and Dawa slipped away having seen Sergeant Phil in the distance.

Anna held Fiona tight, "We said that The Bookery was a target, didn't we? But we all had other things to do tonight."

"Anna, we can't blame ourselves."

Anna released Fiona and stamped her foot, "You're right, whoever did this needs to pay. This is pure evil. They can't get away with it, they can't. Where's Ralph?"

Fiona looked around, "I don't think they're back yet. He was in Sam's car, but I don't know where they were. He'll be here in a minute. Wait, he's there, with Sam, they're coming up the street." Fiona pointed down the hill, as Sam and Ralph ran at full speed towards them.

As they saw The Bookery with smoke billowing from the broken-down door and leaking from the large cracked front window, Sam slowed to a halt, but Ralph kept running. Sam saw him and gave chase, grabbing at his arm and trying to hold him back.

"Wait, Ralph, wait."

"Let me go," Ralph said, trying to shake him off.

"No, hold on. You can't go in there; the police will stop you. Look, there's Dawa talking to Sergeant Phil."

"Where?"

"By The Cookery," Sam pointed and Ralph ran towards them.

"Thank goodness," Dawa said.

Ralph stared at them both, "Is it gone? Everything?"

Phil looked him directly in the eyes, knowing he had to be honest, "It looks like most of the shop has gone, yes. Some of the floor seems to have collapsed down into the basement. The weight of the shelves and the books probably took it down when the fire burnt the floorboards. But from what we can see your flat is undamaged, it didn't reach that far. We will need a proper assessment to see if the flat is safe for you to return to. I'm afraid you won't be going back in there for a few days. I'm sorry, Ralph."

Ralph suddenly felt very cold and rocked slightly on his heels, staring at what had been his dream and his salvation. Gone, all gone.

He felt a hand on the back of his neck. It was cool and soothing as it pressed gently. Then he heard Sam's voice in his ear, "It's not over. The bookshop was *you*. You and Stanley. You're both still here. We can rebuild. Books can be replaced, shelves remade. As long as *you* are here The Bookery can come back to life."

Ralph turned and looked into the crystal green eyes of the man who meant everything to him. He forced himself to smile, "You are what I was looking for in Rye, The Bookery was what brought me here to find you. I still have you." He had a sudden thought and turned back to Sergeant Phil, "Was anyone hurt?"

"No, everyone has been accounted for."

"That's good." Ralph reached up and took Sam's hand away from his neck, but held on to it. He pulled him away from the noise and the mess and they stood on the cobbles in the middle of the street, ash slowly floating down around them like the snow had done when they first acknowledged their love for each other on a cold winter's night before Christmas.

Dawa returned to Anna and Fiona, "It's under control. They think they've got the fire out, and fingers crossed the flat hasn't been affected. It'll take a couple of days to confirm that, but they think it could be fine."

"How did it start? Was there mugwort? Was it through the letterbox?" Anna asked.

"Too early to say," Dawa said.

"It was him, wasn't it? The arsonist..."

"Judy," Fiona called, waving across the road. "Judy was in Let's Screw, she tried to put it out with a fire extinguisher."

Judy crossed the road to stand with them, she looked pale and deeply shocked, "I can't understand how it caught hold so quickly."

Fiona put her arm round Judy's shoulder and felt her shivering, "You did your best. With all that paper in there it was bound to be awful. Why would someone be so cruel as to do this?"

Anna clung to Dawa, her arms tightly around his waist, "Irene was saying today that she thought it was some sort of madman on the loose. I think she's right, you would have to be seriously mentally ill to do something like this."

Judy stepped away, "I need to call the others. Pat

will be very upset. I doubt they'll ever find who did it, random things like this are very hard to uncover."

"Oh, it's not random," Anna said. "We'll find them, won't we, Dawa? They will not get away with this. What's the matter with Stanley? I know he's upset, but..."

Dawa bent down to the little dog who was growling and whining, "Perhaps we should take him over to Ralph, to show him that he's OK."

"Good idea," Fiona said, moving his lead from one hand to the other. As she did so Stanley sensed the slight relaxation of her hold on him, and he took his chance and pulled with all his might. Suddenly he was free.

"Stanley!" Dawa called, making Ralph and Sam turn. But instead of seeing the beagle running towards them he headed straight for The Cookery.

He ran to the door and started jumping up, pawing the handle as he had been shown by Pat in The Bookery. On the third attempt, as Ralph reached him, the door opened and he raced inside.

Ralph turned to Anna, who was just behind him, "Did you forget to lock it?"

"No," Anna said. "I always do it and rattle the handle and come back twice to check it. It was locked."

Stanley barked from inside the café.

They went in and Anna flicked on the lights, "Where is he?"

Stanley barked again from behind the counter and then ran to Ralph and circled him, before disappearing back into the kitchen.

Ralph followed him and was the first to see Irene. She was lying on her side as if she were asleep in bed rather than on the kitchen floor, "Irene," Ralph gasped.

Anna charged passed him and fell to her knees, "Irene. Irene, it's me, Anna. Can you hear me?" They all waited in silence, but Irene didn't move or respond.

"Ambulance," Sam whispered to Dawa, who rushed outside to find Sergeant Phil.

Anna rubbed Irene's cold hand, "Oh Irene, please, please. Can you hear me? Just nod or squeeze my hand." She looked up at Ralph, "She's so cold."

"Dawa's gone for an ambulance, we'll get her some help."

As he said this, heavy footsteps crossed the café and Sergeant Phil was there, quickly moving Anna aside and taking charge. He used his radio to call for immediate medical assistance and began to check the still body of the elderly lady for signs of life.

CHAPTER 19

Rockets, Bon Jovi and a solicitor's letter.

To: helenh@woohoo.com

From: thebookery01@beemail.com

31st May

Hi Helen,

Thanks so much for the card, it arrived yesterday. It made me laugh – the picture of the dog weeing on the flames of a barbecue was perfect! LOL

Even though The Bookery is shut, I'm busier than ever, with two building projects on the go now. I just couldn't let The Bookery go or let the arsonist win. There were about two minutes when I was ready to give up; I sat on the curb and cried, while the shop sat in a pool of dirty water and disappeared behind a wall of grey smoke. But then I saw some of my regular customers crying on the pavement too and I knew that I wasn't the only one who had lost something important. Sam was right, The Bookery isn't bricks and mortar, it's me and Stanley and everything we put into it – and all of that is still here or can be replaced. I brought it back to life once and I can do it again.

Stanley's so confused, he doesn't understand why he can't go to work every day, like before. He is also missing his bed in the window, which looks like a bit of crisp toast at the moment. The hotel the insurers had put us in was nice, but it wasn't home, especially as Stanley couldn't come with us, so he had to stay with Fiona. But the good news is that we've got the all clear to move back into the flat, as it's been pronounced safe! We're sleeping there tonight. I've also been into the shop for the first time. Blimey, that was tough.

I stood for ages outside the door in the downstairs hallway of the flat holding on to the handle. I couldn't go in. Sam and Anna said they'd come with me, but I really needed to do it alone. When I opened the door it smelt so different, I wasn't prepared for that. Wet paper and wood have a horrible smell, then add to that smoke and ash! I stood inside like I did on the very first day I saw it last November, taking it all in. It looked like hell - a cold, dark, barren hell. It wasn't The Bookery anymore, which made it a bit easier in a strange way. The shelves were blackened and charred. The books were in piles of soggy ash. The counter had fallen through the floor and was smashed somewhere in the basement. The stool I sat on every day was gone completely, just burnt up. The fire had even scorched my paintings off the walls, they'd vanished.

I think Sergeant Phil has stopped answering my calls now. Ha ha. I've called him every day to see if they've found who did this. He says they've hauled in every known psycho (his words, not mine) in the area, but they can't be sure it's any of them. Anna is convinced it's something to do with witchcraft, it sounds so far-fetched, but a pentagram fits exactly in the pattern of the locations of the fires. It predicted The Bookery would burn. So maybe Anna has a point. (It's not often you'll hear that from me!). If I got my hands on whoever it is the pointy bits of a pentagram will come in very handy, is all I'll say.

Still, there are positives to starting again. I'm getting shelves that are made from recycled wood, which are fantastic. I'm going to try and use as much reclaimed material as I can throughout the shop. I've sourced a new counter, for instance, that has a multicoloured top made from old wellington boots – it's amazing. This time I won't be doing it on a tight budget either; the insurance company have moved so quickly that they've said we can get started on the preliminary works. I suppose because they're paying me for business interruption and I get money for every day we're closed, the sooner it's up and running again the better it is for them.

I'll enjoy painting everything back again. I might not go with a castle or a jungle this time for the kid's section; I don't want to pretend nothing's happened. I was thinking of maybe a rocket or a pirate ship? I'd like to turn one section into an old timber-frame house, like the ones in Rye. It will have a door you can open to reveal picture books, and windows that open to books on animals and adventure. I might even put some smugglers up on the roof!

Sometimes, I wonder who this new person is. I mean, old Ralph would have crumbled. Sam's worried I'm burying myself in activity instead of grieving for The Bookery. But I don't think I am. Sure, I've got stuck in talking to the insurers, drawing up plans with the architect, finding builders etc, but I genuinely think I'm a different person and I feel proud. Proud of who I have become, thanks to Rye, the Rooftop Club and The Bookery. That's why I can't let it go, it must come back to life. For everyone.

Nothing of The Ceiling of Curious Things survived, which was gutting. You won't believe it, though, I've already got a load of objects brought by local people and regular customers. They leave them on the doorstep with a note or drop them in to The Cookery for me. It's amazing. I have to admit I cried when the first ones arrived. It's the kindness of others that gets to me the most.

Anyway, I'm rambling on now. I'm tired, I think.

Right, Sam's here so we can collect Stanley and go home.

Take care and sorry we haven't made it up to see you yet. Keep your legs crossed and don't have any curries just yet!

Love

Ralph

X

* * *

To: rubyrose@beemail.com

From: annabanana@tallyho.co.uk

3rd June

Mum & Joe,

It was so nice to hear your voice the other day! Are

you down the mountain yet? I hope so or you won't get this email for ages.

Anyway, I wanted to update you and let you know that Irene is on the mend! It's such a relief. Her daughter, Celine, rang me this morning to say she had finally woken up. I popped in after work to see her. She can't speak yet and her left side is still weak, but she can move her fingers and toes a little, which they say is a really good sign.

I can't begin to tell you how awful it is to see her lying in that hospital bed, but it's better than finding her on the floor of The Cookery like that. I still wake up at night crying. She looks so old and frail now. That's not the Irene we all know and fear, is it? Still, the doctors say the stroke could have been much worse and she should make a good recovery in time. They can't assess her speech yet, but Celine said she is able to write stuff on a pad to communicate. She says it's all rude stuff about the doctors mostly, which is a sign that she's getting back to her old self.

Everyone is still in shock after everything. Well, I am. I couldn't open The Cookery, but after three days Ralph forced me to. He actually stood outside my bedroom on the roof terrace and played Bon Jovi at full blast until I got up. I hate Bon Jovi even more now.

Ralph seems to be doing well though. He was devastated on the night of the fire, of course, but by the next morning he was all guns blazing to rebuild as soon as possible. There was no way he was going to let some stupid arsonist ruin the best thing that's ever happened to him (except Sam, of course). He is so much stronger than he was when he first came here and the success of

The Bookery has a lot to do with that.

Anyway, it's getting late and I'm off to meet Dawa for a walk. I'm so pleased you approve of him. I mean, I'd still be with him if you didn't approve, but it's ever so much easier that you like him. He's so kind and funny and safe and protective and interesting and handsome and tall and gentle and polite and strong and has the loveliest teeth and shoes and eyes. Right, I really need to go and see him now. He's a great kisser, did I say that?

Please don't think any more about coming home before you are ready. There's nothing you can do. We're all on high alert for the next fire. We're expecting one more, which we think will be The Chippy Chipper, so they've hired all night security to make sure it stays safe. The police are taking it much more seriously now - about time too! - and have put extra foot patrols around the shops from when they close until morning. We've only got to get through the next 18 days until the Summer Solstice.

Better go or Dawa will wonder where I am.

Love

Anna

Xxxx

※ ※ ※

To: CountessG@fortnum.org
From: MartinRyeCook@zway.com

10th June

Grace,

I've had a letter from your solicitor saying I can collect my things on the 12th at 10am. I will be there.

He says he will also be there to ensure I don't take anything that I shouldn't and that I will be billed for his time.

Good luck with that.

Martin

PS You don't need to be there.

CHAPTER 20

The bed of nails, a tray of cocktails and letting go.

Martin stood on the pavement, his hand hovering over the ornate iron gate. He had walked up this path hundreds of times, but that was before. Now, he had to knock at his own front door and wait for it to be answered.

Grace didn't open the door, but instead an anonymous looking man in a dark suit eased it open slowly, taking what seemed an unnecessary amount of time to do so.

"Earl Martin?" he said, without the tiniest scrap of expression in his voice.

"Martin will suffice."

"Of course. Please enter," he stepped back like an ancient butler and gestured for Martin to come inside.

Martin sighed, this was going to be as difficult as he had imagined. So, he squared his shoulders and prepared to carry out his plan. It had been Fiona's idea, to channel the arrogance and brusqueness of his father, the old Earl of Groombridge. Blast his way through and not take any nonsense from anyone. Martin would struggle with that, but his father would not have given it a second thought. It would be the only way he could get through this without losing the small amount of dignity a man in a raggedy woollen coat, long grey hair, unkempt eyebrows and a motheaten tartan hat could manage.

"This won't take long, so no need to mess about," he said, briskly.

"I... Well..."

"I imagine my wife is hiding somewhere, waiting to pounce if called upon. So, shall we get on with it. Follow me."

Martin set off up the long staircase in front of him, trying not to look at the familiar photographs lining the wall.

"M-my lord," the solicitor stuttered, as he attempted to keep up. "There are certain conditions that must be adhered to. I must insist..."

"Insist away, my good man. It won't make a jot of difference," Martin was beginning to enjoy himself.

"My lord..."

He stopped suddenly at the top of the stairs, turned and looked down at the panicked solicitor, using the height advantage to unnerve him further, "Name?"

"I b-beg your pardon?"

"Your name?"

"Oh, Alexander."

"Mr Alexander, I am here to collect trousers, underwear, shirts, ties, jackets and braces. Other personal items of my choosing will also be coming with me."

"But..."

"But nothing. Take me to court, sue me if you wish. Enjoy yourself, old thing, but do not get in my way," the last words were spoken with such vehemence that Mr Alexander staggered back down a step. "Anything you would like to say?"

Mr Alexander regained his balance and shook his head.

"Excellent. You are learning fast," with which Martin turned swiftly on his heels and headed into the master bedroom. The sight and smell of it made him shudder, but he tried not to show it. This had been the site of so much unhappiness over many years. Here it was, the marital bed, that had been more of a bed of nails for him and his wife, so uncomfortable had their relationship been in recent years.

He shook off the memories and went to the chest of drawers which had been his. He put down the large plastic laundry bags he was carrying and began opening drawers. He had thought carefully about what he would take, determined not to take everything – he didn't want to appear desperate. He was also determined to be long gone before the one-hour time limit came to an end and avoid the embarrassment of being ordered from his own house. Not that he imagined Mr Alexander would be much of a force to be reckoned with on that score.

He picked out decent underwear, all neatly folded and ironed by the housekeeper, who had been loyal to Grace and vile to him.

"May I see?" Mr Alexander said from behind him.

Martin turned slowly and fixed the pathetic man with a heavy stare, "You wish to see my underwear, Mr Alexander? Is that what you are paid for? Inspecting a gentleman's socks? In my day your profession had more respect for themselves. Few morals, but at least a little respect."

Mr Alexander went a puce colour, "Well, perhaps that may not be necessary after all."

"Perhaps," Martin mumbled and returned to his work.

The second drawer contained his collection of pyjamas and he opened it with more care. There they were waiting for him, exquisite paisley silk pyjamas in a range of colours. He picked up the first pair and brought them to his face. He took a deep sniff. "Delicious," he said, as Mr Alexander retreated a little.

Martin carefully arranged all the pyjamas in a laundry bag and moved on to the bottom drawer, where he picked out shirts and handkerchiefs. From the top of the wooden chest, he picked up the tortoiseshell hairbrush and comb set that had belonged to his brother. He ran his finger along the soft shiny surface of the shell, before wrapping them carefully in the silk of a pyjama jacket. Then he moved to the wardrobe and smiled as he opened the door and saw a row of smart jackets and trousers. With each new sight, the memory of the man he was grew a little stronger. His artificial confidence became a little more real. This is what he had needed and Mr Alexander was the perfect person to allow him to enjoy himself.

"Are you a tweed man, Mr Alexander?" he asked,

without looking at him.

"Not really, my lord."

"No, I thought not," Martin said, with a smirk.

He picked out his favourite jackets and trousers, then added some belts and a couple of pairs of braces. He reached out for the ties, but then changed his mind. He was no longer a man who needed or wanted to wear a tie. Instead, he lifted the wooden tie rack from the rail and held it behind him, "My wife said that you want paying. Here."

Mr Alexander didn't know what to do. He let out a muffled sound that could have meant anything, which Martin ignored. He shook the tie rack impatiently and after a moment felt it being taken from him.

"They may improve your prospects," he said, really starting to enjoy himself.

There was room in his bags for a couple of casual pairs of shoes to go with his beloved leather brogues already in his possession.

Finally, he knelt and reached through the hanging clothes to the back of the wardrobe. He felt with his long fingers along the skirting board until he found the tell-tale joint. With a well-practiced flick, the board fell away and he was able to reach into the cavity behind it. His fingers closed around a familiar box shape. He allowed himself a moment and let out the breath he had been holding. It was still there.

Quickly, he pulled the wooden box out and stuffed it down the side of one of the bags, without even looking at it.

"What was that?" Mr Alexander said, dancing around

behind Martin, trying to see what he was doing.

Martin hauled himself back onto his feet, "My shoe cleaning box. I suppose you use a mechanical brush at train stations to bring a shine to your shoes, Mr Alexander?" He looked down his long nose at the useless man, "I do not. I polish, Mr Alexander. I polish."

Martin picked up the bags and left the bedroom, Mr Alexander hot on his heels.

"I should make an inventory of the items you are removing from the house, my lord."

"That will not be necessary."

"But, my lord, under the terms of..."

"They were my wife's terms, not mine," Martin snapped.

"To which you agreed," came a new voice.

Martin nearly lost his footing, but quickly steadied himself as Grace sailed into view at the bottom of the stairs.

"Good morning, Grace, you look... the same," Martin said, before continuing down the stairs, more slowly than before but with the same determination to leave as swiftly as possible.

She reached up one hand to stroke the string of pearls at her neck. She still held herself well, Martin thought, like an old gay bishop admiring himself in the mirror. A thought that made him smile.

"You look a mess," she said, sharply.

"No, Grace, I look like a free man."

"I need to see everything you have taken."

"You need nothing of the sort. You have taken enough from me and my family to last you a lifetime, so you will behave like a human being and let me pass with my belongings."

"Taken?" the shock registered on her face; it had been a long time since anyone had spoken to her like that. She drew herself up to her full height, while Mr Alexander tried to make himself invisible, "You owed me; tricking me into marrying into your pathetic excuse for a family. The years I had to face down the laughter of my friends..."

Martin stepped off the bottom of the stairs and stood directly in front of her, "I married you because I believed I loved you. You married me because you believed that being a countess would buy you class and respect. It appears we were both wrong." He looked into her eyes and saw nothing of the girl he'd met in a crowded bar in Soho with a tray of martini cocktails in her hand. He owed her nothing, but he was not a mean man. He was no longer the man he was then, it was true, but he was beginning to feel him return.

He put his bags down and pulled his tartan hat from his pocket, shook it and placed it carefully on his head, "Now, tell your pet here, that he has one week to send me the divorce papers containing the terms that have already been agreed. The only outstanding matter was the house. One week after I receive the papers it will go on the market and a week after that you will move out. The proceeds of the sale will be split equally between us after the appropriate costs have been deducted. Mr Alexander's costs shall come from your share, just as my solicitor's costs will be taken from mine."

Grace opened her mouth to object, but Martin cut her off, "If that is not to your liking then we will have to go to court. I will insist on a very public court, which will be in the full glare of the press. It has been a while since old time aristocracy fought over their ill-gotten gains, and I'm sure that there will be a vast amount of public interest in the affairs of an alcoholic Earl who was reduced to sleeping on the streets. Not to mention a Countess who started off as a mini-skirted waitress called Gracie Thompsett, who took tips from men when she let them touch her bottom."

Mr Alexander made a small noise from the stairs and Grace's nostrils flared as she turned on him, "Go up to the bathroom, you horrid little man, and do not come out until you are told." She followed Martin as he opened the front door, "You wouldn't dare say a thing. Look at you, you'd be a laughing stock."

He turned in the doorway and smiled, "Oh, Grace, don't you see. I have everything I ever wanted. Freedom. From my history, from my family, from your expectations. I also have my pyjamas. So, it's me who will be laughing. I hope that you find happiness one day." He looked at her for one last time, but nothing of the girl he first met remained. Nevertheless, he leant forward and, although she flinched, she let him kiss her on the cheek. "Goodbye, Gracie."

He walked slowly down the path, the honeysuckle's sweet smell surrounding him. He didn't look back at the large Georgian house, even when he heard the door slam. He breathed in the sky and the trees. He looked at the pavement as a summer shower set in around him and darkened the paving stones. The grass on the verge looked greener than when he had arrived. The air felt fresher. He knew that he was letting go. He would soon be able to live for now, without the weight of his past, his father and his brother pulling him back. He was becoming the man he was always destined to be. It was time to face Robin and share his story.

CHAPTER 21

Yorkshire Balti, the Lion King and Mama Singh.

Dawa placed his knife and fork back on the plate and patted his stomach. His immaculate suit jacket was folded over the end of Anna's green velvet sofa, and his shoes sat neatly by the door.

"That was delicious, thank you. You are an artist when it comes to food. Chicken balti in a Yorkshire pudding, that's a first for me."

Anna blushed, "I'm glad you liked it. I wanted to try and make something with diversity - diverseness, diversion?"

"I really appreciate the effort you make to understand my heritage, but there is no need. Apart from the turban and the beard I'm as British as the next man. I eat custard and Hobnobs like any good Englishman."

"I know, but it's just so interesting. I want to understand everything about you and not get anything wrong."

He reached across the table and took her hand, "Anna, please don't worry. You care so much about everyone and everything, I very much look forward to being the one who gets to take care of you."

Anna felt her mouth open, but she had nothing to say. It was as if he had used some magic words and everything in her head drifted gently away. She had waited her entire life for someone to offer to take care of her and here he was. She couldn't think of what to do, so she cried instead.

Dawa was panic stricken, "What? Have I said the wrong thing?"

She shook her head.

"Are you unwell?"

She shook her head again.

"Please tell me what's wrong."

She wiped the sleeve of her rose-covered kimono across her eyes and took a sip of wine, "That's better. I was struck dumb for a second – which is something of a miracle for me, you must admit. It's just that you are so absolutely perfect that I don't know quite what to do with myself sometimes."

Dawa breathed a sigh of relief, "I was worried I'd said something wrong. I'm not very good at all this and I am certainly far from perfect."

"Oh, trust me you are very good at all this. Very, very good. Although you have forgotten our anniversary."

"What anniversary?"

"It's eleven weeks and three days since you first asked if you could walk with me outside Cinque."

"Damn, I knew there was something special about tonight. Let me think, paper is one year, gold is fifty years. Eleven weeks and three days is eighty days, so that must be... balti! Yes, it's our balti anniversary. I saw the perfect card for that the other day too."

"Mr Singh, I hope you are not taking the micky out of me," she said, caressing his long fingers as she slowly pressed them into the remnants of the thick gravy left on his plate.

He smiled at her as he moved his hands to her face and tenderly rubbed the gravy into her cheeks, "Miss Rose, that is something I would never do."

"I think we'll call that a draw, don't you?"

"I think that's the safest way to handle it," he said, laughing as he went to the kitchen to wash his hands.

They cleared the dinner things together and he insisted on making the coffee, while she sat with her feet up on the sofa.

"I could get used to this."

"Me too," Dawa said, too quietly for her to hear.

"What was that?"

Dawa looked around the cosy room while he waited for the kettle to boil, "I said, which object would you like to tell me about tonight?"

"Aren't you bored with this game yet?"

"Never. With the amount of curios you have in here, I think I will be about a hundred by the time you've told me about them all, one night at a time."

Anna's breath caught in her throat. Since the fire they had spent many nights together here, Dawa's small flat being some way out of town and not nearly as comfortable as hers. Every night he had walked around the room that bulged with junk shop finds and picked one for Anna to tell him about. She thought he was being polite, but now he was talking about carrying on for years. She hugged her Judy Garland cushion tightly to her chest and watched with disbelief as this amazing man pottered about her kitchen in nice stripey socks, making coffee for her.

When he settled on the sofa next to her, he looked around, "How about..."

"Hang on," Anna said. "Before we do that, can we talk about the Solstice Fire Starter?"

"Is that what we're calling him now?"

"Yes, I originally thought of Solstice Sizzler, but that sounded like a sausage. We need to keep working on it. The Solstice is only nine days away, so there will be another fire before then."

"Anna, I admire your desire to solve this mystery, but I don't think we are going to get to the bottom of it. Sergeant Phil..."

"Oh, ignore him. He still doesn't believe in our theory, even after the pentagram and The Bookery and everything. The man's an idiot, so, I've been doing some more thinking. We may have another clue."

"Really? What?"

"I bumped into Louise from The Chippy Chipper this morning and she told me they used to have a board outside the shop advertising special deals. Well, it's vanished! What do you think about that?"

Dawa wasn't sure what to think about it, but knew that 'not a lot' wasn't the answer Anna was looking for, "Well, it's a shame, but what's it got to do with the Fire

Starter?"

"I think... actually, I don't know what I think. I thought you might think something."

"It's an odd coincidence, but I'm not sure how it's related. The main point we haven't yet resolved is why they are setting fire to the shops? What do they gain from it?"

Anna scrabbled to reach her phone, which had fallen down the side of the sofa, "Just a minute, Sherlock, something is coming through."

"Through where?"

"My brain, it can take a while sometimes, give me a minute," she said, as she retrieved the phone and started a frenzy of typing and swiping.

Dawa sat back and drank his coffee. Since meeting Anna his life had gained purpose once again. Spending time with her and sharing her extraordinary, chaotic, colourful life had brought him alive, in a way he wasn't sure he would ever be able to explain. But he had something to ask her tonight and he knew that her reaction might change everything.

"Aha," Anna squealed. "Listen to this. According to this website on pagan ceremonies and stuff, ashes from a special bonfire can protect you from misfortune. What do you think to that?" She looked at Dawa, wide-eyed with expectation.

"Erm, well..."

"To these sorts of witchy people, ashes have special properties, like protecting you from things. Maybe it's the ashes they're after, to use in their ceremony."

"Why?"

"I don't know, but it's the only physical thing that's left from a fire, isn't it. If they manage to get hold of some ashes from each fire, then it might have some sort of significance."

"I can see what you're saying, but The Chippy Chipper is off limits now they have overnight guards there... oh, hang on. Are you thinking what I'm thinking?"

"I hope so, because that'd be ever so romantic if we were both thinking the same thing. It's like a sign or synergy or synchronicity or symbio-something. I always get confused with the Lion King, was he Simba or Symbiosis?"

"I'm not sure, but do you think that the Solstice Fire Starter stole the chip shop's sign so they could burn it to use the ashes on Midsummer Night?"

Anna flung herself at Dawa, knocking him flat across the sofa "Yes, yes. Look at us all synchronised, like those weird swimmers with pegs on their noses. It's a sign that we really are meant for each other."

Dawa laughed as he wrestled his way upright again, "It would seem so. I think you may have hit on something. If the arsonist somehow managed to go back and get some of the ash from the fires..."

"They always say that murderers return to the scene of the crime, so why not arsonists?"

"Good point. So, if they get the ashes from the shops and burn the chip shop sign, they have five sets of magical ashes ready for the Summer Solstice."

"Yes, that's it. We've cracked it!"

"Not really. How does it help us know who is behind it all and what on earth they hope to gain from it?"

"There is only one way to find out. We'll have to be in the field near Romney Marsh at midnight on the Solstice and catch them red handed."

"I'm not sure that's wise. I wouldn't want you exposed to any danger."

"That's lovely, but I've burgled houses in the dead of night, bounced on a very nasty trampoline, driven at breakneck speed across Sussex in a Fiat 500 driven by my barefoot mother, eaten a pickled egg with a man who spits his teeth out... I'm no stranger to danger."

"I think this might be a little different. This is someone who thinks they are some sort of witch or wizard who sets fire to things."

"Yes, but you know Sergeant Phil is not going to help us, he doesn't believe in all of this. It's down to you and me, Dawa."

"Well, if we go to observe and identify the person or people involved, maybe take a few photos as evidence, then we can pass it all on to Phil."

"Yes! I've got the perfect outfit, it's a sort of camouflage, so we can hide in a hedge," Anna sat back on the sofa. "Oh, this is such a great day. I shall always remember our eleven-week-and-three-day anniversary for this."

Dawa shifted on his cushion, "Ah, well, I'm not sure if this is the right moment, but I need to talk to you about something."

Anna looked at him, "That doesn't sound good, you look nervous." Her heart started to race; she'd heard this speech before. The one where blokes say how great she is but then find a way to let her down. She held her breath, surely not Dawa? Not him?

"Anna, I know we haven't been together for long, but... well, you mean a lot to me. An awful lot," he paused, as he searched for the right words.

"But?"

"But what?"

"But, you have a but coming."

"No, I don't."

"You don't?"

"No."

"Oh, sorry to interrupt then."

"That's OK," Dawa said. "I have no buts where you are concerned, Anna, please believe me. You are the best thing to happen to me in a very long time and my only regret is not seeing it earlier."

"I like speeches with no buts," she whispered.

He smiled at her, "Anna, I want to ask you something that is not easy. I want to ask you if you will meet my mother?"

Anna flung Judy Garland's cushion across the room, "Oh thank Judy for that. I thought I was in for the chop, or you had to move to Iceland to escape the mafia or something. Of course, I'll meet Mama Singh, I'd love to."

Dawa needed her to understand what he was asking, "Anna, my mother is... traditional. That's putting it kindly. She is also difficult and can be very hard. I don't want you upset by her, but I think that meeting her is a hurdle that we should get over sooner rather than later.

Whatever she says, it doesn't matter. It doesn't change a thing. But I would rather get it over and done with, then we can get on with our lives."

"Dawa, she's your mother. Of course, I'll meet her. Don't worry about me, I'm great with mothers. They love me. Even my own one does and she knows me really well. When?"

"I was wondering about this weekend. I am not working and if you can get cover for the café for an afternoon?"

"Yes, that should be fine. I've got Janet and Pat, now she can't work in The Bookery. Ralph's also offered to step in if need be. So, I'll do the breakfast and lunch, then he can do the rest of the afternoon with the old ladies. He'll love it. Well, they'll love having him to play with."

"She lives in Brighton, so I can drive us over there and maybe we can have some dinner in town afterwards?"

"Won't she want us to have dinner with her?"

"I wouldn't count on it," Dawa said.

CHAPTER 22

Hygiene rules, three glasses of water and chips on the pier.

Dawa arrived at The Cookery at three o'clock sharp on Saturday, as arranged. He had chosen his pale grey suit and turban, both pressed to a smooth perfection. Although he did it every day, he had rewound the turban three times to ensure there was nothing his mother could find fault with. His tie was a darker grey than his suit and had a tiny pink diamond pattern on it, which pleased him as he knew his mother would hate it and he would have one small victory today.

Janet was sitting at a table in the quiet café with Pat, "Anna's just upstairs titivating."

"There's no rush," Dawa said, sitting at the table with the ladies.

"Now that's a lovely suit," Pat purred. "Such a lovely grey. Isn't it a lovely grey, Jan?"

"It is," Janet said, caressing Dawa's arm. "Is it silk or wool, Darryl?"

"Erm, it's lightweight wool, I think. And it's Dawa, not

Darryl."

"Of course, it is. Silly me. Such an exotic name," Janet said, continuing to stroke his arm. "Where are you from exactly?"

"Brighton," he said, with a fixed smile

Ralph hurried through the door, "Sorry, I'm late, the traffic was really bad from the nursing home."

"How's poor Iris?" Janet asked.

"Irene."

"Yes, I meant Irene. Any better?"

"A little," Ralph said and made his way into the kitchen, swiftly followed by Dawa.

"There's something not right about those two," he said, looking back at the giggling women. "So, how's Irene really doing?"

"Better, I think. She finally spoke today. Apparently, she was blaming herself for not stopping the arsonist. She saw them setting the fire and they think shock set off her stroke. She reckoned that if she hadn't collapsed she could have saved The Bookery. She'd written it all down for her daughter who showed me. So, I made it clear that I didn't blame her for one second. She was furious with her daughter for showing me what she'd written and started shouting at her. It took her about a minute to realise she was speaking again and suddenly went quiet. It was hilarious, especially as her speech is absolutely fine. There's been no stopping her since then."

"I would have loved to have seen her face."

"It was a picture, I can tell you. The problem is, until

she can walk unaided she won't be allowed to go home. She hates being in the home with all the old people, as she calls them, so she's causing no end of trouble. I told her that the sooner she knuckles down and gets on with the exercises and works with the physiotherapists – or physical-terrorists as she calls them - the sooner she'll be home."

"That was brave of you. What did she say?"

Ralph hopped up to sit on the kitchen worktop, "She would only use sign language after that, and you can imagine the sort of signs she was making."

Dawa grinned, "I can."

Janet and Pat both started to applaud as Anna came down the stairs.

"You look sensational," Pat said.

Anna smiled shyly, "Thank you." She turned slowly and looked at Dawa.

He was unable to move. He knew that Anna was beautiful, like the most colourful butterfly he had ever seen, but he had not expected this. She was wearing the traditional Punjabi loose-fitting trousers and long dress top known as Salwar Kameez. It was made from a beautiful soft yellow fabric, and the hem of the dress and cuffs of the trousers were delicately embroidered with purple and gold beading. Over her hair, which he was pleased to see was still its untamed self, she had draped a matching scarf or chunni. She looked exquisite and he knew she had done if for him and his mother. It was rare that he was lost for words, but this was one of those occasions.

Ralph helped him out, "Wowser, I've never seen you

look like this. You look incredible."

She threw the end of the scarf over her shoulder, "Thanks, now get your rear end off my kitchen counter. Hygiene rule seventy-six-A prohibits bookseller's bums on food preparation areas."

"Oh, yes, sorry," he said, jumping down.

Dawa moved round the counter and kissed her on the cheek, "Thank you," he said, quietly. "But you did not need to do this."

"This old thing?" she said, flicking the scarf back around her neck. "I bought it for a sort of date earlier this year, which turned out to be with my own mother."

Dawa smiled, "I remember it well; it was at Cinque. At least, I remember you arriving wearing this and looking incredible."

Anna's normally rosy cheeks became a little rosier, "Really? Blimey, well, we are going to meet your mother and I want to show her due respect. I hope it's alright."

"It's perfect. I only hope she shows you the same courtesy."

"Don't worry, I haven't completely lost my own sense of style," she said with a grin and pointed to her shoes.

He looked down and grinned as he saw that she was wearing purple Dr Martin boots, with shimmering silver laces, "I love them," he said. "And she will love you or she is a fool. Shall we go?"

* * *

It took nearly an hour and a half to get to Brighton in

Dawa's car, and he spent most of the journey trying to prepare Anna for what was to come, but she refused to listen.

"Dawa, I'm looking forward to meeting her. Relax, you're just nervous."

Eventually, they pulled up at a pebble-dashed bungalow on a small estate in the hills that hug Brighton close to the sea. Dawa switched off the engine and took a deep breath, "Are you ready?"

Anna was terrified, but wasn't about to admit it, "I am."

"Just one thing, please don't mention my father."

"Why?"

"He moved back to the Punjab and left her here. He'd had enough of her," Dawa said and got out.

He came round the car to open Anna's door, noticing the net curtains at the front of the bungalow twitch. He reached for the car door and deliberately stood between the window and Anna while she got out, as if protecting her.

"Are you still in contact?"

"Occasionally, just once or twice a year. I haven't seen him since I was a boy. But please don't say anything."

"No of course," Anna said, suddenly feeling even more nervous. "It'll be fine, don't worry." She turned, missed her step onto the pavement, staggered forward and fell face first into the bungalow's front garden. Dawa rushed to her side, not missing the sudden movement at the window.

He carefully helped her up, "Are you OK? Are you

hurt?"

"No, I'm fine. Have I got grass on my knees?"

"No. Well, not much."

"Great. I think my shoe came untied."

Dawa knelt and started to tie her shoelace. His heart sank when he heard a shrill voice from behind him, "Don't kneel on the grass. You'll mark that suit and cheap fabric will never clean properly. Is she not capable of tying her own shoes?"

He looked up into Anna's startled eyes, "Don't worry, I'll look after you."

"Thanks," she whispered, gripping his shoulder tightly as he finished tying her lace. She looked up the garden path to the front door, where a short, round woman in a similar salwar kameez stood with her arms folded across her considerable chest. Her outfit was silver, with black trim, and a black and white chunni covering her head. "Hello," Anna said, with more enthusiasm than she felt. "I'm Anna. Sorry about that, I'm always flinging myself about. Nothing to worry about, I'm fine."

"I am worried about my grass. I pay a man a large amount of money to feed and cut it, I do not want it damaged," and with that she turned and waddled back into the house.

"Twenty minutes and we'll leave," Dawa said, taking Anna's hand firmly in his.

"It's fine, she's probably nervous too. Come on," and she set off up the garden, only to be stopped in her tracks by a shout from the house, "Not on the grass!", and she quickly side-stepped on to the path.

"Sorry," she called, as Dawa led her inside.

"Mama, don't be rude to Anna. We are lucky she didn't hurt herself."

"Humph," was his mother's reply. She stood at the end of a long hallway, like a centurion guard deciding whether she should let them pass or not, "Why did you not tell me?"

"Mama," Dawa said, sounding a warning note. "Aren't you going to offer your visitors some tea?"

"If I had known, I would have prepared quite differently," she paused, gave Anna a long hard look, then gestured to a doorway on her right. "Go in," and she disappeared up the hallway.

Anna and Dawa settled on the hard brown sofa in the plainest room Anna had ever seen.

"Where's all her stuff?" she whispered.

"What stuff?"

"Her books, her knick-knacks or photos or plants or... well, anything. It looks like she's been burgled."

Dawa smiled, "She's afraid that she *will* be burgled, so doesn't leave anything out for them to take."

"But where are the photos of you as a child, family pictures?"

"What are you two whispering about?" Mama Singh snapped, as she slowly made her way into the room with three glasses of water on a tray. "Have you no manners?"

"Only as many as you," Dawa muttered. "Mama, why are you giving us water?"

"Is water not good enough for you now? You think

you are too big a man not to drink water, now you mix with film stars and red-headed women?" She placed the tray carefully on a small coffee table in the middle of the room, took a glass and carried it to the armchair that faced the sofa. She lowered herself down slowly, until the last second where she let herself go and practically bounced onto the tight brown cushion beneath her.

"Would you like some water, Anna?" Dawa asked.

"No, I'm fine thanks." she said. She smiled her best smile at Mama Singh, "You have a lovely house, Mrs Singh."

"Do you have a house?"

"Yes, well, I have a flat above my café."

"Anna has two businesses in Rye, she's very successful," Dawa added.

"One business is not enough? Is it not making enough money, so you need two?"

"Well, I was offered the opportunity to open a second café. The first had been so successful that I thought it would be good to expand."

"I see that money is important to you. More important than my son's happiness?"

Anna gripped the crumpled fabric of her dress tightly, "Not at all. I love your son. I hope I make him very happy. I know he makes me happy."

Mama Singh sniffed loudly, "But you will not keep him happy. Red-headed, pale women do not have the capacity to be faithful, unlike Sikh women."

Dawa leapt to his feet, "Mama that's enough. I've brought Anna here to meet you out of respect, but you have shown her not one ounce in return."

"Dawa, please," Anna said, taking his hand. "It's OK."

Dawa had known this would not go well, but he had not anticipated his mother being quite so evil so quickly, "No, Anna it is not OK. Mama, let's be clear, I did not come here for your approval. I came here for you to have the opportunity to meet the woman I intend to marry, if she will have me."

Anna and Mama Singh both let out sharp sounds of shock.

"You have chosen to treat her with the utmost disrespect, even though she has come here today in clothes of your own culture that make her look more beautiful than I even imagined. If you cannot see that and are not prepared to get to know her, then we will leave and you will not see us again."

Mama Singh had gone very red in the face and the glass of water shook in her hands, but she sat silently and would not speak.

"Very well, goodbye," Dawa turned and went to the door, which he held open for Anna.

Anna looked at Mama Singh, "I don't know why you want to hurt your son. It seems bonkers to me because he is really terrific, but that's up to you. But I will make you a promise, I will never ever do anything to hurt him. And if you ever change your mind... well, come and find us."

She turned to Dawa and saw a tear slowly trickle down his cheek. She wiped it away with the edge of her head scarf, "Let's go and have fish and chips and candy floss on the pier," she said and took his hand and led him out of the house.

They drove to Brighton seafront in silence, with so much to say but neither knowing where to begin. Dawa parked near the pier and they walked hand in hand beside the sea and up to its ornate entrance lined with old-fashioned food stalls.

They stood together both overwhelmed by the sudden noise and lights around them.

"What do you want?" Anna asked.

Dawa smiled, "You."

"I was thinking cod or plaice, but that's a much better answer." She reached up and put her hands around his neck, looking deep into his eyes, "She has no idea what she is missing," and she kissed him. For a long time.

Neither of them was especially hungry so they opted to share a portion of chips and settled on two blue and white striped deckchairs halfway along the pier.

Anna speared a chip with a little wooden fork, "Well, that was a short visit, wasn't it?"

"I'm sorry it got out of hand," Dawa said. "I did try to warn you what she was like."

"I'm sorry too, I don't think I handled it very well. Going tits first into her garden, for a start."

"On the contrary, I think you handled it perfectly. But it's over now, we don't need to worry about her again. I have done my duty." He picked at a chip, "I can say that she is not representative of all Punjabi women. I have some smashing aunts you are going to really like, and they are going to love you."

"I can't wait to meet them."

He shifted round on his canvas deckchair until he was facing her, "May I ask you a question?"

"If it's, do I want to go on the dodgems? The answer will always be yes."

He smiled, "No, it's not about dodgems. You said something to my mother about liking me and wanting to make me happy. Was that the truth, or just something to shut her up?"

Anna waved her little fork in the air, "Oh, no, it was the absolute truth. Except I didn't say I *liked* you. I said, I *loved* you." She scratched her ear with the fork, waiting for him to kiss her.

Dawa didn't, he stared at her instead, "Truly?"

"Yep, completely truly. I love you Dawa Singh," she closed her eyes and pouted slightly inviting the kiss. When none came, she opened one eye, but Dawa was gone. He was no longer sitting next to her on his deckchair.

She looked around fearfully until she saw him kneeling at her feet, "What are you doing down there? I thought you'd done a runner. Did you drop a chip?"

"Anna, I spoke my mind in my mother's house. I didn't know I was going to say it until it was too late, but the moment I did I knew it was completely true. I know it's way too soon and this probably makes no sense to you and I don't expect you to answer straight away. I am sure you will not be ready to for some time, but..."

"For the love of Biggins will you say it," Anna squealed.

Dawa took her hand in his, "Anna would you, one day, do me the greatest honour and agree to be my wife?"

Anna dropped her fork, which fell through the gaps in the floor of the pier and floated away into the sea below, "Dawa, I absobloominlutely will be your wife. One day. Any day. Yes!"

She slipped off the deckchair to hug Dawa, but only got part way as her chunni caught on the wooden frame, "Aaah, I'm attached," she yelled. "I'm hanging by the chunni." She clung tightly to Dawa as she fought to free herself, meaning he couldn't get round to free her.

Seeing their predicament, an old man in a smart blazer came to their rescue and unhooked her scarf from the back of the chair, "There you go," he said.

Anna collapsed on the floor, "Thank you. That was close, I'm sure I could see a bright light at the end of a tunnel."

"That's probably the ghost train over there," the man said and carried on with his stroll along the pier.

"Sorry," Anna said, settling down in front of the still kneeling Dawa. "I spoil everything."

But Dawa was laughing too hard to do anything but take her in his arms and hold her. After a few minutes he had recovered enough to speak and he took her face in his hands, "You couldn't spoil anything. You make everything better and more colourful than I could ever have imagined. I love you, Anna."

Anna held on to him tightly, vowing to absobloominlutely never let him go.

CHAPTER 23

A glorious Sunday, the Queen's handbag and triangles of toast.

Ralph began Sunday in the usual way, growling at the alarm, throwing his phone on the floor and Sam elbowing him out of bed to turn the noise off.

He scrambled to pick the phone up and staggered out of the bedroom, where Stanley was ready for him on the landing.

"Morning, Stan, hang on." He went into the living room, where he always left his running gear if Sam had a late night at the restaurant. He got dressed, swallowed a glass of water and grabbed Stanley's lead.

"Come on then," he said, and they headed down the stairs, through the narrow hallway and out on to the High Street.

"Morning!" a bright voice shouted in his ear and Anna bounced in front of him.

"What the..." Ralph said, staggering back against the door frame. "Anna?"

"Well done, double word score. Well, one word, but

have double points," she said, jogging enthusiastically on the spot. "Isn't this time of the morning glorious?"

Ralph stared at her, "What the hell are you doing? And when did you ever use the word glorious?"

"Glorious? It's a glorious word, I've decided I haven't used it enough. Glorious! Which way do we go?"

"Wait, wait. What's going on? You don't run, you don't get up at this time in the morning unless you're baking. Why aren't you baking? Why are you wearing a track suit and leg warmers?" Ralph was struggling to process what was happening on what should be a slow easing into a quiet Sunday morning.

She smiled at him, "I thought I'd go for a run with you. It'll be a nice change. I thought we might jog past the station. The café opens early, I could treat you to breakfast."

Ralph frowned, "That's not going for a run, that's going for breakfast."

"Is it? Well, if you insist let's do that then," she took his arm and led him along the High Street. "I'm not sure I've got the right bra on to jump about too much, so breakfast is a much better idea."

Once they had settled into a corner table in the empty station café and ordered their food, Ralph sat back and crossed his arms, "Well?"

"Well, what?"

"What's going on?"

"Nothing's going on," Anna said, fiddling with her hair. "We're having breakfast."

"Why?"

"You're grumpy this morning, aren't you? How's Jane Scott's portrait going? Is it a masterpiece yet?"

"Don't remind me. I've made a start, but with everything that's happened I haven't been in the mood really."

"Blimey, Jane Scott won't be happy."

"She's not. She texts almost every day wanting to see what I've done. I've told her she can't see it until it's finished, which could be years at this rate."

"And The Bookery? With all that paper over the window no one can see inside. How's it going? Can I see it?"

"Nope. Same thing, no one will see it until it's finished. It will be a big reveal. I'm going in today to finish the artwork and Sam's hanging the new Ceiling of Curious Things."

Anna gripped the ketchup bottle and wailed, "But that was my job. Please can I do it, I did the last one. Please."

"Well, I wanted it to be a surprise for you, but I suppose we could do with the extra pair of hands."

"Yes!"

"Oh, you remember little Elliot from the football team who won the painting competition? Well, he knocked on my door the other day, with his mum. He's spent weeks making a model of the Queen on her wedding day from kitchen paper and wool. It's amazing. She even has a big black handbag, which I'm not sure she actually had on her wedding day, but he said it was so you could tell it was her. He loved the Queen. He wanted me to have it in case I could use it in The Ceiling of Curious Things. I said it would have pride of place, where everyone would see it."

"I love it! I'll hang it right in the middle. Dawa's working the lunch shift and Marcia, who's one of Sam's kitchen team, is going to cook today, so I'm free all afternoon. This weekend just gets better and better."

"Spit it out, then. What's going on?"

Anna couldn't hold it back any longer, "Well, there is something, BUT you have to promise to keep it a secret. We've agreed we're not going to tell anyone yet."

"But you're going to tell me?"

The young waitress arrived with their coffees, which she took her time to cautiously unload from her tray, much to Anna's frustration.

"That's fine. Just leave them anywhere. No, that's his. That one's mine," Anna's frustration made the girl anxious and spill some coffee into the saucer.

"Oh, I've messed that one up," she said. "I'll get you another."

Anna quickly grabbed the saucer, "No, no, just leave it. Please, I have to tell my friend I'm getting married and I need you to go away. Sorry. Didn't mean to be rude. But can you go away. I'll drink it out of the saucer. Thank you. Goodbye."

The poor girl took her tray and tiptoed away, crushed.

Ralph sat forward, "You are *what*?"

"Eh?" Anna said.

"You're getting married?"

"How did you know that? It's a secret."

"You just told me and that poor girl, who you've frightened half to death," Ralph shouted, frightening the poor girl half to death again.

"Did I? Oh, poop, I wanted to tell you properly, build up to it."

"Who are you getting married to?"

Anna stared at him, "Dawa, of course."

"Well, I suppose that's something."

"What does that mean?"

"Well, knowing you it could have been anyone if you'd got over excited and... Sorry, that's not fair. I'm just a bit tired," Ralph sat back and scrubbed his hands through his hair.

"You've spoiled it now. I wanted to tell you all about his awful mother, she's worse than Sam's mum. She is horrid and quite racist. I know that's a terrible thing to say, but she is. Plus, she has a room in her house with nothing in it. Well, it has furniture, but no pictures, no ornaments, no photos, nothing. She was horrible to Dawa, and he lost his temper and told her she was being rude to the woman he was going to marry. I nearly fell off the sofa at that point, but that happened later from the deckchair when I got all tangled up..."

"Wait, wait," Ralph said, rubbing his face hard to try and focus. "Slow down. So Dawa told his mum he was going to marry you?"

"Yes. Isn't that the most romantic thing, ever?"

"What did she say?"

"Nothing, she just sat there and stared at him. Then we went and had chips on the pier."

"Wow, Anna, that's... quick, don't you think?"

Anna shook her head, "I know it seems like it, but in terms of hours we've spent with each other it adds up to more time than I've spent with any other man in my life. Apart from my dad, but he's dead so he doesn't really count. I worked it out on a piece of paper. I've got it here." She rummaged in her tracksuit pocket and pulled out a scruffy piece of pink paper, "So, we've spent two hours walking and chatting most nights for twelve weeks, add on the time he comes to the café in the morning, then the walk on the marshes and other things, which all comes to about two hundred hours. If you date someone normally I reckon the first six weeks you might see them for three hours a week, then six hours for the next six weeks, which is one hundred and forty-four hours. That leaves sixty-six hours from my two hundred, so that's at least another eleven weeks. So, that's twenty-three weeks dating time in total, which we can round up to six months. So, although we've been seeing each other for twelve weeks, it's actually the equivalent of six months."

Ralph stared at her in wonder, "How on earth does your mind work?"

"Do you want me to go through it again?"

"No, please, no."

"My point is, lots of people get engaged after six months, right? So, it's not actually so strange for us to get engaged after twelve weeks."

Ralph smiled, "I think I get the gist. Is he really the one?"

"Yes. He's like no one I've ever met before. He makes

me feel... I don't know, brave and sane and whole."

"Then congratulations," Ralph said, reaching over the table and giving her a hug. "I think it's amazing."

"Thank you. Watch out she's coming back." Anna smiled warmly at the waitress as she returned with their breakfasts, "Sorry about before. I was a teeny bit tense, I hope I didn't upset you."

"No," said the waitress through tight lips. "Two breakfasts," and she dumped both plates on the table with a crash and walked away.

"I think she might be upset," Anna giggled.

Ralph picked up a triangular slice of toast from his plate, "This deserves a toast."

She picked up a slice from her plate too and held it up to his.

"To Anna and Dawa, a match made in heaven and Rye," he said and they bashed their toast together. Stanley popped his head up to the table level and barked, celebrating whatever everyone else was celebrating.

"Thank you, Stan," Anna said, giving him her piece of toast. "I thought, you might think it was crazy."

"Well, I wasn't expecting it, that's true. But when you know someone's right, you know. I can't deny that, can I, with Sam? But maybe you should have a long engagement. Take your time until the actual wedding, really settle in with the relationship."

Anna speared a piece of bacon. "I was thinking of July."

"July?"

"Look, as much as I want to talk about wedding

dresses and whether you'll look better in peach or pink as my bridesmaid, we need to talk about the arsonist."

"Peach or... hang on..."

"Focus, Ralph, we need to talk about catching the person who burnt your shop down. Dawa and I think we've solved the mystery."

"You know who it is?"

"Not exactly, but we think we know more or less what's going on."

Ralph cut into his sausage and dropped a piece down to Stanley, "Anna, I've told you, this whole pagan witches and spells thing is pretty far-fetched. It's the police who should be getting them. I appreciate you are trying to help, but..."

"It's the ashes they're after. People believe they have powers to protect you from misfortune and things like that."

"Right, so they've done all this for a few bits of ash?"

"We think so, and we need to be there on the Solstice next Friday to see who it is when they have their big ceremony."

"*If* they have their big ceremony."

"Oh, they will, I know, I feel it in my waters. So, we all need be there, on the marshes."

"Friday? That's the night before The Bookery re-opens, so I'll have to see if I have everything ready. Can't we get the police to go down and find them?"

"As if they're going to believe us about pentagrams and ashes and stuff. No, it's down to us."

"Well, I hope you're right and we can bring it all to an

end."

"I am right, trust me. Oh, and I need you to answer one question."

Ralph looked at her warily, "Go on."

"When you're my chief bridesmaid, would you prefer peach or pink?"

"Hang on, there is no way..."

The waitress passed their table.

"Excuse me," Anna called. "I'm sorry about the misunderstanding earlier. Can I ask you something?"

The girl looked worried, "What?"

"Do you think my friend here would suit peach or pink?"

CHAPTER 24

Fine tweed, two brothers and an old-fashioned valet.

Martin, Fiona and Jack walked the short route from the bus stop to the nursing home in silence through the soft warmth of the Sunday evening. It was turning out to be quite a different evening to the one either Fiona or Jack had expected.

Firstly, a stranger with Martin's voice had met them at the bus stop in Rye. He was wearing a fine tweed suit, was clean shaven and had neatly trimmed white hair, cut with a crisp parting. When they realised it really was Martin, he had run his fingers along his smooth chin, still feeling a little exposed without his rough stubble of recent months, "I'm sorry you get to see more of my face, like this, old things," he'd said. Fiona had said it made him look younger. Jack had just stared.

Secondly, feeling stronger and much more like the man he was before brandy became his best friend, he had said that he was ready to face his past and would really like them to meet Robin and his brother. Fiona had thought that Martin's brother had died some time ago, but said, yes, nevertheless. Jack shrugged, pretending not to be desperate to find out more about Martin, who was an Earl, but was also a tramp and a cook and a teacher and proper posh.

When they arrived at the nursing home, Erin opened the door as usual, but this evening she had a tray of tea things for them.

"He's all ready for you," she said. "I've put the extra chairs in his room that you asked for. I've laid up a tray too, if you'd like. I thought it might be nice for everyone to have a cuppa while you chat."

Martin bowed slightly, "You are a mind reader."

Erin stood back and looked him up and down, "I must say, I almost didn't recognise you when you came in. If it hadn't been your voice on the intercom, I wouldn't have known you. You look so dapper."

Martin blushed as he picked up the tray, "I have had what I believe is called a make-over. Although in reality it is more of a make-back. Back to who I was, a better and braver man."

"I bet you're proper hot in that furry suit, aren't you?" Jack said, getting a poke in the ribs from Fiona.

"I think he looks smashing," she said, marching him down the corridor to where Martin was knocking on the door of Robin's room.

Martin opened the door and stepped back for Fiona and Jack to enter. As before, the light was soft and warm, and the rich furnishings made it feel unlike the somewhat sterile atmosphere elsewhere in the home.

Jack let out a low whistle, "My dad's room ain't like this."

"Well, Robin does own the place, so he is allowed certain privileges," Martin said, putting the tray of tea things on a side table. He stood at the end of the bed and smiled at its occupant, "I've brought the friends I told you about."

Fiona and Jack waited behind Martin and watched the man in the bed slowly pull himself up on his elbows to a higher position on a large pile of pillows. His hair was pure white and smoothed back across his skull. His face was very thin and pale, his cheeks sunken and his eyes rimmed with red then dark blue, making them look hollow and a little lost. But he fixed his guests with a warm smile and beckoned them to come closer.

Fiona stepped up beside Martin and Jack took a small step, staying behind Fiona's shoulder, "Hello, Robin. I'm Fiona. This is Jack. We're very pleased to meet you."

Robin nodded, "And I you. I'm sorry it's taken so long for us to meet." He transferred his gaze to Martin, "Phillip has taken some time to come to his senses."

Jack whispered to Fiona, "Who's Phillip?"

"Shush, just listen."

Martin laughed, "My first name is Phillip. No one calls me that, except Robin."

"Why do we call you Martin then?"

"Martin is my family name, at school we were all known by our surnames alone and it stuck."

"Please sit down," Robin said. "I have manners, even if he doesn't."

"Yes, sorry, old things, do sit," Martin said, not put off by Robin's teasing manner. "Tea anyone?"

"Yes, please," Fiona said.

Jack shrugged, "Alright."

Martin poured the tea while they looked around the room at the gallery of paintings on the walls.

"I see you are admiring my collection," Robin said, his voice clear but weak.

"They're lovely," Fiona said. "Are you a collector?"

"Not really. I rescued them when the artist threw them all away."

Fiona got up and moved along the wall looking more closely at the landscapes beside the bed, "They are very good. I don't know much about art, but whoever did this was very talented. They're signed, PM, I think. Is that right?"

"Yes," Robin said.

"Shit," Jack said, getting up and looking at a big seascape. "PM? Is that you? Phillip Martin?" he asked.

Martin handed a mug of tea to each of them, collected his own and sat down before he answered with a simple, "Yes."

"Martin?" Fiona looked back at the paintings. "You did all these?"

"He was very good," Robin said. "They were done over many years, so you can see his skill developing through time."

Fiona returned to her seat beside the bed, "They are lovely, Martin. I can't believe you tried to throw them away."

"Who's this?" Jack said, from the end of the bed, pointing at the large portrait that faced Robin. It was of a man in his twenties sitting on a park bench, his legs were crossed and he looked directly out from the painting through tortoise shell glasses, a delicate smile held across his lips.

Martin didn't turn to look and Robin shut his eyes.

In the awkward silence Fiona beckoned to Jack to return to his seat. He shrugged and dropped himself back in his chair between her and Martin.

"That's Matthew," Martin said, quietly. "My brother."

"He's very handsome," Fiona said.

Robin smiled and opened his eyes, "Oh, yes, he was. Very. Will you tell them or shall I?" he asked Martin.

"I think I need to," Martin said, taking a sip of his tea and then a deep breath before turning to them. "He was my older brother. There were five years between us. He was the heir to the title and the estate. I was the spare, in case anything happened to him. In those days we had the big house, Manor Place, and a number of farms and houses around the area."

"You owned them all?" Jack said, wide-eyed.

"They had been in the family for several hundred years. When I was ten my mother died, from cancer we believe. She had never been a well woman and rarely left her bedroom from what I can remember. Possibly because my father was one of the most unpleasant people you can imagine, so I can't say I blame her."

Jack snorted, "I know what that's like."

"Indeed," Martin said, giving him a small nod of acknowledgement. "My childhood nanny encouraged my passion for art. My father did not. He told me it was a waste of time and not something someone like me should be spending their time on. Nanny, however, disagreed and set up an easel for me in her bedroom, in case he came into the nursery. Well, somehow, he found out, so Nanny had to go. I got a male tutor after that and Matthew, who was fifteen, got a valet."

"Me," Robin said.

Jack looked at Fiona, "What's a valet?"

"I don't think we have them anymore," she said.

Robin shook his head, "More's the pity. A valet was a servant who was responsible for a gentleman's appearance and clothes. Often, he became something of what we would call a personal assistant in today's parlance."

"What's parlance?" Jack asked, but was quickly shushed by Fiona.

"I was only nineteen when I joined the household. In the 1960s and 1970s domestic service was dying as a career, but if you had nothing it could be a good way to survive. You get a roof over your head, food, a uniform and a little pay. It wasn't much, but it was more than I'd grown up with."

Martin put his hand out and laid it gently on Robin's foot beneath the damask bed cover, "He was a breath of fresh air from the moment he arrived. He stood out straight away, mostly because he had bright red hair – all turned white, now he's so old."

"Careful," Robin warned with a shaky grin.

"We knew we could trust him when he confessed that father had told him one of his duties was to report back on everything we did and everywhere we went."

Robin pushed himself further up on his pillows, "It was wrong. They're father was a brute. I was there to take care of Matthew, I was not employed as a spy. So, each week I would make up all sorts of boring stuff for their father. Some of it true, most of it nonsense."

"Good for you," Fiona said, standing and helping adjust Robin's pillows for him. "Is that better?"

"Much, thank you. I wish I could get up and sit with you, but it's my heart. It's running out of steam and I find it hard to do much these days."

"It's fine, you rest," Fiona said. "Tell us when you want us to leave."

"No, no, you have so much more to hear," he said, looking at Martin. "Are we telling them everything?"

Martin nodded, "Yes, I need to get rid of it all."

Robin smiled, "Good. Get on with it then, don't drag it out, I'd like to live to hear the end."

"I know, I know. Well, having Robin around was great for us boys. We had a pretty miserable life. Matthew was always quiet and rarely spoke in front of my father. He hated him to such an extent that he chose to stay quiet and keep his feelings locked up inside. His silence used to drive father mad, which made Matthew even more determined."

Jack slurped his tea, "What was he like then, your dad?"

A dark shadow crossed Robin's face, "The Earl ruled everything. Meals were at a particular time, lateness was punished severely. He once made Matthew hold a boiling silver teapot with his bare hands for exactly the same number of minutes he was late. He wasn't allowed to hold it by the handle, he had to clasp it with both hands around the middle. Dinner was the same, he never spoke to them, except to read out the results of the tests he set for them each day. Mathematics, geography, history. They were not allowed to use his library and look up the answers, and of course there were no computers and so on then. For every answer they got wrong they would receive a wallop from the walking stick he kept by the fire."

"No," Fiona gasped, tears gleaming in her eyes as she looked at Martin, his head hanging low to his chest.

"Shit," Jack added.

Robin looked at them, "That was just the tip of the iceberg."

Martin hesitated and looked at Robin. "Maybe you should tell the next part."

"No, no, you're doing quite well. Go on."

"Well," Martin continued. "On Matthew's eighteenth birthday, my father threw a party. Not a proper party that you or I would recognise, but more of a reception for the great and good of the area to come and pay homage to the future Earl. Matthew was dead set against it, but of course he didn't say anything. He started to talk to me in earnest about making his escape. Then the night before his birthday he sat me down and told me that he was leaving. I remember being so excited. We'd talked about it for years, this was our chance to get away from the stifling house and the bullying of our father, the restrictions on everything boys want to do and be. But he told me he couldn't take me with him. I didn't understand it, we'd sworn to take care of each other. I can see him now, with tears in his eyes, holding my shoulders tightly as he looked me in the eye.

He said, 'Phillip, if I took you, he'd come after me twice as hard. You're only thirteen, he'd accuse me of kidnap. He'd use the law and the police to find us.'

I knew he was right. I started to cry; I couldn't seem to stop. He held me for ages until I could control myself, then I said, 'But who's going to look after you?'

That's when he smiled, a grin covering his whole face. 'Well, that is the big news, little brother. Robin is coming with me.' That made me feel better, at least he wouldn't be alone."

Robin's gnarled fingers tightened on the bed sheet, "We packed as much as we could in two bags. I had saved some money from my wages and we left the house about an hour before the party was due to start."

Martin looked out of the window at the gathering dusk, "When the clock ticked towards eight o'clock, the guests for Matthew's party started to arrive. Lady this, Lord that, the Lord Lieutenant of the county, a judge, a bishop, police chiefs and so on. All toadying to my father, the biggest landowner in the area. When Matthew failed to appear, I was sent to find him. I went out of the room and sat on the stairs. Matthew had told me what to say, but I couldn't do it - I was too scared. After half an hour father charged out of the drawing room shouting and bellowing at me. I looked at him, the words I'd practiced going round in my head, but I couldn't say them. So, I took over where Matthew left off, I said nothing.

I won't go into details, but suffice to say he did everything he could to find out where they'd gone.

But I genuinely didn't know where they were, so I had nothing to say.

Matthew was never mentioned again. It was as if he never existed. Life went on exactly as before, breakfast, dinner, the awful tests each night. Silence and bitterness laying like a heavy blanket over the house. Until they caught Robin."

CHAPTER 25

Two silver cigarette cases, love letters and Raffles, the gentleman burglar.

Everyone looked at the man in the bed, "Spotlight, please," Robin said, with a thin smile. "We thought we'd made it. We got jobs in a hotel on the coast of Norfolk. It was menial stuff, but we got paid and they gave us accommodation thrown in. It saved them some money, because of course we only needed one room. The manager turned a blind eye to that, as it was cheaper for him."

"What?" Jack said, spitting out a mouthful of tea. "You and Matthew were queer? Sorry, I mean, gay boys?" and he smiled proudly at Martin.

"We were," Robin said, quietly. "I thought he was the most exciting person I had ever met, not to mention..." he gestured to the painting on the wall. "He was beautiful."

"Jack," Martin said. "You must understand that in those days and for a long time afterwards it was illegal to be gay in this country. Men were sent to prison for simply loving someone of the same sex."

"Shit," Jack said, flopping back in his chair. "I mean, it ain't my scene, but that's insane. Prison, for that?"

"Yes, so you can see why the hotel was such a refuge for us," Robin continued. "We had a marvellous few weeks of freedom, but then the old Earl tracked us down and they arrested me and I was accused of theft."

"Theft?" Fiona said. "Why? You didn't steal Matthew?"

Martin's laugh was hollow, "We had all underestimated my father's desire for revenge. He reported to the police that when Robin left the house several items of silver also disappeared. When they arrested him, they searched his belongings and miraculously found two silver cigarette cases."

"How?"

"Don't forget that the people invited to Matthew's birthday party included senior police officers and a judge or two. It was much easier and more common in those days for money to change hands within the establishment, and *problems* like Robin were made to disappear."

Robin ran his hand carefully across his eyes, "In my case, for three years at Her Majesty's pleasure."

"Y-you went to prison?" Jack stuttered.

"Oh yes, not without a fight, but what could we do? The judge had been another guest at Matthew's party."

"The night before Robin's sentencing Matthew turned up at Manor Place. I was asleep but I heard him practically breaking the door down and demanding to be let in. Father took a gun and faced him in the hallway. I stood at the top of the stairs and watched it all. Matthew was beside himself. He shouted and swore at father, used everything he could to persuade him to drop the charges. He promised to come back, to do everything father said, be the dutiful son, anything. Father just stood there, his hunting rifle over his arm. In the end Matthew ran out of steam and Father asked one question, 'Why are you willing to do all that for this man, this servant?'

Matthew stepped close, within inches of Father's face, and said, 'Because I love him.'

Father said nothing then spat in Matthew's face. Matthew fell back and Father lifted the gun. I shouted from the top of the stairs and started to run down. Matthew saw me and called my name. Father turned and as he did so the gun went off. I'd never heard a sound like it, ricocheting around that dark old hallway like the end of the world.

Matthew leapt on Father's back and brought him to the ground. I wasn't hurt, of course, the shot had hit the woodwork somewhere on the wall. I shouted at Matthew to run. I told him I would find him one day soon. He turned and ran out of the hall and out of my life.

The next day Father disinherited Matthew. I had to watch while he signed the papers in front of witnesses. I was now the new heir.

I told him I didn't want it, but he ignored me. I was given no choice, no freedom, not a moment to myself. Any talk of Matthew or Robin was banned. Somehow, I survived for the next three years. There wasn't a word from Matthew, nothing. I rang the prison and found out the exact date and time Robin would be released. It was three days after my sixteenth birthday."

Robin shifted on his pillows, "And there he was. This scrawny youth, with a rucksack on his back, trousers at half-mast somewhere near his calves and this awful tweed jacket hanging off his shoulders. He was standing in the rain outside the prison gates. He had two pounds in his pocket and a bar of chocolate for me. That's when we joined forces, as it were. We shared the same quest - to find Matthew."

"Hadn't Matthew written to you or visited you in prison?" Fiona asked.

"He visited me once not long after I was sentenced, but I told him that I didn't want to see him again. All I could think was that Matthew needed to get away and keep himself safe. I was so afraid that his father would come after him next, for more revenge. He wouldn't listen of course, so every time he requested a visit I refused. It broke my heart and I was a fool, but I thought I was doing the right thing. For him.

After about a year the letters suddenly stopped. Up until then he had written to me every week. I only wrote back once, to tell him I loved him, but he must leave me alone," Robin closed his eyes, exhaustion overtaking him. "Please, Phillip, carry on. I'll rest and listen."

Martin touched Robin's foot lightly, watching him for a moment, then carried on with the story, "Matthew understood why Robin had tried to push him away, but he wasn't having any of that, of course. He was a young man in love and injustice coursed through every vein in his body. So, he fought for Robin and carried on writing."

Fiona wiped her eyes, "But he stopped eventually,

Robin said. Why?"

"At the time, we had no idea, so we began our search for him. You must remember there was no internet or social media to track people, it was very easy to simply disappear. We got all sorts of part time jobs and we scrapped enough together to pay rent each month, and in-between we kept searching. We were forced to keep moving every time my father's hounds caught up with us. He was determined not to let his only remaining son and heir escape him. After a year or two we both had no money and no jobs. We would spend hours in the local library scouring the papers for work, or just reading books in a place where we could be warm without having to pay the bills. That's when I read about AJ Raffles, the gentleman burglar. That was it, sweet revenge, and it would solve our immediate problem.

I didn't tell Robin, as I knew he would be entirely against it. Also, there was a risk of being caught and the last thing I wanted was for him to go back to prison."

"You were a burglar?" Jack said, his eyes wide with astonishment. "A Lord and everything?"

"I was, Jack, but the only things I stole were my own, in a way. I went back to Manor Place, our family home, in the dead of night but this time not through the front door. Having grown up there I knew exactly which windows were always left open, which doors were unlocked at night and which floorboards creaked. So, I managed to get in easily. I knew exactly what I was looking for; the silver cigarette cases that Robin had been accused of stealing.

I knew that they were kept in my father's dressing room. The trickiest part was not waking him, as I had to cross his bedroom. I could have gone for anything else in the house, but, like a fool, my mind was set on those two cases. I was sure that when he found them missing my father would know the significance of only those items being taken. It would be like a calling card, just as Raffles always left his calling card when he stole something."

Martin looked at Fiona and Jack's expectant faces. He knew this part would be hard and was quite prepared for things to change when he revealed what happened next, "Do not judge me too harshly, dear things. I have lived with my actions for so many years, that I find it hard to face them again now, but I must."

He took a deep breath and began to recount the moments after he stepped through the door to his father's darkened bedroom, "The curtains were pulled across the window, but there was a gap and a shaft of moonlight across the room. I could see the dark bulk of him lying in the bed. I tiptoed slowly around the room, keeping to the walls and shadows as best I could. Finally, after what seemed like an age, I reached the door to his dressing room. I had to step into the shaft of light to reach the handle. As I did so my father's voice barked, 'Phillip.'

I froze. My breath stopped. I was pretty sure my heart had stopped too. I didn't respond, I think I was hoping he had said the word in his dreams.

'Phillip,' he said again. 'Have you come to kill me, boy?'

My eyes had adjusted to the darkness and I saw him properly. A shadow of his former self. The big brute who dominated our lives and bullied us mercilessly was a thin skeleton, lost in a giant bed. All the fear of him fell away at that moment and I felt nothing but anger.

'Would you blame me if I did kill you? After all you did to me and Matthew and Robin?'

'Don't utter the names of those abominations in my house,' his voice a whisper of its former power.

'He is your son. I am your son. Why would you choose to ruin our lives?'

'I chose nothing of the sort, you managed to ruin them yourselves,' he began to cough and I was afraid he might start to wake the house.

I went to the cabinet beside his bed and poured him a glass of water, 'Here,' I said holding it out to him, but he waved it away.

'I want nothing from you. Ring the bell, I need the bloody nurse and my cursed tablets.'

His face had gone even paler, and I could see his lips turning blue as he struggled to regain his breath, 'The bell... idiot.... the bell.'

His hands grabbed weakly at the sheets, fisting them into balls at his side. He gasped for breath, like a fish struggling on the riverbank.

I don't remember consciously making the decision, but I found myself walking to the armchair that sat in the corner of the room, sitting down and waiting.

Fiona reached out her hand and laid it on Martin's, "What were you waiting for?"

"For him to say, please. For once in his life, to ask me for something and to say please."

Jack leaned forward, "And did he?"

243

Martin nodded, "Eventually. He knew that was what I wanted, and he struggled against it for as long as he could. But in the end he gasped, *Help me, please.*"

"And did you?" Fiona asked.

"I did. I pocketed the two cigarette cases first, then rang the servants bell and walked out of the house. This time I used the front door and walked calmly down the long drive and away from him. He died the next morning in hospital. I do not regret my action, nor am I here to ask anyone's forgiveness. I did what a young man needed to do at that moment in time, and I have had to live with it for the rest of my life."

"You didn't kill him, Martin, you rang the bell. The servants would have gone to him," Fiona said, tightening the grip on his hand. "But he killed himself by the choices he made. For any parent to treat their children as he did is unforgiveable. I'm not saying he should have died for it, but if he had behaved with more humanity then he may have received more back from you, from the universe, from God... from whoever was looking down on him. So, you were not responsible."

"Thank you," Martin said, with a brief nod. "The upshot of it all was that twelve hours later I was declared the new Earl of Groombridge. He had not changed his will, as I thought he may have done."

Jack looked at Martin with awe, "So you're proper rich, then?"

Martin shook his head, "I'm afraid not, old thing. Through my father's mismanagement of the estate, combined with inheritance laws and taxes, there was next to nothing left. The house had to be sold along with its contents to pay off the debts. The land and estates had to go too. It soon became clear that there would be little left for me to inherit except the title, which was something I was supremely uninterested in. It had brought me nothing but misery since birth. But then everything changed. After the announcement of my father's death in the papers, one of his old friends got in touch. He knew where Matthew was."

CHAPTER 26

*A proper memorial, Raffles returns
and an old wooden box.*

Fiona could barely dare to ask, but she had to, "Was Matthew alright?"

Martin took a deep breath, "I'm afraid his old friend led us to where he had been buried."

"No," Jack gasped.

"He had developed cancer. We think it was the same as the one that killed our mother, but there were few details. He had died with nothing, so his friend had scraped together enough money for a funeral but couldn't afford a headstone. There was a simple wooden stake in the ground where he lay with his name on it.

I couldn't leave him like that, he needed a decent headstone to be remembered properly. But we had nothing, as I'd sold the cigarette cases for a pittance to pay our back rent and bills. I was desperate, so, I contacted the family solicitors. They told me that everything was being held until all debts had been paid off and they were not in a position to release any funds. Everything in the house had been catalogued and valued and they believed there would be nothing left at the end.

So, back I went to the world of Raffles, the gentleman burglar. There was only a skeleton staff left in the house by then and I already knew I could get in and out easily. I only took things that were unlikely to be missed easily, none of the Gainsborough paintings or big pieces. I took candlesticks, coins from a collection, other pieces of silver. Quite a haul. I ended up with a good sum of money. Enough to pay for a proper memorial for Matthew, with plenty left over."

"I'm so sorry," Fiona said, through her tears. "It seems so unfair."

"It was. I was consumed with the unfairness of it all. My father, the tight society that had protected him and sent Robin to prison for nothing, leaving Matthew to fend for himself alone. If it wasn't for Robin, I'm not sure what I would have done, I had so much rage in me." He looked carefully at Jack, "That is why I understand your situation, my young friend. I was you many moons ago. Luckily, Robin took me under his wing, perhaps as a way of dealing with his own grief."

Robin opened his tired eyes at that, "Actually, it was something Matthew said in one of his last letters. He asked me to watch out for his little brother. He must have known he was dying, you see. So, I brought Phillip home from whichever pub or gutter he'd fallen in to, sobered him up and tried to keep him in one piece. In the end we went back to Manor Place to meet the executors of his father's will. The big surprise was that the sale of some of the famous paintings had raised more than was expected, so not everything had to be sold. There was one property left from the estate. An old timber manor house in the village of Tenterden."

Fiona gasped, "This nursing home?"

Martin rubbed his newly shaven chin, "Yes. As Robin was, in my mind, Matthew's next of kin I felt it should have gone to him, but he wouldn't take it. So, I did the only thing I could, I got the papers drawn up and signed it over to him, then disappeared. We only met again a few months ago - and that is my other great regret, for which I will forever be sorry."

Robin held out his hand to Martin, who moved round the bed and took it, "It broke my heart a second time to lose him as well. But I knew he'd be alright, he needed to run away so he could come back stronger. So, I got on with turning this place into a business using some of the money from Phillip's escapades as a gentleman burglar. That's when St Matthew's was born."

Fiona gasped, "Is that its name? I didn't know."

Martin stroked the fragile hand in his, "It was only a short while ago that I plucked up the courage to come and have a look at the old place. Not imagining for a moment that Robin would still be here, let alone as a resident, but here he was. And that, my young friends, is the end of our tale. I am sorry to have taken up so much of your time, but it was something that had been inside me for too long and I really needed to set it free. To set young Phillip free. Now his story is out and lives with you, as I hope a little of Matthew and Robin will too."

"It will," Fiona said, wiping her eyes with a tissue. "It always will."

"There is one more thing to do. Robin? Are you

awake?"

Robin's eyes fluttered open, "I'm not dead yet, if that's what you mean."

"I didn't, old thing, but it's good to know."

Martin stood up and moved to the door, where he had left the bag he had brought with him. He picked it up and placed it on the bed. He reached inside and pulled out the dusty box he had taken from behind the skirting board in his house and held it out to Robin, "I think these are yours."

Robin looked at him and knew exactly what the box contained, "No? I asked you to burn them."

"I know you did. I also know that you didn't really want me to."

Robin reached out a pale hand and touched the box, "His letters?"

"Yes," Martin said. He turned to Fiona and Jack, "I think that's enough for one night. Let's leave Robin alone with Matthew for a while."

Stunned, Fiona and Jack stood, quietly putting their mugs back on the tea tray.

"Good night, Robin," Fiona said and kissed him on the paper-thin skin of his cheek.

"Night," Jack said, his voice hoarse.

"I'll meet you outside," Martin said, as he closed the door behind them. He sat gently on the side of the bed, "I'm sorry I didn't give them to you earlier. I hid them, like I hid everything from that time. Once Matthew had gone and it was all over, I had to start again. Every time I thought of what happened, I froze. I felt like I'd failed him and I couldn't face that. I had to turn away, so I failed you too. Do you understand?"

Robin looked at him, a lifetime of caring for people showing in his old eyes, "Of course, I understand. I know you are asking for forgiveness, Phillip, but I can't give it to you. Because there is nothing to forgive. You didn't fail him or me."

He looked at the box on his lap and caressed it gently, "You will tell your other friends the story, won't you? I really would like it to be told, so we are not forgotten."

"Of course," Martin said. "I'm sorry it took so long for me to be able to speak about it all."

"Enough apologies," Robin said, with a smile. "Leave me alone with Matthew," and he pulled the box towards him.

Martin hesitated then leant down and kissed him on the forehead, "Goodbye, my friend."

"Goodnight, Master Phillip," Robin said, as the door to his room clicked quietly closed.

Fiona watched Martin walk up the corridor towards them, noting that his step seemed lighter than the previous times she had seen him trudge down it to visit Robin.

"That's quite a story," she said, as Martin reached her and Jack.

"Yeah, I thought my dad were messed up, but what you lot went through is a different level," Jack said.

Martin nodded, "But it's all gone now. I've carried it around my entire life, touching everything, tainting it. Not now. I believed my lowest point was being an outcast lying on the street with nothing to hold me to this earth. I realise now that I have been through far worse, so this was a wake-up call to turn the page and begin a new chapter. Which has already begun. I cook in the café, which I love. I have friends, whom I love. And I have a place in this world in which I fit quite comfortably. So, my past is over. I can move on."

Fiona looked at the new man who stood before her, a little taller, a little more handsome and a whole lot happier than the one she first met, and she could think of no words to say, so she hugged him hard.

They travelled home in silence and all got off the bus in the High Street.

Jack looked awkward as he stood on the pavement, "Erm, you know you said about my graphic novel stuff? That you might wanna see some more of them? Was that true?"

"Of course," Martin said and turned to Fiona. "Jack has created the most beautiful graphic novel. It is quite brilliant."

Jack shuffled his feet and pulled his beanie hat lower, "Yeah, well, whatever," he said. "Anyway, I brought you some of the other ones." He swung his duffle bag around his shoulder and reached inside to pull out three scruffy notepads, "Read 'em, if you want."

Martin took them, "Thank you, I will. I am excited to see what else you have created."

"Right," Jack said, feeling a little bit of something he hadn't yet got used to or knew what to do with. Pride. So, he walked away, "Night."

Fiona and Martin watched him disappear around the

corner.

"I have an old acquaintance," Martin said. "Who is a publisher and is always on the lookout for new talent. I have a feeling he will be as excited by Jack's work as I am."

"Well," Fiona said. "It really has been a night of surprises."

Martin looked above them at the night sky, "*There are more things in heaven and earth than are dreamt of,*" he said.

"Hamlet?" Fiona said, following his gaze up to the heavens.

"Indeed. There are also more chickens on earth than there are people."

Fiona laughed, "Who said that?"

"Omelette," Martin said.

Fiona took Martin's arm as they laughed, "After all you've been through, I feel like I'm finally seeing the real you. I mean, I liked the you from before, but this one smiles and laughs more. You know, neither of us had the best fathers in the world, did we? But if I'd got to choose one now, I'd chose you."

Martin kept his gaze on the stars, feeling Fiona's arm through his and thinking that at this moment Rye was the most magical place on earth.

* * *

In the small hours of the morning, Robin felt more tired than he had ever known. He had found the strength from somewhere to read every single one of Matthew's old letters. He lay in the warm light of the one lamp still lit beside his bed and looked out at the stars. This earth really was a magical place, he thought. Matthew's letters had come back to him just when he needed them most. As he had read them Matthew's voice came back to him too, something he thought he'd lost for ever. He could hear him so clearly and now he could see him through the window, laughing and smiling... oh, that smile. He hugged the box of letters close to his chest, knowing that Matthew's touch and voice and heart were all held within it.

Robin closed his eyes, a gentle smile on his lips, and took a final contented breath. One letter held tightly in his hand, the last one he had received from Matthew telling him that he would always wait for him, *'here or in another life.'* After so many years Robin and Matthew were finally reunited.

CHAPTER 27

A new house for Stanley, tiny
hats and big surprises.

A few days later and the longest day of the year was hot and sticky. Stanley, not usually too keen on heat, was excited. In fact, he couldn't contain his excitement. He didn't know where to run first. Every day when they walked through the hallway beneath the flat he had sniffed and scratched at the door to The Bookery, but had never been allowed in. But today was different.

As they went into the hall Ralph didn't bend down to attach his collar. He wasn't pulled and encouraged past the internal shop door. Today, the door had been unlocked and even before it was half open he had curved round it and shot through.

The smells and sights were overwhelming, so Stanley's nose stayed close to the floor as he took in all the new deliciousness that came at him. The books were there smelling new and clean and bright. He could smell paint and spent some time around the bottom of what he didn't know was a rocket, but the children would. It was big and red and silver, and its body was packed with books.

Stanley continued to a house with a dark timber frame. He nudged a small red door and stuck his head inside to find more lovely smelling books tucked away. He'd come back to that, he thought, that needed further investigation.

He had lost the dark, slightly mouldy smell that usually filled the middle of the shop at the back. He went to investigate the big hole and the metal stairs he knew he wasn't allowed down. He peered through the balustrade and had a good sniff. Clean. Light. Fresh. All new.

There was a stool behind him, on which Ralph now sat. He did a couple of turns around it, to let Ralph know he was enjoying himself, stuck his head under the counter, which smelt odd. Kind of rubbery, like the smell you got from people's feet when they were out in the rain.

Then he trotted down the step to the bottom of the shop, this was his domain and he'd missed it. He had a quick check of the lie of the land. The big floor had something in the middle of it. It was round and quite high, but if he got on his hind legs and reached up he could just get his nose on it, where he got the whiff of more books.

Something caught his eye, glinting above his head. He stopped and looked up. Yes, there were things flying around above his head. They weren't doing much except bobbing about in the breeze, but they were all shapes and sizes and colours. Even from this far away he could smell that some were quite old and a little bit dead to be honest, but there had been curious things hanging from the ceiling before.

Finally, he worked his way along the front window. He found a gap and jumped up into the window display. The colours that had warmed the windows before had gone. Above his head swung lights on long strings, they made a nice glow and he could feel some warmth coming from them too, so that was good.

He tripped his way between some interesting smelling books that people could see from the street and liked the feel of the velvety fabric under his paws. Then he came to his bed at the end. Except it wasn't his bed. He stopped and looked at it. He looked to where Ralph had been sitting. Ralph was still there.

"Go on, Stanley. It's yours. In you go."

Stanley looked back at the small, square house in front of him, with an open arch in the middle. It had a bright roof and walls with some flowers growing up it. He sniffed at them, but they smelt like paint, so they weren't really that interesting. Slowly and cautiously, he put his nose through the hole at the front and sniffed.

Hm, not bad. He inched his way in and smelt the cushion that was on the floor of the little house. Not like his bed before, but he could make something of it. He stepped fully inside, found that he could turn around quite easily. So, he did. Several times. Then he flopped down onto the cushion that was now his.

Stanley lay his head on his paws and found that he could see the world going by like before, but he had a bit more privacy and he could get some shade from the sun without going to lay under the counter where Ralph sat. Yes, this would do nicely.

By mid-afternoon, Stanley was entirely at home in the new shop and so was Ralph. It had been a mammoth undertaking, but incredibly, with a huge effort The Bookery would be ready to welcome customers again in the morning.

He had a long list of small jobs to do, but his task for the afternoon was to repaint the sign that ran along the bottom of the shop window. He had marked it out with a chalk pen and was slowly painting the words in bright blue. He saw a pink reflection of something in the glass and turned to see the tiny figure of Psychic Sue standing beside him. Her white hair and big glasses topped a pink pinafore dress, which she wore with pink leggings and purple glitter jelly sandals.

"I knew you'd fix it. You're a fixer, I could see that," she said.

"Thanks, Sue. You look well."

"I do, don't I. It's a special day for me, I'm off to see my new home in Bexhill."

"Oh, no, are you leaving Rye?"

"Yes, it's time for a fresh start. My friend Destiny is an estate agent and found me a lovely flat on the seafront," she said, pushing her glasses back up her nose and hauling an overstuffed tote bag back onto her shoulder. "It was going to be too much for me to reopen the shop, the energy was all wrong in there now. I'm putting it up for sale and moving on. I inherited a bit of money from my son, so I can afford to retire. When do you reopen?"

"Tomorrow morning, if I can get all the last little jobs done."

"You will. You know it's the Summer Solstice tonight, don't you? A time for rebirth. I'm off to my new life, you're starting again – it's all meant to be. Perhaps tonight the person who set fire to our shops will be revealed too."

Ralph smiled, "Maybe, but I won't be there to see it. I reckon I'm going to be here all night, sorting things out."

"Well, good luck. I'd better get down to the station. No train waits for no woman... or something. Tally ho!" and she marched away down the High Street.

She passed Sam who was coming the other way carrying a large cake box, "Tally ho!" she shouted at him and turned the corner.

"She's in a good mood," he said, as he got to Ralph.

"Yes, she's retiring and moving along the coast."

"Good for her," Sam said, blowing out his cheeks. "When do you think we'll have time for a holiday?"

"In about ten years," Ralph laughed and tried to look in the cake box. "Can I see?"

Sam held the box away from him, "No, you'll have to wait for the surprise reveal later. Is everyone still coming?"

"Yep, it's just Dawa and Anna who don't know. I'm not sure how long I can stay though; I keep thinking I've finished, then I remember something else and the to-do list never seems to get any shorter."

"You need a break, come and have a drink and some

cake, then we can both come down and get it all done," Sam stood back to look at the finished window. "That looks amazing. But wasn't the wording different before?"

"Yes, it said *Let your adventure begin....*"

"I love the new one, *Let the adventure continue...*"

"It's true though. The adventure is clearly not over yet, there is always something new to deal with or enjoy. I can honestly say that the new look Bookery excites me even more than the first one. I'm not saying I'm grateful to the arsonist, but this feels like a great new start."

They stood side by side and took in the clean bright window, the shining shop behind it and all the unusual colours and paintings and hanging curios that would entice people back into The Bookery.

"Well, Mr Bookseller, I am very, very proud of you, but if I don't put this cake down my arms are going to fall off. Don't be long."

"No, I've got the last few letters to do, then I'm done."

* * *

Half an hour later, Sam was back in the restaurant pottering around in the kitchen, although he knew he wasn't staying long. He could see Dawa through the glass porthole in the door effortlessly greeting guests and seating them for their evening meal, none the wiser as to what was about to unfold.

Dead on time, as arranged, Graham, the head waiter who was supposed to be on his night off, came through the restaurant door. Sam shot out of the kitchen as Dawa returned to his reception desk.

"Graham," Dawa said. "I thought you had the night off?"

Sam slid in behind him, "He did," he said, as he took Dawa by the shoulders and started to propel him around the reception desk and towards the door. Sam had forgotten how big a man Dawa was and didn't find it easy to manoeuvre him, especially as Dawa wasn't a man who liked to be manoeuvred.

Dawa fought back as he saw Graham take his place behind the desk, "Sam, what are you doing?"

"Taking you away for the night, so please don't make it difficult," Sam said, straining to move him any further. "Just... let... me... get... you... out."

Dawa stood his ground, digging in his heels, "Not unless I know where we are going."

Sam sighed and came round in front of him, "Do me a favour and trust me. It'll be fun."

"I doubt that, if you won't tell me where we're going."

"Don't be miserable, it's a nice thing. We're doing a nice thing."

"Why?"

"Because we're nice people and we like you... when you're not being difficult. Please just come with me," Sam said, hearing himself starting to plead. Then he pulled out his emergency joker, "Anna will be there."

Dawa's face lightened, "She will?"

"Yep, so please come."

"She didn't mention anything to me."

Sam was back behind him pushing hard and Dawa was slowly edging towards the door, "Well, she doesn't actually know about it either. Ralph is with her now, and I bet he's having a much easier time getting her up to the rooftop."

✽ ✽ ✽

"Is it a surprise party? For me and Dawa?" Anna shouted, as she ran out on to the rooftop, followed a few seconds later by a red-faced Ralph. "I hoped someone would do something. Hi, Martin. Hi, Fiona."

Ralph held his hands up to Martin and Fiona, "I told you it wouldn't be hard to get her up here. The moment I mentioned the words 'a bit of surprise' she was like Usain Bolt – and was off and running."

"Where's Dawa?" Anna asked, looking around. "Oh, you've decorated it!" She clapped her hands and reached up to touch the bunting that said *Congratulations* in big silver letters. Another banner behind Fiona declared it an *Engagement Party* in gold. The little iron table was covered in a gold cloth, with champagne flutes and a silver wine cooler which held ice and a bottle of champagne.

"Of course, we have, old thing," Martin said. "This is a very special occasion."

Anna hugged Martin, Fiona and then Stanley, who had been quite happily asleep under one of the deckchairs, "Thank you, thank you,"

"Oh, I can hear someone now," Martin said, pointing towards Ralph's flat.

Sam appeared looking frazzled, but threw his arms out and announced, "Ta da! Dawa Singh, ladies and gentlemen. The man of the moment!"

Everyone cheered and Anna wolf whistled, as Dawa stepped out on to the terrace looking stern, "I hate surprises."

Sam put his hand in the small of his back and pushed him forward into the arms of the group, "Well, you're marrying the wrong woman then."

Anna gave him a big hug and a kiss, "Isn't this amazing? We were only talking the other day about having some sort of engagement party, weren't we?"

"Were we?" Dawa said, still taking in the banners, bunting and all the fuss that he was not used to.

"Well, *I* was," Anna said. "Were you there? Oh no, I was talking to Irene about it when I visited her."

"Well, I think we should open the champagne, don't you?" Ralph said. "Martin, will you do the honours? We bought you some sparkling grape juice, which is under the table."

"Thank you, old thing," Martin said. "Well, here goes." He removed the foil from the bottle and expertly popped the cork, which flew across the terrace towards the bar, hotly pursued by Stanley.

While the glasses were filled, Sam slipped back into the flat and returned with the cake he had been working on all morning, "Ta da, number two!" he shouted, as he presented the cake to Dawa and Anna. It had two layers; the largest was round with white icing and gold polka dots all over it. The smaller layer on top was also white but had gold icing dripping down the sides. On top of that were two large, fat, white icing letters standing on end. The D had a tiny blue turban sitting on top of it, and the A had its own sweet little yellow beret.

Anna looked at Dawa, her eyes filled with tears, "It's amazing, isn't it? No one has ever made me a cake. I always do them for other people."

Dawa put his arm round her and kissed the top of her head, "Well, you deserve it. Thank you, Sam, it's excellent."

Sam put the cake down on the table and handed Anna a large silver knife, "You need to cut it together."

Anna put her hands behind her back and shook her head, "No, I can't cut it. It's too beautiful. I want to look at it for a while."

"Said the actress to the bishop," a deep transatlantic voice said from behind Sam.

"Oh, yes," Ralph said, moving quickly to Sam, blocking the view of the visitor behind them. Then they both stepped apart and shouted, "Ta da number three!" to reveal Joe and Ruby waving small silver and gold flags on sticks.

CHAPTER 28

*A new candle, camouflage
dungarees and a midnight sky.*

Anna screamed as she flung herself at her mother, "Well," Ralph said. "That'll scare the birds off the roofs."

Anna hugged Ruby, stepped back to look at her properly then went in for another hug, "You look fantastic, all tanned and relaxed and young and... gorgeous! I wanted a chance to use that word again, I don't use it enough and you do look gorgeous."

Ruby did look great, in relaxed linen trousers and a blue and white striped t-shirt, with her blonde hair slightly longer than before falling gently over her shoulders, "It's so lovely to be home."

Anna moved on to Joe, who looked more handsome than ever with tanned skin, a little more grey sprinkled through his short hair and beard, and his clear blue eyes sparkling in the string of lights that swung in the breeze above him, "Hey there, crazy lady," he said as he hugged her.

"I can't believe it," Anna said, taking both their hands. "You're actually here!"

"Finally," Ruby said. "It feels like we've been travelling forever. We couldn't stay away, not with so much going on here."

"We've had a great time, but we missed home, didn't we?" Joe said and smiled at Ruby. The sort of smile that meant their love was a strong as ever.

"Well, we missed you," Ralph said. "Where's my hug?"

"And mine," Sam said.

After everyone had hugged and caught up a little, they all found a chair and a glass and sat around the table together.

"This is the best night of my life," Anna said. "Except maybe that Christmas I got the Barbie Hair Salon, that was pretty good too."

"When we rang Ralph and told him we wanted to surprise you, he told us it was perfect timing because you were having a rooftop engagement party," Ruby said, taking in the cake, the bunting and Anna sitting on Dawa's lap.

"I'm sorry I didn't ask your permission, Ruby," Dawa said, seriously. "It all happened rather quickly."

"Oh Dawa, there was no need. Once Anna had decided you were the man for her, my permission became irrelevant."

"Still, it was the respectful thing to do," Dawa said.

Ruby smiled at him, "I appreciate that. Don't worry, you'll pay for it as my son-in-law for the rest of your life."

"Yeah, don't get on the wrong side of this woman," Joe said, shaking his head. "We only had one fight in the entire time we were travelling, but it was a doozy."

"What did you do?" Anna asked him.

"Hey, why assume it was my fault?"

Ruby and Anna looked at each other and both said, "It was."

"OK, maybe it was my fault. It was a good joke though."

"Dare I ask what it was?" Martin said.

"We'd rented a motorhome and were sitting under the stars in the middle of the Rockies. It was beautiful. Ruby turned to me and said, where have you been all my life? And..."

"And he replied," Ruby continued. "Well, I wasn't born for a lot of it!"

There was a shocked gasp from everyone and Joe looked at them all, "Hang on, guys, I thought it was funny."

Anna ignored him, "What did you do, Mum?"

"I'll tell you what she did," Joe said. "And you tell me if this is in proportion to the error I made. She got in the motorhome, started the engine and drove away. The door was still open, so all sorts of stuff fell out, but, oh no, your mother kept on driving and driving and driving."

"That seems fair enough to me," Fiona said.

Ralph nodded, "Me too."

"Yup," Sam said.

"Wait, wait, there's more. She left me there the whole night. Ten hours I sat alone with nothing but a camping chair and a bottle of beer. I could have been eaten by bears."

"Serves you right," Anna said.

"Thank you everyone," Ruby said and winked at Joe. "He learned his lesson."

"I certainly did, no more jokes from me."

Anna's eyebrows shot up, "You promise?"

"Yup, not even one. But let me ask you this, why can't ponies sing?"

Everyone groaned, "I thought he'd made a promise," Martin said to Ruby.

She laughed, "Oh well, you can't keep a good man down," and she leant over and took Joe's hand. "Go on then, why can't ponies sing?"

"Because they're a little horse."

Fiona giggled and everyone looked at her, "Sorry, but it was quite funny."

Joe frowned, "*Quite* funny? That was comedy gold. Some sort of welcome home party this is."

Anna cuffed him on the shoulder, "Hey, this is our engagement party, don't go turning it into your party."

Martin stood and lifted his glass of grape juice, "Which reminds me, may I ask you all to raise your glasses to toast Anna and Dawa. It is a pleasure to be able to celebrate your engagement with you both. You are two very special people who have had the good fortune to find each other in this turmoil we call life. Henri Matisse, the French artist, was right when he said, *He who loves flies, runs, and rejoices; he is free and nothing holds him back.* May all your days ahead be free with nothing to hold you back. Ladies, gentlemen and small dogs, I give you Anna and Dawa."

"Anna and Dawa!" everyone chorused and toasted the happy couple.

As he sat down Fiona shyly rose to her feet, "Erm, sorry everyone, but before you carry on with the party... oh, dear, I'm not very good at public speaking. But what I wanted to say is that most of you know that Martin's lovely friend, Robin, passed away in the early hours of Monday morning. Some of us have now heard the story of him and Matthew, Martin's brother, and what they went through as young men. I had the privilege of meeting Robin and I know he wanted his story and especially the memory of Matthew kept alive through us. So," she bent down and pulled a candle in a small glass jar from her handbag. "I thought it would be nice to keep their flame burning alongside Auntie B's here on the rooftop, as a memory of absent friends and family." She set the candle on the table and lit it, "Perhaps we should raise a glass to Robin and Matthew as well?"

Martin stood and carefully placed a kiss on Fiona's cheek, "Thank you, that is an incredibly kind thought." He raised his glass and looked up at the sky, "To Robin and Matthew."

Everyone followed suit and stood, throwing their voices high into the sky, "To Robin and Matthew!"

Martin smiled at the young friends around him, "I think the thing to do now is party-on. Is that the correct phrase?"

"Absobloominlutely!" Anna said. "This really is the best party I could have imagined."

Joe held out his hand to her, "So, let's see the engagement ring? I hope he's splashed out."

Anna looked down at her empty ring finger, "Oh, well, we haven't had a chance to sort that out yet. It's all been a bit of a whirlwind."

Dawa shifted forward on the deckchair, dislodging Anna from his lap, "It's funny you should mention that, and this is why I was so reluctant for Sam to drag me here until I heard you would be here too." He slipped off the chair and knelt on one knee.

"Oh my," Anna whispered. "I think I'm going to faint."

Ralph dashed forward with his arms outstretched, but she quickly waved him back, "No, no, don't spoil it. It was just a figure of speech, I'm fine. Sorry, Dawa, carry on."

Dawa smiled up at her, "Anna, you are the brightest star that has ever shone on my life. So, just to be sure that I'm not dreaming and this is all real, I want to ask you again, will you marry me?" He raised his hand and opened his palm to reveal a small pink box.

There was silence across the roof terrace as everyone looked at Anna. Even Stanley raised an eyebrow and one weary eye to see what was going to happen next.

"Dawa, I have thought about this every moment of every day since you said that I was the woman you were going to marry. I've thought of every reason you shouldn't marry me – it's quite a long list, by the way – but I haven't come up with a single reason why I shouldn't marry you. So, yes, of course, I'll marry you."

With shaking hands she took the small box from Dawa and opened it. Inside was what looked like a perfectly round golden pebble, that shimmered with tiny fragments of glitter running through it. Anna drew in a sharp breath.

Dawa stood nervously, "I hope you like it. I took Ralph with me to help choose, as I knew that nothing ordinary would be right for you. It is called goldstone, made and shaped by a local artist. The ring itself is rose gold. I know it is not a normal sort of engagement ring, and I can always take it back if..."

Anna looked up at him, "You are taking it nowhere. It's the most gorgeous thing I've ever seen." She lifted the highly polished goldstone up towards the fairy lights and its smooth round surface sparkled against the darkening sky, "It's perfect. Can you put it on?" she said, holding out her left hand to Dawa.

He took the ring and slid it onto her finger, "Phew," he said, looking at Ralph. "It fits."

"That's a relief," he said. "When you were out of the café I had to sneak into your flat and raid your jewellery box to find a ring to get this one sized."

"It's the best ring EVER, thank you, both of you," she hugged Ralph then returned and kissed Dawa, while everyone cheered and clapped. "What a perfect night. Everyone is here. My rooftop family is complete. I couldn't want anything else in the world. Except, of course, when we catch the rotten arsonist later on. What a night!"

"Anna, about that..." Dawa began.

"I won't be coming, I'm afraid," Ralph said, moving away to the bar for another beer.

"What's this?" Ruby asked.

"I told you in the emails, about the pentagram and the lunar magic and the ashes from all the fires. Well, tonight is the night that it all comes together – the Summer Solstice. We need to be on Romney Marsh at midnight when they'll perform their ceremony so we can catch them."

"That sounds like a job for the police, not you, Anna."

"Agreed," Dawa said. "Look, I spoke with Sergeant Phil earlier and he said that we should not go out there. They've got extra patrols all around the area."

Anna frowned at him, "But will they go to that spot, where the circle of fires had been, at the right time? I mean, do they even believe our Holmes and Watson theory?"

Dawa looked at Ralph, Anna gasped, "Not you too? Et toots Dawa, or something Shakespearean. We worked it all out, we need to be there tonight."

"It's too dangerous, Anna, you can't."

Ruby took her arm, "Anna, listen to Dawa, please. You have no idea who will be out on the marshes on a night like this."

"Wait, wait, does anyone believe me?" She looked around the rooftop, but was met with embarrassed faces and silence. She sat down on her deckchair, all her excitement at the party and the adventure to follow ebbing away, "Oh, I see. Just me then. I really thought we could catch them."

Dawa knelt at her side, "I'm sorry, Anna, but it's best to leave it to the police. I do think we are on to something and I want them caught as much as you do, but this person is dangerous. We have done what we can. Let's enjoy the party and wait for the authorities to do their job."

Anna sighed, "I had an outfit all ready and everything. Oh, well, we'll just have to stay here and have some more champagne and cake instead."

Everyone cheered and the celebration continued as Dawa and Anna cut the cake.

By eleven o'clock the party had thinned out. Ruby and Joe were overtaken by jetlag and had gone to their hotel to sleep. Martin was escorting Fiona back up the hill to her flat, and Ralph and Sam were taking Stanley round the block for one last walk before heading back to The Bookery to finish the to-do list. The night was warm and Dawa and Anna were sitting in deckchairs looking up at the moon.

Dawa yawned, "It really does feel like the longest day of the year. I'm shattered."

"Just a few more minutes," Anna said. "I love that it's only us left. Shut your eyes, I'll wake you up in a minute if you nod off."

"Are you sure?"

"Of course, relax. I'm quite happy if you're beside me."

"Me too," Dawa said and he closed his eyes.

Anna waited a few minutes until she could hear the even breathing of sleep from him. Then she got up and trotted silently to her flat.

Twenty minutes later she was parking her small pink car in a dark spot at the back of Rye Cemetery. She was convinced that her theory about witchcraft was correct, and she was not about to rely on the sceptical Sergeant

Phil to catch the culprit. But she needed to hurry if she was going to get into position before the potential arsonist arrived to begin the ceremony. Her heart beat fast in her chest as she killed the car's lights and watched darkness descend around her.

"Right," she said to herself in the rear-view mirror. "Nothing to be frightened of. You can do this." She put her hand on the door handle and looked out at the line of shadowy graves that awaited her. "Stop looking at me," she shouted at the silent stones. Before she could change her mind, she shoved open the door and launched herself out of the car, determined not to be put off by her fears. As she slammed the car door, she caught sight of a set of headlights bouncing down the track to the car park behind her.

"Damn, damn, damn," she muttered, as she did a crouched run through the cemetery. The lights grew closer and swept across the row of headstones she was hobbling behind and she flung herself onto the ground. She was glad she had decided to change into her camouflage dungarees as she lay on the damp grass, hoping she couldn't be seen.

The car slowly turned into the car park and took its time turning round and reversing neatly into a designated disabled parking space. "Hm," Ann grunted, as she crawled towards the gate that led on to the fields. "Another thing to report them for, if they're not really disabled."

She made it through the cemetery gate and into the neighbouring field, which was still and quiet under the dark midnight sky and watery moon. She kept tight to the hedges, pulling her black woollen hat down low on her head, allowing the large red pompom to do its own thing on the top.

As she approached the field in which they had found the burnt grass patches, her stomach began a series of somersaults. She may not have thought this through in quite as much detail as she should have done. Her mother and Dawa were right, this was risky and dangerous and not nearly as exciting now she was alone. She turned around, ready to get back to her car and safety as quickly as possible but stopped in her tracks as four shadowy figures, swathed in long dark robes, made their way slowly towards her.

CHAPTER 29

*The Solstice Ceremony, maiden's
ashes and a large cow pat.*

"**P**oop, poop, poop," Anna cursed, as the shadowy figures processed through the cemetery. "Dawa, where are you?" She couldn't risk getting her phone out as the screen would light her up like a lighthouse and give the game away. She could do nothing now but follow her plan, find a hiding place and wait to see what happened.

She fought her way into a space near the centre of a dense hedge and squatted down, holding her breath as the dark figures processed towards her. With their robes skimming the ground it looked like they were floating across the field.

Finally, they all stood in front of Anna's hedge, forming a tight circle. She could hear the mumble of voices, but they were too low to make out what was being said. Despite the shivers coursing up and down her spine she inched forwards in her hedge hideout. As she did so the strap of her dungarees caught on a twig which broke with a loud crack. The mysterious group whipped round and faced the hedge. The robes had large hoods worn low over their heads, so she could see nothing but blackness where their faces should be.

"Did you hear that?" a voice hissed from inside one of the hoods.

"Shush," said another, sterner voice. "Listen!"

The four shadowy figures stood still and silent as they scanned the hedge for more activity.

"It's nothing," the stern voice said. "Come sisters, let us begin. You know what we must do."

With that the four robed figures turned away from the hedge and began to fan out in a large circle. Each one pulled plastic shopping bags from under their robes and lay them on the ground marking out the pentagram. The stern witch, who seemed to be wearing a smarter silk robe than the others, placed a fifth bag at the top of the pentagram. The leader had called them sisters, so Anna assumed they were all women. Certainly, the voices she had heard so far were all female.

They all then drew from each bag a disposable aluminium tray with a tiny barbecue inside and a small cloth bag tied with string. When they had finished, the witches stood and waited silently. At the centre of the circle stood the witch in her silken robe, who was clearly the leader, with her own small barbeque and a large paper cone of what Anna could now recognise as mugwort. She raised her arms and declared loudly, "Sisters, we begin."

"Oh, you gave me a start," one of the hooded figures yelped.

Anna frowned, she knew that voice, it was strangely familiar.

"We are calling on the great goddess at this sacred time to make us visible, to make us live again," the leader intoned. "Let us begin our ceremony with fire to light the way. Then we will make our offering and leap through the flames to release the future each of us are due. Light the fires, sisters, then prepare the maidens' ashes."

Anna was so engrossed in the ceremony that she failed to hear soft footsteps behind her and knew nothing until a hand was thrust through the hedge and clamped across her mouth. She froze for a second then began to struggle, "Keep still," a deep voice hissed in her ear. "It's me, Dawa."

She twisted round to see the large shadows behind her turn into Dawa, Ralph and Sam. Dawa stepped lightly into the hedge beside her. He released his hand from her mouth, "Sorry, I didn't want to frighten you and make you shout out."

"Well, I'd hate to see what you did when you do want to frighten someone," Anna panted. "I nearly died."

"Anna, this is crazy, coming out here alone. What were you thinking?" Ralph hissed, as he crouched behind her and Dawa.

"I had to know if I was right. I thought I'd just take a quick look, but I hadn't really taken into account the darkness and the graves and it generally being terrifying out here at night. How did you find me?"

"When I woke up and found you gone," Dawa said. "I checked the flat and saw your kimono, so I guessed you had changed. It was obvious you couldn't resist coming here. I'm sorry to say this, you know I love you, but this was a really stupid idea. Let's go."

"No, no. Let's stay for a few more minutes, they haven't taken their hoods off yet. We need to see their faces. Those bags on the ground contain maidens' ashes apparently. What does that mean?"

Dawa peered through the hedge at the witches who were attempting to light the coals, "Maidens' ashes? They must be the ashes from the five fires in town, but what do they have to do with maidens?"

"Well, I'm a maiden which means single, right? Psychic Sue is a widow, so technically single. Ethel is single. Louise at the chip shop broke up with her boyfriend, Adam, a few months ago. So, we are all single ladies – cue for a song, but not right now."

"What about Ralph?" Sam asked.

"Oh, good point. Wait, what are they doing?"

The witches had all gathered around the final barbecue, the others all now alight, and some sort of argument had begun, "It must light. Try it again."

"Yes, sorry, it's a bit awkward you see."

Anna gasped, "I know those voices."

Ralph turned to her, "Me too. It can't be."

"Come on, follow me," she stood up, anger powering her forward out of the hedge, the others hot on her heels. "Evening all," she called loudly.

The witches spun round to face her.

"Do you have any spare sausages? I'm quite hungry and really fancy a barbeque."

There was a tense silence, the robed women lit by the eery glow from their small fires stood unmoving.

"Nothing to say for yourselves, ladies?"

The leader stepped forward, "Leave this place, you are not welcome here."

Anna's face hardened, "I bet I'm not, but I'm going nowhere until I know which of you burned The Bookery."

"She knows," one of the robed figures gasped.

Ralph stepped up beside Anna, "Who was it? Come on."

There was silence again, then three hooded heads turned slowly and looked at the witch in the smart silk robe. After a moment's hesitation she reached up and pulled back the hood, to reveal the immaculate blond bob and angry face of Judy McMurray, manager of Let's Screw, "No one died, the shop's been rebuilt, there's no lasting harm done."

Sam took two large strides and quickly pulled back the hoods of the other women revealing Susan, Janet and Pat all looking tearful and pale in the moonlight.

Anna looked from one to the other, "You were all in on this? But we gave you jobs. We were nice to you. We thought of you as friends, and you tried to burn our shops down?"

Susan threw her hands over her face and began to sob. Pat rushed to her side and embraced her, while Janet took a step towards Anna, "I am so sorry. We didn't mean it to go this far. Judy told us we only needed a small amount of ash from each shop. They were meant to be tiny fires, so we could get a bit of burnt door mat, something like that. It's the magic of the Summer Solstice, you see, we needed it."

"Silence, sister," Judy ordered, turning on Janet.

"No, Judy, not this time," Janet said, stepping away from her. "It's quite straightforward really, Anna. We are all single women of a certain age. Either divorced, widowed or never got lucky, but there's still plenty of life left in us all, so we wanted some companionship. Men, in short."

Susan blew her nose on a tissue, "It was Judy who persuaded us that drastic action was required. The Summer Solstice was a magical time, she said. The ceremonies go back to the stone ages, she said. Bonfires are supposed to boost the sun's energy, banish demons and lead maidens to their future husbands."

Anna stared at her, "You did all this to find men? That's the most ridiculous thing I've ever heard."

"Enough, sisters," Judy yelled. "They understand nothing. Run, run." She gave Dawa an almighty shove that caught him by surprise, and she took off in the other direction, hitching her robe up above her knees.

For a moment Pat and Susan looked at each other then they turned towards the car park and started to scuttle across the grass.

Dawa turned to Sam and Ralph, "Oh dear. Which would you like to take?"

Sam smiled, "We'll do the slow ones heading for the car park."

"Fine," Dawa said, with a grin. "Leave Judy to me." He turned to Janet, who stood forlornly in the middle of the pentagram, "And you, are you going to start running too?"

She shook her head, "No, I don't run very well. I'll wait here with Anna."

"Let's rendezvous in the car park," he said. "Anna, can you bring Janet and all this with you?" he indicated the barbecues and cloth bags.

"Yes, leave that to us. Try not to hurt Judy too much."

Dawa set off with long strides into the darkness where Judy had disappeared, while Sam and Ralph began a slow jog towards the car park. Anna looked at Janet, "I can't believe it. How could you do this to us?"

Janet started to extinguish the barbecues with her robe, while Anna picked up the cloth bags.

"It all got out of hand," Janet said, miserably. "My sister can be very persuasive. Not that it's all her fault. We got carried away."

"We'll have to leave the barbecues here to cool down," Anna said.

She led the way back to the car park, with Janet walking slowly beside her, "You have no idea what it's like to become invisible? Have you, Anna? I doubt it, with your ridiculous clothes and orange hair and your exclusive club up on the roof."

Anna turned to her, "Now hang on..." but she stopped as Dawa appeared out of the darkness pulling a bedraggled Judy by the arm.

"Look what I found lying in a cow pat," he said.

"He pushed me," Judy moaned. "That's assault."

"You fell over your own feet. You were lucky the cow pat was large and wet so it would cushion your fall."

They had reached the cemetery by now, where they found Sam and Ralph standing over Pat and Susan who sat on the ground leaning against a couple of gravestones.

"I've spoken to Sergeant Phil," Ralph said. "He's on his way."

"Can't we settle this between ourselves?" Judy asked, as Dawa pushed her down next to the other women. "There's no need for the police to be involved."

Anna threw her arms in the air, "No need? Are you kidding?"

"Oh, shut up, Anna," Judy snapped.

Dawa's deep voice rumbled across the graveyard, "Don't speak to her like that."

"You can't frighten me, Dawa Singh," Judy said, staring round at their captors. "You have no idea, none of you. We have had enough. Enough of being invisible women. You say you thought of us as friends, Anna? But not once did you invite any of us up to your stupid rooftop. And you know nothing about us, do you? Susan, for instance. Tell me what she did before she came and dressed up in pretty caps and aprons and served tea for you. Go on."

Anna looked at Susan, who was twisting the chain attached to her green glasses round and round her finger, looking wretched, "I... well, I'm not sure."

"No, because you didn't bother to ask. Like everyone else, you didn't think of us as real women, just silly old ladies who wanted a bit of company. You had no idea that she had been a pharmacist and ran her own chain of chemists across Kent for more than thirty years. Janet has worked in your own café for weeks, what about her? Did you know that she was a senior intensive care nurse with more than forty years' service, who only stopped working when she had to nurse her husband through terminal prostate cancer? That Pat was a research chemist, with an MBE? That I managed a portfolio of properties for a global bank?"

"No, I... I had no idea."

"Of course you didn't, because once we retired we became invisible. Balmy old women to have a giggle at, who could come and keep your shops running while you got on with the real business of living. Our time was over, right?"

"I'm sorry..."

"Anna," Dawa said, taking her hand. "Do not apologise. Please can we get back to the point. Why did you start the fires?"

Judy stuck out her chin and looked defiantly at Dawa, "I doubt you will understand, but ashes from midsummer bonfires are very powerful. We needed to gather ashes from the property of other maidens, bring them all together on the solstice night and throw them on new fires. This would bring renewed strength to us as well as good fortune. We would ask the goddess for decent, intelligent companions to share our retirement years and reward us for all the years we have given to society."

Janet moved to stand beside Judy, "It was all fully researched, we even spoke to an expert in witchcraft. We would set the fires, using a special herb that would increase the potency of the magic."

"Mugwort," Anna said.

"Yes, how did you know?"

"We found some when she ran off from Ethel's place.

That's what started us tracking you down."

Pat raised her hand, "That was me, actually. I was the one you nearly caught at Ethel's shop. I dropped the mugwort when Stanley came after me."

Judy laughed, "I went back to the shops in the morning after the fire to help tidy up. I'd pretended to be all shocked and helpful, and everyone kept thanking me and saying how kind I was. But really I was gathering some of the ashes into a dustpan, tipping them into my pocket and bringing them home. Then we would keep them in bags..."

"I made those," Susan said, proudly. "I make peg bags too."

Anna shook her head, "Even if we bought into your magic, the big thing I don't understand is why The Bookery? You said the ashes had to be from a maiden's property, but Ralph is not a maiden."

Judy waved her hand dismissively, "Time was running out, so we had to stretch the point a bit. Ralph was single, he was probably going to marry a man, like us, so that meant he qualified as a maiden."

Susan shook her head, "That was just an excuse, all Judy wanted was to set another fire without being discovered."

Judy's defiance faded slightly as she turned to Susan, "That's not true."

"Yes, it is and you know it. You found it exciting to fool the police and everyone else. The Bookery would be your coup de théâtre. You could set the fire then quickly slip into Let's Screw and pop out again as the heroine who put the fire out and saved the day."

Janet swallowed hard, "You have to believe us, we never intended to actually burn the whole shop. Judy always planned to come straight back with the fire extinguisher and put it out quickly. Didn't you, Judy?"

"Of course, I did. But that Fiona woman appeared outside with the dog, so I had to wait and see if she'd seen me or if she'd go away, but she didn't. I waited too long and the fire had got a real hold and I couldn't stop it. For that I am sorry."

Anna looked at the dishevelled group, "You give women a bad name, I mean, all that to get a man? As if that's the answer to your loneliness. I was desperate for a man for years. I'd have taken anyone. Sometimes I went on the most ridiculous dates just because a man – *any* man bothered to ask me. Then I realised that I was worth as much – no, *more* on my own, just as I am. I knew until I accepted my strength and independence as a woman, I would never meet anyone who was my equal. But even at my lowest, I would never, ever have hurt other people."

"We didn't want to do it," Susan said, through her tears. "It was Judy."

Anna stamped her foot, "No. You could have stopped her. Any of you, but you didn't."

"She's right," Janet said, quietly. "We can't blame Judy. I stole the chip shop sign. Susan started the fire at The Copper Kettle. We all hid some of the ashes. We planned the fires together. We are as guilty as she is. All because of some silly idea about dancing around a fire at the Summer Solstice. It seems so ridiculous now, when you say it out loud."

Dawa looked behind them as blue flashing lights

approached, "Well, there are going to be plenty more occasions for you to say it out loud, but this time it'll be to the police."

CHAPTER 30

No bail, no disguises and no regrets.

Ralph sat back in his chair, a strong black coffee energising him after the meagre couple of hours sleep he had managed after talking to the police and finishing work in The Bookery, "I still can't believe it. Has the world gone totally mad?"

"If you did my job, you might well think so," Sergeant Phil said, wiping ketchup from his plate with a finger. "All four of them have signed full confessions. They spent the night in the cells and we'll take them to court to see a magistrate this morning. Not for a few hours yet, though, it's still too early."

"What do you think will happen to them?" Sam asked.

"Three of them will probably get bail and sent home. I'm not so sure about Judy McMurray. She's still adamant it was all in a good cause and, as she seemed to be the brains behind it and the one who set the worst fire, they may not grant her bail. So, she'll be held in prison until her trial."

"Prison?" Anna gasped.

"It's possible. That's more than likely where she'll go for a while anyway once she's sentenced. The others might get shorter or suspended sentences," Phil said, pushing his chair back. "I'd better head back and get ready for court. Thanks for the bacon sandwich, Anna, much appreciated."

"You're welcome."

Sergeant Phil paused in the door of the café, "And well done for working out what was going on. I'm sorry I didn't take it seriously enough. You're quite the detective."

Anna blushed, "Oh, thanks. Ta. I was Watson, Dawa was Sherlock. We did it together. Bye."

Martin took his mug through to the kitchen, "I must get back up the road to The Copper Kettle, Fiona is holding the fort alone preparing today's cakes and scones. We will all have to struggle through without our new helpers for a while, I suppose."

"Yup, there's no way they're coming back to work," she said.

"I'll have a ring round some of the staff from Cinque," Sam said. "One or two of them are always looking for extra hours, I might be able to send them your way to help out."

"That'd be amazing, thank you."

"Dawa can be with you until after lunch, as well. We can cope without him until later."

"Yes, he said he might be able to do that. He's got his own pinny already."

"Where is he anyway?" Ralph asked.

"Bloody hell," Sam said, as the bell above the door to the café heralded a new arrival.

Anna stared, "Dawa? What have you done?"

Dawa stood in the doorway with the light of the early morning sun behind him. His shoes were their usual smart and shiny selves, just as Anna liked them. His long firm legs were encased in smart navy-blue chinos. He wore a crisp white shirt, that set off his light brown skin beautifully. It was above the collar where things had changed.

Where a dark, thick beard had previously sat, there was now a smooth, square jaw with a strong cleft chin at its centre. The turban that had been part of Dawa's life for so long was gone. In its place sat short, lustrous hair with an almost satin sheen, in a neat, tailored cut.

Dawa shrugged his shoulders, "Morning all."

"You... you look..." Sam stuttered.

"...Incredible," Ralph said, finishing his sentence.

Sam nodded slowly, too stunned to form proper sentences, "Yeah, that's it. I mean... it's... you're..."

"Back off you two, he's mine," Anna said, as she walked towards Dawa. "Can I?" she asked.

"Of course," Dawa said.

She ran a finger carefully along his jaw line as if she couldn't quite believe what she was seeing. Then she stood on her toes and reached up to touch his hair, delicately, so as not to disturb it, "It's soft. You're skin, your hair. It's gorgeous – I'm finding lots of cracking uses for that word. But why? I hope you didn't do this for me. Your culture is so important to you."

Dawa smiled down into her concerned face, "I did it for me, Anna. I had my hair cut yesterday, but kept it hidden under the turban. I wasn't sure if you would like it."

"I wondered why you fell asleep with it on last night. You could have given me some warning."

"Us too," Sam said. "I almost didn't recognise you."

"It's simple. I am not the man I was before I met you, Anna. The old Dawa was hanging on to something in his past that my mother finally drove away last weekend. I was born a member of the Sikh community and I have come to see that the outward show of beard and turban are not necessary for me to be who I am or to be proud of my heritage. They are important for other people and that's fine, but they no longer mean anything to me. I will be proud to take you as my wife, but as I am, with no disguises or adornments. Just Dawa Singh. After your words last night to those women about finding yourself first before finding your equal, I knew that this was the right thing to do."

Anna reached her hand around his neck and pulled him down so that she could kiss him, gently and slowly as she wanted to do for the rest of her life.

"Ahem," Sam coughed. "We're still here, you know."

"I think we should go," Ralph whispered.

Anna pulled away from Dawa, "Erm, I don't think so. Sam is going to get on the blower and find me some staff, then he's going to get in that kitchen and help me sort out pies, gravy and a mountain of mash."

Dawa chortled behind her until she turned to him, "And you, Mr Singh, are going to put on your

Thunderbirds pinny and start cleaning tables and get ready to serve the hungry people of Rye."

He saluted, "Yes, ma'am."

"And you," she pointed at Ralph. "You need to clear off and open your lovely, shiny new shop."

Ralph did as he was told, but when he arrived at The Bookery there was a queue waiting outside, "I'm so sorry," he said, as he hurriedly unlocked the door.

When he pushed it open there was a spontaneous round of applause, and he stood back to let them all in. Stanley galloped out of his new little house in the window to greet the customers like old friends, which many of them were. By the time lunchtime arrived the pace of new customers slowed, and Ralph sank into his new upholstered stool behind the counter, "Well, Stanley, Rye doesn't seem to have forgotten about us."

He looked up as a thin lad in skinny jeans and a hoody slid through the door, "Erm, hi," he said.

"Hi, Jack. Everything OK?" Ralph said, managing to grab Stanley's collar before he fired himself at Jack, lips turned back and teeth bared. "Hang on. Stan, pack it in." He took him to the door of the flat and pushed him through, shutting it firmly behind the little dog.

"Everything OK, Jack?" Ralph asked again.

Jack shuffled his feet, "Erm, nah. Not really. I, erm, need to talk to you."

"Is something the matter?"

"Kind of. Martin said I should tell you, but I didn't wanna, but I do now."

"I didn't realise you knew Martin."

Jack nodded, "Yeah, we met at the old people's home. My dad's there."

"Oh, right, I see. So, what do you need to talk to me about?"

"Well, it's kind of why that dog don't like me."

"Go on."

"He thinks I'm... dangerous, maybe."

"Dangerous? Why would he think that?"

Jack had clearly thought long and hard about what to say and he was determined to say it all as quickly as he could, "OK, right, so last year I wasn't in a good place, right. I was pretty messed up most of the time. One night I was pissed up on cider and stuff and... how did Martin put it? Yeah, angry at the world. Well, that included you and the other one. Sam. I saw you in the street. Together. I don't know what made me do it, but I thought I'd take it out on you. My anger and my feelings. So, I shouted at you, bad stuff. Said things I shouldn't. You ran off, so I came after you. With a knife. I know it's bad and you should call the police and everything, but I've changed. I don't do it no more. I've got the building job and my dad's in the home, so he don't get at me no more. I'm sorry. That's it. Yeah. I'm sorry."

Jack stood in the middle of the shop, his arms tight by his side, fists clenched and shaking. He stared at the floor, until the silence became too much and he glanced up at Ralph, "What you gonna do?"

Ralph didn't know what to say, let alone what to do, "I have no idea. So, Stanley remembers you from that night? The night he bit you."

"Yeah. It proper hurt. I got scars there if you wanna

see them," Jack started to reach for the waist band of his skinny jeans, but Ralph held up his hand.

"No, no, that won't be necessary. We thought you were really going to hurt us, Jack," Ralph said, remembering his fear as he and Sam fled through the streets.

"I don't think I would have actually done anything," Jack said, moving closer to the counter. "I was all mouth. I don't do it no more. I've got a proper job. I'm learning loads from Chaz. I do my comics too. Martin's read 'em all."

"Comics? What sort of comics?"

Jack hesitated, then shyly pulled the curled notebook from the back of his trousers, "Like this. It's rubbish, but I do 'em in the evenings when I'm at home on my own."

"May I see?"

Jack reached out to Ralph and handed him the book, then stood back, like a pupil reluctantly giving his homework to a teacher.

Ralph took his time looking through it. He was immediately impressed by Jack's talent and imagination, but he didn't say anything. He wanted to make the lad sweat a little bit, just as he and Sam had on that cold winter's night.

Ralph suddenly snapped the book shut and shoved it under his arm, "Come with me," he said. More of an order than a request. He slipped off his stool and made his way down the stairs behind the counter and into the basement.

Jack didn't know what to do, but he couldn't run away - he wanted his drawings back. So, he followed Ralph cautiously down the stairs.

He blinked in the light of the basement, surprised it wasn't dark and dingy. Instead, it was a clean, white space, with good lighting above and natural light from a long thin window along one wall.

Ralph was waiting for him at an artist's easel at the back of the room, "Do you ever use paints?" he asked.

"What?"

"Do you only draw with pen or can you paint too?" Ralph said, sternly, pleased that he was making the boy nervous.

"Yeah, I've painted."

"Excellent," Ralph said. He pulled a large blank canvas from a small pile leaning against the wall behind him and put it on the easel. He pointed to a jumble of paint tubes on the table next to him, "There are plenty of colours there for you and brushes in those pots. I want you to paint this." He flicked through the scruffy notebook and folded it back at a page near the middle and held it out to Jack, "I love this image. The Japanese cherry blossom falling on the man lying asleep under the tree."

"He's dead, not asleep," Jack said.

"Oh, is he?" Ralph took a closer look. "He looks asleep. Anyway, paint me that picture and if it's good enough, we'll say no more about you threatening us," he held out the drawing.

"You're joking, right? How am I supposed to paint that? It's just a few scribbles."

Ralph put the notebook on the table and started to

make his way back upstairs, "I don't know who's told you that. Your drawings are fantastic. I'll talk to Chaz and tell him you're doing a job for me this afternoon. So, it's all yours."

❋ ❋ ❋

Joe straightened the white framed picture in its new position above the driftwood mantlepiece. The greens and golds shimmered in the sun bouncing off the sea outside the window of the beach house.

"That is such a beautiful painting," Ruby said, sipping her tea as she stood by the large open window. "It means so much more now I've been to Canada and met your family, and we visited your mum's grave."

"I know," Joe said, stepping past her into the garden. "It still gets me that Auntie B painted it for Mom, but never got to give it to her. But by going there I think we sort of closed the circle, don't you?"

"Yes, I do. And you have your family back. They'll love it here when they come and visit next year, and they can see Ginger's picture."

Joe looked back at Ruby, "So, no regrets?"

"About what?"

"Anything. Me, Canada, moving in here?"

Ruby smiled and tucked a lock of hair behind her ear, "Not a single one. You?"

"I've decided not to do regrets. Although, I regretted rubbing baked beans in my eyes... but that's just Heinz-sight."

Ruby groaned, "Joe, be serious. This is a big move for us, moving in together."

"I am serious, I'm not doing regrets anymore. I'm only looking forward and everything I see there has you in it. You, this town, this beach, this house, our friends, the shop. It's time for me to put down some roots and this is where I want to do it."

Ruby put her mug down and moved into the garden, leaning her head on Joe's shoulder. They both looked across the beach to the sea, "There really is no place like home, is there?"

"Nope, and this is it. Our home."

CHAPTER 31

A new baby, a new outfit for Stanley and Independence Day

To: helenh@woohoo.com

From: thebookery01@beemail.com

3rd July

Hi Helen and little baby Layla!

It's all happened so fast, I can't believe we missed all the excitement and weren't there with you!! I'm so pleased you're both OK and things were pretty easy. (Can seven hours in labour be described as 'easy'? Probably not, but I'm a bloke, so I have no idea.)

We will be up as soon as we can to see you both. I need to get my new staff member settled in first though. Do you remember me talking about one of the under-ten footballers, Joanne Ringrose? Well, her dad, Howard, was made redundant recently and applied for the job in The Bookery. I really like him and I think he's going to be great. So, once he's had a couple of weeks here, we can leave him and come up to meet Layla. We can't wait.

So, the latest news. Judy is on remand in prison, the others got bail. They all pleaded guilty and will be sentenced in the Autumn. Pat came into the shop to apologise. She seemed genuine, but I didn't know what to say. So, she bought a Jeffrey Archer book and left.

Joe and Ruby are settled back into his beach house down at Camber Sands, and we all went over there the other night for a party. Ruby is working in The Cookery with Anna, which seems to be going OK. No fallouts yet. Irene had another minor stroke, it gave us all a fright and it's set her back quite a bit. They say it'll be months until she recovers, if she ever does. It's awful. As much as she frightened me to death, I really miss her next door.

Dawa has persuaded Anna, with a bit of help from Ruby, to wait until later in the year to get married. So, they've chosen Bonfire Night, the 5th of November. Anna says it's because they get a free firework display on their wedding night! At least it gives me time to get out of being her bridesmaid, I thought she was joking at first, but she's not. Oh, and Ruby has offered them her house in Winchelsea as their wedding present. Dawa is insisting he can't accept it as a gift, so he is selling his flat and is going to force Ruby to take some money for it. I can see a fight happening there before it's all sorted.

I told you about Jack, the builder's assistant, who turned out to be our homophobic attacker from last year, didn't I? Well, I got him to do a painting of one of his graphic novel images, and it was stunning. He is so talented, and a publisher friend of Martin's has asked for a meeting with him to talk about developing some of his ideas. I think his luck is going to change from now onwards. It took him ages to finish the painting for me, so he used to come into The Bookery on his days off and the occasional evening. I'm going to sell it in the shop and give the proceeds to a local charity that helps teenagers. Martin helped Jack a bit, being an old art teacher, which was great, and I've got him helping me with Jane Scott's portrait. It's a complete nightmare and I've started again, twice. I'm sure she won't like it, she won't look twenty for a start, which is what she wants. I've painted her simply, without any of the nonsense she asked for, like English roses surrounding her and the Hollywood Hills in the background. The thing is, she is actually really beautiful – if you don't know her. Ha ha. Anyway, I want to finish it ASAP and send it off to her. I'd rather I wasn't there when she saw it.

We can't wait to get into our apartment, which Chaz says will be finished soon. When we've moved in there will be someone new in my flat and someone new in Anna's when she moves up the road to Winchelsea. So, that will mean the end of the Rooftop Club.

Except, of course, it won't. We're all still in Rye and we are family now. So, wherever we are we will be The Rye Rooftop Club.

Oh, blimey, I've got Anna banging on the door of the shop now, waving a tuxedo and top hat in Stanley's size! Another wedding idea I've got to try and crush. Gotta go.

Send more photos of Layla soon, she is gorgeous (which is Anna's favourite new word, BTW)

Love

Ralph and Sam

XX

* * *

To: CountessG@fortnum.org

From: MartinRyeCook@zway.com

4 July

Grace,

Today is the 4th of July, Independence Day to our friends across the pond. It is our Independence Day too as we are now divorced.

I wish you luck and a better life than I was able to give you.

Martin

CHAPTER 32

*Paper roses, two town criers
and a surprise guest.*

Rye Town Hall sits at the top of Market Street, directly opposite The Copper Kettle. The Georgian building sitting on stone pillars has been through many lives since the first hall was burnt down in the 14th century by the French, who were keen on a bit of marauding back then. On this bright, chilly afternoon of Bonfire Night, it was preparing to host a less incendiary activity, as Ruby and Ralph walked Anna up the hill from The Cookery to get married.

The Town Crier, resplendent in his maroon and blue coat, tri-corn hat and white gloves, rang his large bell and welcomed them in a loud voice, "Oyez, oyez, oyez. Let it be known that on this afternoon, the 5th day of November, in the fine and ancient town of Rye, Miss Anna Rose shall be betrothed to Mr Dawa Singh. May their solemn union be long, happy and fruitful, and may God save the king. Ladies and gentlemen, please, will you join me in three cheers for the bride? Hip hip - Hooray! Hip hip - Hooray! Hip hip - Hooray!"

As the crowd of well-wishers and curious shoppers

cheered, Stanley barked with excitement as he led the way in front of Anna and Ruby. He was enjoying all the attention in his doggy-sized replica of the Town Crier's coat and hat, complete with feathers. He had refused to wear the little bell around his neck, which Ralph thought a blessing as he walked along behind him. He was more conservatively dressed in a light blue suit, colourful paisley patterned shirt and a buttonhole of a summer daisy and sprigs of parsley. Anna held a single rose, to signify her last day as Miss Anna Rose, surrounded by just about every green herb she could find. Parsley, coriander, rosemary, dill, sage, thyme, tarragon, mint, basil and even a sprig of mugwort, fought for air in her billowing bouquet.

Ruby had been holding back tears all day. A day she never thought she would see, not because she didn't think Anna would ever marry, but with so many years lost in their relationship she had simply never expected to be invited into her daughter's life again. She wore a simple cream trouser suit, with a rose-pink silk blouse underneath. Her hair blew gently around her face in the afternoon breeze and as Joe watched out of the window of the Town Hall he thought that she was probably the most handsome woman he had ever had the privilege to know or kiss, or both. There being any number of women he had kissed but not known.

Anna looked around at the crowd who cheered her and she was as happy as she had ever been, and yet there was something else. A feeling that was unfamiliar. As she stood and smiled at the crowd of happy faces around her, at her elegant mother and her handsome best friend, she realised what it was. She felt entirely calm. This was exactly what she should be doing and

Dawa was exactly the person she should spend the rest of her life with. She knew both these things beyond any doubt. So, for the first time in her life she was absolutely calm and sure of herself.

She felt the gentle breeze blow the long white silk of her full-length kimono, and heard the rustle of the pale pink tissue-paper roses that adorned it. They covered the bottom of the kimono, then as it rose to her waist they thinned out gradually, until the last one sat alone on her shoulder. Beside it was a tiny origami crane, a symbol of good luck, made from bright green paper. As it wobbled and bobbed about it looked like it was pecking at the paper rose.

Her bright copper curls shone in the Autumn sunlight, as did the simple string of crystal stars that ran across her forehead and into her hair, where they were woven through the curls and down her back.

Her shoes were a gift from Irene for her birthday a few days ago. They had provoked a flood of tears from Anna when she pulled back the silver tissue paper to reveal a pair of white Dr Martin boots, with a tiny pie delicately painted on the front of each one. She declared them perfect, before cancelling the whole wedding if Irene couldn't be there. After much shouting and slamming of doors, Ralph managed to talk her round by getting Joe to arrange a live video feed to Irene's room in the nursing home, so she wouldn't miss out.

Once the wedding party had arrived at the Town Hall, the Town Crier whisked them inside and up the stairs to the elegant ceremony room.

Sam stood at the front next to Dawa, acting as his best man, both wearing blue suits to match Ralph's. Sam had a paisley shirt and a daisy and tarragon buttonhole, while Dawa wore a white shirt, silver tie and a buttonhole of two bright daisies. Sam winked at Ralph as he and Stanley walked down the aisle, making Ralph blush and Stanley bark as they took their seats amongst the other members of the Rooftop Club, two of Dawa's aunties and other Rye friends. Dawa fiddled with his buttonhole for the hundredth time as the music began, the doors opened and Anna gently sailed down the aisle on Ruby's arm to the strains of the Nolan Sisters belting out *I'm In The Mood for Dancing*. He cried when he saw her, so she cried, even though she was trying hard not to. As she reached him, she whispered, "I'm so relieved you're here."

"Where else would I be?" he asked, holding her hand tight.

"I don't know. I did think you might have decided you'd better things to do than marry me."

He lifted her chin and looked deep into her eyes, "I can only think of one better thing than marrying you today, Anna, and that is spending the rest of my life with you."

Anna cried again, as did Ruby and Ralph and Martin and Fiona and Sam and Joe and Psychic Sue and Dawa's aunts and Sergeant Phil and Rosie, Anna's old waitress who had come back from her European drumming duties just in time. Jack didn't cry, but he was still pleased as punch to have been invited to his first wedding, especially as he was sitting next to Rosie, who looked hot in her cut-off denims and leather waistcoat.

The registrar brought things to order and began the ceremony.

"Ladies and gentlemen, welcome to Rye Town Hall. We are gathered here today to celebrate..." but she could get no further as a wild banging began on the doors of the ceremony room.

Everyone turned and looked at the fragile grade-two listed doors rattling and thundering in their frames. Someone was attacking them from the outside - bang, bang, bang. Muffled shouts could be heard, but no one could make out what was being said, until eventually one voice became clear above the others.

"I OBJECT!"

The Registrar looked at Dawa, who looked at Anna, who looked at her mother, who looked at Joe. Joe got up and hurried down the aisle, with Ralph close on his heels. They reached the doors as the voice yelled, "Can't you hear me? I OBJECT!"

They took a door each and yanked them open, to reveal an aluminium crutch waving in the air on the end of which was Irene, sitting in a wheelchair like Boadicea in her chariot.

"About time," she grumbled. "Didn't you hear me knocking? I've probably wrenched a kidney with all that palaver. Come on, Gladys, get me in," and she pointed her crutch into the room, narrowly missing Ralph and Joe who had to duck.

An embarrassed looking petit blonde in a blue nurse's uniform started to push Irene into the room, "I'm so sorry," she said. "She's caused such a fuss at the home, threatening to call the FBI and sue us for kidnap. She insisted I brought her."

"Stop talking, Gladys Emmanuel, get wheeling," Irene

ordered.

The nurse grimaced at Ralph and Joe, "My name's Christine. Everyone calls me Chris, but she insists on calling me Gladys, for some reason."

"I think it may be from an old TV show," Ralph said.

When Anna saw Irene coming down the aisle, she flew to her and fell on her knees in front of the wheelchair. "Careful," Irene said. "Gladys here is a terrible driver, she'll run you over and you'll have wheel tracks all up that kimono."

"Oh, Irene," Anna blubbed. "You're here."

"Well, I'm not one of those holigrams, am I," she sniffed. "Did you think I'd miss your wedding? Have you married him yet, am I too late?"

The Registrar approached cautiously, "I'm afraid we don't usually do the bit about objections to the wedding these days."

"I'm not objecting to the wedding; I was objecting to it starting without me. Nurse Gladys here drives like Stevie Wonder, we crept along as if she couldn't even see the end of the bonnet. But I'm here now, so you can carry on."

"Thank you," the Registrar said, looking a little shaken.

"You're welcome, but don't take forever. It's fish fingers for tea back at the doo-dah and if I'm late, her with feet like flippers will be on seconds already."

"It's good to have you back," Joe said, bending down and kissing her on the cheek.

"Oh, you're here, are you? Finished galivanting and

remembered where your home is, have you? Good, about time. Ralph, push me up the front, I won't see a thing from the back. Gladys, take a pew and rev yourself up for the ride home, see if you can get over twenty miles an hour this time."

With Irene in place at the front of the room, Anna knew that everything was perfect and she was ready to marry Dawa Singh, which she did with many tears and no further interruptions. She vowed to make Balti Yorkshire Puddings for him whenever he wanted, love him unconditionally and not buy more than two new knick-knacks a month, unless he specifically agreed to more. In return he vowed to care for her, walk at her side forever and wear nice shoes until he breathed his last breath.

Back outside the Town Hall, the Town Crier introduced the new Mr and Mrs Singh to the small crowd who cheered and threw confetti.

Sam had never seen Dawa look so happy, partly helped by being able to see more of his face since he'd shaved his beard off, but he was proud of the man who had been like a guardian, friend and brother to him since his father had died. As everyone crowded around Anna, he found a moment to take Dawa by the arm and lead him to a quiet corner of the street away from the others, "Dawa, I just wanted to say thank you for all you've done for me over the years. I know you never expected to take me on when you started working for Dad, but you have been more than my best friend for the last few years and I'm not sure I have ever thanked you."

Dawa swallowed hard, "There's no need, it was..."

But Sam stopped him with a hand on his shoulder,

"No, Dawa, I need to say this. Although I am your best man today - you are the best man I have ever known. I think of you as a father as well as my friend and I love you." He pulled Dawa into him and hugged him for the first time since he was a boy. After a moment Dawa put his arms around Sam and held him tight, "Your real father would be proud of you, just as I am," he said into his ear.

Ruby stood with her back to The Copper Kettle her arm hooked through Joe's, "Today has been perfect, hasn't it? There were times when I would never have dreamed that anything like this would happen. I mean four years ago I was a miserable old woman surviving on white wine and regrets. Look at me today; my beautiful daughter has married an incredible man, she asked me to give her away, and I'm with you. What did I do to deserve it all?"

Joe put his arm around her shoulders, "Ruby, you've really gotta stop asking that question. You re-entered the world as your real self after a long time hiding away and that was enough. You have got everything you deserve. Many would say you didn't deserve me, but that's another discussion."

She laid her head on his broad shoulder, "I think I probably do deserve you - I did some pretty rotten things in my past."

"Charming, but not inaccurate. We'd better get going to start things at the reception, hadn't we? I'm on bar duty, remember."

"Yes, we should. I need to get the cake up on the rooftop too."

As they slipped away, Ralph and Sam started to

follow them, walking hand in hand, "Is Anna going to be happy with this?" Ralph said.

"Please stop asking that. We've gone over and over it. Dawa agreed to it, didn't he?"

"I know, you're right. I just don't want her to be disappointed."

"She won't be. The Rooftop Club is so important to her, how could she not want us to be together on the rooftop for her reception. Come on."

CHAPTER 33

Shiny floorboards, burnt orange cashmere and a housewarming gift.

Stanley loved his new home above Cinque, the smells of cooking from the kitchen below and beer from behind the bar being an intoxicating mix for him, so he barked with joy as he ran up the stairs to the new apartment.

Sam paused at the bottom of the stairs, "What are you doing?" Ralph asked.

"Come here."

"Wait…"

But Sam had scooped Ralph up into his arms, "Ooof, no wedding cake for you!" he wheezed.

"Put me down."

"It's a day of traditions, so you, Mr Bookseller, are being carried over the threshold," he said, as he took each stair one heavy footstep at a time. "I forgot all about it when we moved in, but this seems like as good a time as any. Jeez, this seemed like such a good idea a minute ago."

Ralph laughed as he clung to Sam's neck, "Well, you started it, so you've got to finish now. Come on, only four more steps."

Sam struggled up the final steps and as he reached the top rolled Ralph out of his arms and onto the varnished wooden floor of their new apartment, "Welcome home," he panted triumphantly.

Ralph lay with his face on the shiny floorboards, "Not quite how I imagined it, but thanks anyway."

"Isn't it beautiful?" Sam looked at the light space, exposed warm brickwork, clean white walls dividing the bedroom and bathroom from the rest of the open-plan apartment. The kitchen behind them was made from reclaimed wood and copper, the dining and seating areas were defined by tall green potted palms and free-standing bookshelves. Ralph's portrait of Sam hung between the two large warehouse windows that looked out over the streets of Rye. They had put so much love into it and now it was truly a home for them both.

"Halloo," echoed up the staircase from below. "Anyone home?"

They looked at each other, "No!" they said together.

They heard light feet and sharp heels staggering up the stairs, "Samuel? It's your mother, I'm coming up ready or not. There you are, looking very smart the pair of you. Paisley is very on-trend now, well done you."

Jane Scott leant on the balustrade at the top of the stairs to steady herself. She was wearing a long dress in burnt orange cashmere with a plunging neckline, and a long floating scarf in white wrapped loosely round her neck. She looked like she had just walked off a Greek beach instead of one of Rye's wintery streets.

"Dawa said he thought you might be here. I must say he's scrubbed up well now all that hair has gone. I never thought of him as handsome – to be honest I never think of staff at all, but I suppose he is not quite proper staff." She moved into the apartment, "This is lovely, boys, quite lovely. You've done such a good job. A tad bland for my taste, but you will learn. I'm sure we could get a decent spread in one of the classier magazines, with some accents from accessories or better fabrics. Elle Decoration might not go for something like this, but we could try." She turned to them with a smile and winked, "Cat got your tongue, boys?"

Ralph and Sam stared at her, too stunned to speak. They had thought they'd got her out of their lives, or at least at a sufficient distance for her to cause no further harm, but she insisted on popping up just when they didn't expect her.

Sam finally found his voice, "No."

"I beg your pardon, darling?"

"I said, no."

"That's what I thought you said. No, what? Am I allowed to sit? No one has offered me a chair, but I'll sit anyway." She sashayed over to one of the reclaimed wooden dining chairs and eased herself gently on to it. "Hm, more comfortable than it looks. I hope I won't get splinters."

"No, to everything," Sam said. "No to photo spreads. No to magazines. No to your taste. No to your interference. No to whatever it is you have come here wanting. Just, no."

Jane eyed her son for a long moment, before crossing her long legs, "Good heavens, that's an awful lot of nos. Ralph, are you able to translate?"

"What do you want, Jane?" Ralph said, standing close to Sam for safety and support.

"Want? Just to see my late husband's dear friend married and celebrate your new abode. Is that not enough?"

"Not for you," Sam growled.

Jane used a long red fingernail to adjust her perfect bobbed hair slightly before standing up, "I see. What you are telling me is that I have been a terrible mother and more than that, a complete bitch."

Sam felt himself wobble slightly, so much so that Ralph reached out to hold his arm, "I... well, since you mention it... I mean..."

Jane moved towards him, "Sam, my darling boy, let's be frank with one another. I have been an absolute monster for most of your life. In fact, I'm surprised you even let me in the door."

"I didn't, you let yourself in."

She blinked at him, "That is a very fair point. It will not happen again. This is your home and it is not for me to enter uninvited."

Sam looked at Ralph, panic written across his face, "What's happening?"

Ralph shrugged, "I've no idea."

"I have spent quite some time thinking over the last few months. Since I went public with the issue of domestic abuse..."

"Which was a lie."

"Which was a carefully crafted media... oh, what the hell, it was a lie. But since then, I have talked to a lot of people who have suffered greatly in their lives. Genuine suffering, I mean, and it has made me think. With the help of Dr Shultz, I have been doing a lot of work on myself. Externally there is nothing that currently needs doing, but internally he has led me to believe that there are some improvements to be made."

"I'll say," Sam muttered.

"I heard that," Jane snapped, then took in and released a long breath. "Look, darling, I am here to apologise. I have damaged our relationship by thinking of you as a tool to develop my life and career goals. Whereas now I have come to see that you have your own autonomy and your own right to live a full and generous life outside of my own expectations and needs."

"Go on then," Sam crossed his arms tightly over his chest.

She frowned slightly through the tight grip of Botox, "Go on then, what?"

"Apologise. I haven't heard you say it yet."

"Oh, yes, I see. Well," she straightened her back and flicked her hair. "Samuel, I apologise for not being a better mother. I apologise for trying to use you in ways you were not comfortable with. You are my son, of whom I am immensely proud and if I have made life difficult for you in the past, then I am truly sorry. There. How was that?"

Sam scrutinised Jane's face. Beneath the surface of

carefully applied make-up and expensive procedures, he wanted to see something genuine. He had so rarely looked at her in this way he didn't know what was real and what was not. "Fine, I accept your apology. But don't expect me to trust you straight away, Dr Schloss will explain why, I'm sure."

"Dr *Schultz* has already said that it will take time to build trust and I accept that. Action not words is what is needed. So, let us begin now. I have brought you both a housewarming gift."

"Oh, right. I mean, thanks," Sam looked around. "What is it?"

"It's downstairs. Would you be a dear and bring it up? It's in some purple wrapping by the front door, my nails wouldn't allow me to drag it up here."

Sam disappeared down the stairs, leaving Ralph standing awkwardly in front of Jane, "Erm, I think it was very brave of you to apologise, Jane. Thank you."

"Hmm? No need to thank me, dear. The universe has made it clear that I need to be a better mother. I have listened and will be rewarded, I'm sure."

"Rewarded? What do you mean?"

But before she could answer, Sam returned carrying a flat square parcel, "This had better not be what I think it is," he said, his face grim and hard.

"I don't know what you mean, darling. Now, I thought you might need a few things for your walls, so I have brought you something that is very precious to me. I have had it framed by two lovely young boys in Covent Garden. It's so beautiful I can hardly bear to part with it, but as I want to show you I intend to make things right – well, it's yours now. A token of my love for you both."

Sam held the parcel tightly in his arms, "Mum..."

Ralph looked confused, "Shouldn't we open it, Sam?" he tried to take it from him. "Sam, let go."

Sam released the parcel to Ralph, who laid it on the long kitchen counter. He undid the shiny purple paper to reveal a layer of bubble wrap, which he peeled apart to reveal an ornate gold frame surrounding his own portrait of Jane, "Oh, no."

"It's such a clever, clever painting, Ralph. When you sent it to me it completely... took my breath away. All my girlfriends adored it, they said it was extraordinary and how brave I was to have such a starkly honest portrait of myself done. Every line and wrinkle clear as a bell for all to see, the whole story of my life written large over my face, every single year. Aren't you clever? I mean I had intended for it to go on public display, for everyone to see, but I realise I couldn't do that as I want you to have it. You can imagine how hard it was for me to part with it, but it will look so lovely tucked away in here, as a memento of our new closeness as a family."

"For crying out loud," Sam muttered, his teeth grinding audibly.

Ralph took Sam's hands, both of which were balled into fists and gently unfolded them finger by finger, "Sam, look at me. Please, look at me. That's better. I think Jane has been very kind to give it back to us. But I think we shouldn't hide it away here. For a start Rye Gallery have asked a couple of times if there is any chance of displaying it for all the locals and tourists to see..."

"Oh, no," Jane gasped. "Do you think...?"

"Then after a few months there, we could hang it in the restaurant downstairs. I mean it's always packed and so many people will see it. We could even arrange an unveiling for the press. I know I'm always a bit shy about my work, but this was a prize portrait and of such a famous person. I'm sure we can get quite a bit of press coverage and splash it all over social media."

Jane ran her hand through her hair, dislodging its normal slick order, "But, but, this is a private family matter. You don't like going public with your private life, you just said. It should stay between us. Look, there's a lovely blank space on the wall..."

"No, no," Sam said, seeing Ralph's ploy and beginning to enjoy himself. "That's by the toilet, that won't do. We'll get it down to the gallery on Monday and put it in the window. Then there's a lovely spot right inside the entrance of Cinque where everyone who comes in and even those outside will see it. Thanks, Mum," he gave her a long kiss on the cheek, then took her gently by the arm and guided her to the stairs. "It's been lovely to see you, but now we have to get back to Anna and Dawa's wedding reception. Let me know you got home safely."

"But, darling, I'll come with you..."

"No, that wouldn't be appropriate. For a start Anna is the star attraction today, not you. And then there's the rather crucial fact that you are not invited."

"But..."

"Adios Mother. Give my love to Dr Strangelove."

"Schultz!" Jane called from the bottom of the stairs where Sam closed the door firmly behind her.

CHAPTER 34

The rooftop, red roofs and The End.

The rooftop terrace was packed with people chatting and laughing under yards of silver bunting and white fairy lights. Flickering white candles were spread around the edge of the rooftop, and the whole thing shivered with light and life, as the sun set, leaving a soft, comfortable glow on the frosty roofs of Rye below.

Ralph leant on the railing looking down at the town, alive with excitement on what was known locally as Rye Fawkes Night.

"Hello, you," Anna said, as she appeared beside him, wrapped in a bright yellow shawl.

"Hello, Mrs Singh."

"Mad, isn't it? I'm Mrs Singh. A proper grown-up Mrs."

"How does it feel?"

"Gorgeous."

"Good. I hope you didn't mind the change of reception venue."

"I couldn't understand why Dawa was leading me

towards Cinque instead of the shops. I had set my heart on one last party as the Rooftop Club, with the old bar, the knackered pot plants and the deckchairs I couldn't get in to or out of."

"I know, I'm sorry."

"No, don't be, this is so much better," she turned around and gazed happily at the large oblong roof space on top of the warehouse that housed both Cinque and Ralph's new apartment below. "How you got the old bar here without it falling apart, I will never know."

Ralph laughed, "Oh, it fell apart. Joe spent ages rebuilding it, but used all the original fruit crates and wicker panels. It's much sturdier now."

"And the deckchairs are here and the old plants, with all those new ones that aren't half dead. The lighting is gorgeous, where did you get the lamppost from?"

"It was an old lamp from the High Street, Jack found it in a reclamation yard. We had it refurbished so it works, and all the other strings of lights are plugged into it."

"It's so beautiful. I can't believe you even brought Auntie B's table over."

They looked across to the little iron table, where Martin and Fiona sat chatting with Jack and Rosie over two lit candles that flickered in memory of absent friends and family.

Anna sighed, "It's the perfect end to a perfect day. A new roof for the Rye Rooftop Club. It feels so right, not to end something on my wedding day, but to start something new."

"We had a code lock put on the gate at the bottom of

the external fire escape, so you can get access whenever you want, even if we're not here. It's alphabetical and the code is A-U-N-T-B."

Anna gulped and hugged him, "Auntie B! She's come with us too. How brilliant!" She let him go and leant on the railing that ran around the roof, "Do you remember the night we stood on the old rooftop, not long after you arrived? We were looking at all the roofs of Rye around us. I asked you to imagine who was living under them."

"I remember. I said it was two people wearing slippers and eating soup – snug and warm and happy."

"I asked you who they were, and you wouldn't tell me. You changed the subject."

Ralph nodded.

"Was it you and Sam, or you and another man? You hadn't come out then, had you?"

"No, not then. Do you really want to know who it was?"

"Yes, please."

"You and me. Two friends who can sit and eat soup in their slippers. Easy and uncomplicated. That's all I wanted then. To have someone who I trusted to simply be myself with," he paused, as he found himself engulfed in white kimono silk and yellow shawl again. He whispered in Anna's ear, "I'm very lucky I found you that night I arrived, coming out of the supermarket with your squirty cream and brandy. You brought me up the hill to The Bookery; it was like you were bringing me home."

She stepped back and he handed her a tissue, "Thank you. I've done nothing but roar all day. I'll have to stop soon or I'm going to shrink my face - which might not be a bad thing thinking about it."

"Shush, you look beautiful. You always look beautiful."

"Stop it or you're going to set me off again. So much has changed, hasn't it, since the day you arrived, just over a year ago, with one bag and lovely eyes?"

"Yes, it has, but look what we've got now."

Ralph took her hand and they stood together watching everyone enjoying themselves on the terrace. They saw Sam and Ruby laughing at Stanley, as he tried to lick a piece of wedding cake icing from a particularly tricky corner of his eyebrow. Psychic Sue had joined Fiona and Martin at Auntie B's table and was attempting to persuade Martin to let her read his palm. Jack was sitting cross legged on the floor wrapped up in Rosie's tales of band life on the road. Joe was behind the bar, entertaining Dawa's Aunties with his jokes and usual charm, as he made brightly coloured cocktails for them. Dawa waved at them from a deckchair where he sat next to Irene, who he had carefully carried up the stairs, much against her wishes and advice from Chris, her nurse. Irene looked tired but happy, smiling and telling Dawa off for something.

Anna smiled, "Look what the old rooftop has done. It's brought us all together and set us on new paths. Who knows where they will lead, but we will always be a family of friends."

Ralph nodded, "It's time that we moved on and let new people have the chance to go up and breath the air on the rooftop above the shops. The first time I met Auntie B, she told me that up there you can breathe more freely. She said, there you can open your heart, bit by bit, and find your way."

"She was right, wasn't she? You did find your way. We all did."

"Yes, but now it's time for the rooftop to work its magic on new people who need it more than we do."

Anna sniffed, "Yes, I suppose we must pass it on. What was that lovely Dickens' quote Martin said in his speech when we cut the cake, *Happiness is a gift and the trick is not to expect it...*

"*...but to delight in it when it comes.*"

At that moment the first firework of the night exploded in a rainbow of stars above their heads. There was a loud cheer from everyone as they rushed to the edge of the roof and surrounded Anna and Ralph.

The sky filled with colour and light. Anna gripped Dawa's hand on one side and Ralph's on the other. She looked at Dawa, "Thank you for finding me." Then she turned to Ralph, "Thank you for finding us." Then she looked up at the sky, "Thank you, Auntie B, for still guiding us on."

Ralph smiled at Sam, who appeared at his side, then along with everyone else he looked out over Rye's jumble of red roofs. "Thank you," he whispered to the ancient, magical town.

THE END

Thank you for reading Book Three in The Rye Rooftop Club series.

If you enjoyed the book, please review it on Amazon.co.uk so other readers can find their way to Rye and meet the Rooftop Club.

You can read more about Psychic Sue in the light-hearted thriller with more twists and turns than a seaside helter-skelter!

Death and The Seagull

By Mark Feakins

ACKNOWLEDGEMENTS

Thanks to all my friends and acquaintances who have had their names recycled for this third and final book in the Rye series. Although I have borrowed their names, I have not used any of their characteristics and any peculiarities of the characters named after them are entirely of my own creation.

Thanks again to Martin and Andy, my insightful team of early readers for their continued enthusiasm and guidance.

ABOUT THE AUTHOR

Mark Feakins grew up on the Sussex coast and was a frequent visitor to Rye.

He moved to London to attend drama school and, after a brief time as an actor and running a number of theatres, he travelled further north as Executive Producer of Sheffield Theatres.

He has a degree in Librarianship, danced around a maypole on BBC TV's Playschool and won Channel 4's Come Dine with Me in 2010. Mark now lives happily in the region of Valencia in Spain, with his husband Martin.

E: markfeakins@gmail.com
Facebook: My Writing Life

Books by Mark Feakins:

The Rye Books

The Rye Rooftop Club
The Rye Rooftop Club: Mother's Day
The Rye Rooftop Club: Summer Solstice

Other Books

Death and The Seagull

Printed in Great Britain
by Amazon